Cassandra
IN RED

Cassandra
IN RED

a novel

MICHAEL COLLINS

DONALD I. FINE, INC.

New York

Library of Congress Cataloging-in-Publication Data
Collins, Michael, 1924–
Cassandra in red / by Michael Collins.
p.   cm.
ISBN: 1-55611-316-1
I. Title.
PS3562.Y44C36   1992
813′.54—dc20   91-55190
CIP

Manufactured in the United States of America

10 9 8 7 6 5 4 3 2 1

Designed by Irving Perkins Associates

To Juli Stone,
life and happiness

Evil is common,
and most people who commit evil are asleep.

—HANNAH ARENDT

I
THE ROAD

They listen in the night.

"Where the fuck did he go, Scorpion?"

"The bastards'll hear us!"

"Shut up! All of you!"

When Wolf speaks, they freeze and listen to the silence. They all freeze in the dark night under the shadows of the palm trees, the oaks, the maples with red leaves. All the weird trees.

"Jesus, Wolf, we could be walking bareass into a trap."

They move on, invisible in their dark clothes, only their alert eyes white in blackened faces.

"Maybe we should get the fuck out of here."

"You want to sleep in your clothes another goddamn night, Roach?"

Wolf's sharp voice. "Down!"

Weapons at ready, each facing away to cover front, rear and both flanks.

"Over there, Wolf!"

It is a voice, voices, singing.

"Scorpion with me. Roach and Spider cover our tails."

They move through the dark trees toward the voices that seem to sneer at them.

"We got to rag one, Scorpion. We don't, they never stop hitting on us."

1

Night was day in the glare of floodlights. The flat white faces of the police as pale and empty as the painted faces of actors in an old silent movie. *The Cabinet of Dr. Caligari*. Motion stiff and angular, slow and deliberate under the trees that looked like painted backdrops in the garish day of the floodlights. In the distance, beyond the perimeter of tape and the uniforms of the patrolmen, rows of featureless faces like masks stared at the Victorian gingerbread bandstand, its filigreed conical roof topped by a weathervane, as artificial as a stage set in the flood of white light.

"Found her inside," Sergeant Gus Chavalas said. "Under the band platform."

"Stabbed fifteen, thirty times. They go crazy, those goddamn bums." Detective Max Miller dug his thick hands into the bucket of popcorn, watched the video on the small screen. "The place looked like someone'd spilled a tank of blood."

"The Park Department man always comes to work around five or six," Chavalas said, "goes home early."

"Damn good hours," Max Miller said. "He can work his second job and still get home for dinner."

"He saw the door under the bandstand open," Chavalas said. "It's supposed to be closed. It doesn't lock, and he knows people sleep in there sometimes, so he went in to make sure whoever had been in there was gone."

"Did he know she slept in the park?"

"He says he never saw her there before. He admits he can't be sure, but he doesn't ever remember a woman sleeping there. He found her, called us."

"Still dark as the chief's heart when we got there," Miller said. "She'd been dead four to six hours the coroner says. Last night somewhere eleven P.M. to one A.M. No one saw anything, we ain't found anyone yet who'll say they were there. They move around the

damned town like ghosts if they don't want you to see 'em or hear
'em. Kill each other and fade out of town."

On the flickering crime-scene video the park, the masks of the
curious, the painted faces of the detectives, and the glare of floodlights on the dark green wood of the bandstand began to fade into
the dawn. The trees emerged with the real day. And the faces of the
crowd drawn to the blood even at the crack of dawn on a Wednesday
in January. There is something wrong with a world or a species or
both that finds nothing as exciting as other people's trouble and
pain and death.

"No knife, no evidence, no witnesses," Chavalas said.

The park was in the heart of the city. On the edge of the upper
eastside of elegant and massive old Victorians, rambling new
ranches, two-story *haciendas* and modern apartment complexes. A
double park: the large city park two blocks wide and one deep, and
the new memorial gardens with benches and fish pond where the
old El Mirador Hotel had been. Paths for walking on warm summer
evenings, on long afternoons. Grass for sunning, eating lunch, toss-
ing a frisbee or throwing a ball, playing with the dog and the kids.

The exotic trees brought from across the world, in a city where
little of the lush green and color is native to the semi-desert of dusty
oaks and brown grass and gray chaparral where the Chumash Indians lived. It was here the crowds of the Sixties and early Seventies
gathered to hear the speakers on the bandstand denounce war, rac-
ism and hate. Here the Kiwanis Club holds its pancake breakfast for
the public every Fiesta August, where the historical parade to cele-
brate the city's Hispanic past ends. Where, across the street in the
fine memorial gardens, a snapping turtle and piranhas were found
in the fish pond, causing a wild brouhaha among animal lovers,
environmentalists, parents of small children, and the city, much to
the delight of the irreverent and the frustration of the city fathers.

Now they had another problem in the park.

"She was lying on her back, sleeping bag open, her pack at the
head, a book in the dirt like she'd been lying on the bag reading
when the killer came in."

"Cassandra," Miller said. "Iron Cassie they called her down on
lower State. No last name. She looked sort of Mex. Dark skin and
eyes, big lips, dark hair. You don't often find a Mex on the streets."

"Reilly," I said. "Cassandra Reilly. One of the dark Irish. From the
Spanish Armada back in the sixteenth century."

"The family hired you, Dan?" Chavalas said. "How'd they know?"

"One of her street friends hired me, Al Benton."

Miller said. "King Al of the streets? The Marx of City Hall? Guru of the gutter?"

"Benton have a hometown for the woman?" Chavalas asked.

"Not that he mentioned."

Miller stood, headed for the door. "I'll put the full name in the loop."

"How'd Benton know about her so soon?" Chavalas said. "He's got money to pay you?"

"He heard it on the morning radio. I hope he's got money."

Miller returned, picked up his bucket of popcorn. On the TV screen dawn light was full over the park, a yellow wash of sun behind the crowd of watchers that had grown with the coming of morning on the crime scene video. They brought the body of Cassandra Reilly out through the heavy wooden door under the bandstand. The gawkers strained to see, the patrolmen held them back, the detectives cleared the way to the wagon, and there was an unreality like watching the news on television. I knew this was real, as real as if I had been there this morning, but I felt detached, distant, watching a movie about something I couldn't be sure had ever happened. Maybe it was the warm room with the afternoon sun outside, the chairs we sat in, Detective Miller and his popcorn.

"She was wearing jeans, a man's wool plaid shirt, baseball jacket, work boots, a navy wool cap pulled down over her ears. The street uniform for a winter day even in beautiful Southern California. Short hair and not much showing. I'm not sure anyone could have known she was a woman unless they did already, or unless she spoke, and I don't know what kind of voice she had."

"Rough and whisky," Miller said. "The merchants down on lower State didn't love her. Feisty, hardnosed, and never stopped talking. One of the leaders in the streetbum drive to push their rights. Along with Fortune's client. King Al Benton, the derelicts' Darrow."

Chavalas looked at me. "Is Benton accusing anyone?"

"Not yet."

On the video screen the body was gone, most detectives had left, and the patrolmen were starting to disperse the crowd. "Coroner says she wasn't raped. No evidence of recent sex activity. No wallet or purse or money, nothing valuable on her or in her pack. She could have been robbed. Looks like she had a wedding ring."

"Benton says she had some money, the ring, a big blaster radio, maybe other stuff," I said.

"Then that's it for sure," Miller said. The tall, lean detective looked into his empty popcorn bucket, tossed it into the wastebasket, and stood up. "They'll steal from anyone, even each other. Especially each other. They kill each other over a bottle of white port. We'll work on it, but nine-out-of-ten the killer's six states away by now. He confesses, someone tells us who he is, or we never find out. We solve it quick or never."

Miller left the small room, Chavalas and I sat and watched until the park was empty and the screen went blank and silent. The Sergeant continued to stare at the vacant screen. "Miller's by the book and the headlines all the way, but ninety-nine out of a hundred he's right."

"Is this the one percent?"

Chavalas got up, turned off the VCR. "What does your client say?"

"He doesn't know. I get the idea he's confused, even scared. He wants to know."

Chavalas put the video away, returned to his chair. "No hard evidence, but there was something about what we found in that park had a funny feel. Sort of military. Two, maybe three people down behind trees. Marks in the dirt, some cigarette butts. Boot prints around the door and on the other side too, as if covering all flanks. More butts up on the bandstand floor above the door, cuts in the railing like someone was doodling with a knife to kill time."

"A lookout?"

"Could be, Dan." He stood up. "A lot of veterans on the streets. Vietnam, Nicaragua, probably Iraq by now. Trip-wire types, loonies."

I stood to follow him. He didn't walk to the door, looked at me. "When we got there you could tell she was a woman. The knife had ripped the heavy shirt open, her bra was showing, one bare breast. Someone had spit on the breast."

2

"Military macho and anger at women. They go together," Kay said. "We're too pushy. Feminist bitches taking their fun away."

We were in my office in our Summerland house. She is Kay Michaels. Tall, auburn-haired, she runs her own actors-and-models agency. Her own boss in all things. I run my business, my own boss. There the resemblance ends. We live with each other. It's what we both want, except that we still rent the hacienda-style house and she'd prefer to buy. There must be some Native American in me, I have trouble with ownership. Only what I can carry. Maybe socialist genes from my Polish grandfather.

"Chavalas wonders about the ex-soldiers on the streets."

"Wouldn't they be anti-military?"

"Some, not all. A lot of trip-wire survivalist types came home from Vietnam, went into the forests and mountains. They're older now, out of the mountains and down on the streets."

The sun was low outside in what passed for winter in Santa Barbara—there is a difference in seasons in Southern California, definite and noticeable, it's just not as much difference as the snow belt. We waited for my client. In jeans and a purple turtleneck, Kay was stretched out on the office couch.

"The misfit mercenaries, Dan? Overage juveniles couldn't make it in the military, walk around playing at soldier? Fantasy Foreign Legionnaires, imaginary Green Berets with scrapbooks of John Wayne and Rambo?"

Al Benton stood in the office. The side door had opened and closed so quickly I barely heard it. A tall emaciated man with the bony face, solemn aspect and slow manner of a country church deacon, Benton was nervous.

"Someone after you, Benton?"

"I sure as hell hope not."

He sat in my only armchair. "Like I said before, damned if I want anyone to see me with you. They'd want to know where I got the money, why I'm spending it this way."

"Where did you, and why are you?"

He was dressed in grimy surplus army pants, a wool plaid shirt over a denim shirt with a ragged old turtleneck under that, work boots, and a navy watch hat. The street uniform.

"Contributions. We get 'em from all over to help the cause. Civil rights people, groups. It's a damn good chance Cassie got killed because of what she was doing. I could damn well be next."

Kay said, "And you wouldn't want it broadcast that you get money for your cause from outside Santa Barbara."

"Not too much. We met?"

"Al Benton, Kay Michaels," I introduced. "What was Cassie doing?"

"I told you, helping me lead the fight for the rights of the street people. She was tough, free and a hell of a talker. Good on a street-corner, good in front of the City Council. A lot of people who run this town didn't like Cassie."

Kay said, "Do you really think the City Council or the Mayor killed her, Mr. Benton?"

His long, bony face considered her. "I've traveled a lot around this country, Miss Michaels. You'd be surprised at what I've seen people with power do. Do and have done." He looked back at me. "Then there's The Lower Town Protective Association, right, Fortune? I know for a damn fact they've hired muscle to harass us, lean on us, discourage us. Maybe someone got too eager to please Hatcher."

I said, "Anyone besides the merchants and City Council?"

"How do I count them? Like I said, Cassie was tough, had a big mouth. She didn't have a doubt in the world about what we're doing. Hell of a lot of people don't like someone that sure of knowing what's right and telling them."

"Street people?"

He rubbed the stubble of gray beard on his lean jaw. "Some. The belligerent assholes gonna demand their rights, yeah, man, yo! and all that shit. You got to kick butt, stand up to the bastards, burn the fucking place down they don't let us in. Cassie told them confrontation never works in the long run. They don't like that, they're all Crockett at the Alamo." He seemed to see the massed faces of angry street people in the office. "I didn't always agree with Cassie, I've had some confrontations when I didn't see any other way, but no one stuck to what she believed and worked harder for it. That's why the macho screamers on both sides were afraid of her."

"But not you?" Kay said.

"Not me."

I said, "You have any names, Benton?"

He shook his head. "They come, they go. First names, the handles, that's all you get most of the time on the streets. Funny thing about the streets, you're not alone much, always someone around, always someone else to hang with. Everyone's alone but no one's alone."

"She had no individual enemies, no private life?"

"A boyfriend."

"He have a name? Somewhere I can find him?"

"Jerry. Not so sure you can find him. I heard they'd had a big fight, he wasn't around the last times I saw Cassie. She didn't want to talk about him."

"You know what they fought about?"

"No."

"Jerry's all the name you have?"

"Jerry, that's it." He sat back in the big armchair where I like to listen to music. "He's younger than Cassie, maybe ten years. Nice looking, if you like the pretty-boy type. Smallish guy, a little heavy, and sort of spooked. Cassie said he was one of the walking wounded, but to me he was plain damn sullen."

Kay said, "How long had they been together?"

I said, "Casual? Sometimes? More permanent?"

Benton shook his head. "That's all I know about her and Jerry. I saw them together a lot, and I saw her alone a lot. On the streets is one of the few places left in this goddamn country with real privacy. No one knows, no one asks. I worked with Cassie here and up in San Francisco, and all I know about her is she was pushing forty, married once with no kids, had a set of parents somewhere she stayed away from."

"You know anything about the husband? Was his name Reilly, or was that her maiden name?"

"Not a clue, Fortune. Don't even know if it was an early marriage or late, long or short."

Kay said, "You know what put her on the streets?"

"All she ever said was that only boys could join the Foreign Legion to hide when their lives were a mess or dead, so she went after her own legion."

"Did she often sleep in Alameda Park? In that bandstand?"

"I never heard of her sleeping there before. That park's great for the lunches the kids throw in the trash at the Catholic school across Anacapa Street. Always good stuff to eat there."

"Where did she usually sleep?"

"At the tree or on the beach with Jerry."

"Where did she and Jerry sleep on the beach?"

"Some hideout. You need those on the streets too."

You need those off the streets. The private places, the solitary havens. They don't have to be physical, they can be in the mind, the imagination. As real and needed as any hidden spot on a beach. Places where the world does not intrude, for you and another, or you alone. Cassandra Reilly had a hidden place for her and Jerry. Maybe it had become too crowded.

"You know any group that operates like soldiers and had something against Cassandra?" I told him what Chavalas had said about the attack in the park last night.

He stood up. "Shit, what's going on? We got some goddamn vigilantes in town?" He'd dealt with vigilantes before, did not like what he'd heard. "I better go warn the people."

Kay said, "What about hating women? Is there much of that on your streets?"

"There's plenty of that everywhere. A lot of guys feel cheated, robbed of their place these days. The streets are no worse, maybe a lot better." He went to the door. "I'll call in tomorrow."

"Where do I look for this Jerry?"

"Anywhere the people are. The county nurse, she might know more about Jerry than anyone. Cassie talked to her a lot."

"Does she have a name?"

"Janet Steiner. Try the Rescue Missions. On the beaches. Even around City Hall."

"I'm going to need somewhere to get in touch with you. At least a message drop."

Benton hesitated. "Okay, call 662-7890. Say it's Dan, nothing more. I'll get back to you."

Then he was gone. For a slow-moving man he could appear and disappear as if the doors never opened or closed. Maybe it was all the street training on how to get in and out of places fast. Kay stood and walked to the windows. After a time she returned to the couch, lay down again.

"He walked through the alley. He didn't walk all the way from downtown, Dan. Someone has to be driving him around. Someone he didn't want to know he'd visited you. Is he telling the truth, Dan? All or part?"

"I have to figure he is until I learn different."

"What was Cassandra Reilly to him?"

"I think she was useful," I said.

3

In Alameda Park the crime scene tape was still up around the bandstand, but the police and the curious were gone. Evening strollers were out with dogs. On a bench an older woman still read in the fading twilight. A man and a boy sat on a blanket spread on the grass against the chill that settled over the city with the dusk in January. The boy played with a pull toy, the man looked at his watch. On Anacapa Street the homebound rush hour traffic flowed in a steady stream toward the freeway.

I stood inside the door of the room under the bandstand, studied the walls, the floor, the ceiling. The dirt floor was marked where Cassandra Reilly had been—in a far corner away from the door under the bare bulb of a wall socket. An electric outlet was directly under the wall socket. A double outdoor outlet with waterproof covers. One of the covers was up. I heard Al Benton's voice: *"She always had some money, the ring, a big blaster radio, maybe some other stuff."* The police had found no money or rings, and no portable radio. But someone had used the outlet recently. It could have been the park

man, or it could have been Cassandra Reilly listening to her portable. Which meant that the radio had been stolen too.

I searched the room step by step. After three complete circles of
the windowless room, I found nothing more. The police don't miss
much or often.

Outside the bandstand the park was already dark. No one read on
the benches, the twilight dog strollers long home. The watch of the
man on the blanket with the young boy had finally pointed to the
right time and they had gone wherever they were supposed to go. I
walked to the exit at Anacapa Street. The traffic flow had dwindled
to nothing.

The movement in the darkness came from my right. The dark
shine of chain that whipped out of the night. It slashed and tangled
on my upraised arm. My only arm. I pulled it, kicked at the shadow
behind the chain. A human shadow.

"Ahhhh!"

The shadow vanished, the chain dangled loose on my arm. A hard
blow slammed against my back. Hard and heavy and solid. A club
and a masked face. Ski mask. White eyes and black ski mask and
teeth and the long, thin gleam of a knife that caught the distant park
light. I dropped, rolled, flailed the chain in the air like a steel whip.

"Shit . . . fuck . . ."

A masked face in front of my foot. I kicked a scream in the night.
Slashed the chain into another mask with white eyes and a flash of
mouth. Kicked and slashed at anything that moved. A face, a leg, an
arm, a . . .

Slashed at nothing.

The sound of running footsteps faded. I sat on the path and
breathed, breathed, breathed. Hammer of the heart. The pain of my
solitary arm and cut hand. The bicycle chain dangled from my arm.
The hammer slowed and the pain eased and I breathed slowly.
Breathed, and the park reappeared like a slow vision of night trees.
A path and the shadows of benches and the dark bandstand with the
yellow tape. The sudden sound of traffic beyond the exit between
low stone walls.

After a time I stood up. Two or three of the ski-masked men in
black. A knife, a club, a bicycle chain, and they had run without
much fight. As if they had never faced real resistance that fought
back, wanted to hurt them, would hurt them.

Drunks? Street militants? Or hired muscle intended only to intimidate street drunks and discourage panhandlers?

The office of The Lower Town Protective Association is on the basement floor of an office building off lower State Street.

"Ski masks and dark clothes," I said, leaned across the desk. "They sound like anyone you just might know, Hatcher?"

I'd worked for Ellwood Hatcher on a problem of unlicensed street vendors selling bogus brand merchandise. Most of them had turned out to be artisans who sold their own handicrafts. There was little merchandise that was either bogus or competed with what the stores sold, and I got tired of hassling small people who were just trying to make a living.

"We hire people to discourage bums and drunks from scaring our customers and pissing in our doorways. Shouldn't we?"

Hatcher likes his work at the Association. A labor of love. He often stays after the five-thirty posted on the door. This time he was still there past seven P.M. writing reports to the clients and letters of rage to the City Council and police.

"This isn't Indian Territory. Vigilantes and hired guns are illegal these days."

"We don't do anything illegal."

"That's not what the Legal Defense Society thinks."

He typed a few more lines on his computer screen. "Why would I hire people to attack you, for Christ sake?"

"Because I'm working on the Cassandra Reilly murder."

Hatcher is a medium-sized man with the body of a weightlifter. An ex-paratrooper, he spent five years on the road himself. Drank, took drugs, skidded down to zero. His own goddamn fault, he says, and his own goddamn way back by kicking the habits and working his ass off on construction to save money and start over. Now he owns a shoe store, leads the Protective Association, and hates the bums on the streets.

He typed. "You accusing me of that?"

"They tell me you didn't like her."

"I didn't like her."

"She got in your hair."

"She got in my hair."

"Maybe some of your hired muscle got carried away, a little too gung-ho for the cause of safe and sane streets."

"Bullshit." He hit save and exit and turned his chair to face me. "You say any of that again without more than shitass speculation and we sue you." He gave me the cold, intense stare he practiced for the City Council. "Who hired you? Iron Cassie have money stashed? Maybe with that nut she shacked on the beach with? The lawyer for her trust fund?"

"Al Benton."

"Jesus!" He shook his head. "I should have guessed. She was the best weapon Benton ever came up with."

"Why?"

"She was smart, she was tough, and she believed the shit she was saying and doing."

"You sound like you knew her pretty well."

"I knew her too damn well." He seemed to look for a window on the night and Cassandra Reilly, but there were no windows in the basement office. "I don't know who killed her or why, but I'm not sorry she's gone. We're in a war in this country against people like her. She wasn't violent or physically dangerous, but she was the worst. She scared the hell out of me."

"She wasn't dangerous, but she scared you?"

He still looked at his non-existent window. "Smart, sober—and crazy as a loon. Life isn't something to be survived, she told me once. The world had gone to pot because of the Hebrews and Greeks. Male force dominated the world and destroyed human potential. Male force was going to destroy us all. Male force divided everything into winners and losers, masters and slaves. Her exact words, Fortune. I told her that was human nature. She said it was my human nature not hers. She could spout that crap all day, people who should know better listened. That's scary."

"What was her side of human nature?"

"Christ, who knows? Love and brotherhood. They never spell it out, put it into anything you can get a grip on."

"She opposed confrontations, Benton says. You say she didn't believe in force. How did she fight you so hard?"

He turned away from his imaginary window. "She knew how to go for the jugular—money. Where it hurts most, right? Love and guilt, brotherhood and the cash register. She handed out fliers, put up posters, talked to the customers. Christ, could she talk. To the

Council, the mayor, the businessmen. She got the bums to talk to people on the street one on one. Free speech, right? She drove everyone crazy, especially customers, made them stay away from the stores. And talk to the City Council? She could make herself look like Joan of Arc and Mother Theresa, the drunks and bums like refugees from a goddamn war. She made *us* look like the bad guys."

"Maybe you are the bad guys, Hatcher. Get those bums out of *our* town. Put 'em in jail. Let 'em starve."

He leaned across his desk at me. "That's the exact shit she used to spout. Well, let me clue you, Fortune, it's not those street pissers and winos who're the victims down here. It's *us*. The merchants, the people who work, the business owners. We can't walk our own streets. We can't use the parks we pay for, the beaches and recreation areas we fund. Most arrests aren't for sleeping or vagrancy but for drunkenness and pissing in public. We're the ones not free, goddamn it."

I said, "Treat the drunks, shelter the sick, put up public toilets. This town doesn't have a single public john. Police won't solve homelessness, Hatcher. Help and jobs will."

"And who pays for it? If they're nuts or sick, put them away. If they can work, send them where they can get jobs. Most of them don't goddamn want to work. That's what I told Crazy Cassie, and that's what I tell you."

"But she didn't listen, did she?"

"None of my people were near that park."

"Maybe you better ask them."

"Why should I?"

"Because if the police or I find them first, it's going to make you and your organization look bad. Real bad."

Al Benton leaned back on my office couch. It was past ten, the sea wind outside in the Summerland night. I could hear Kay in the kitchen doing my job while I talked to Benton. We'd lingered over dinner, were thinking of more, when he finally knocked and slipped into the house.

"What other 'stuff' did she have?"

"Mad money and a credit card." He closed his eyes. "She was almost ready to come in from the streets. Go on working for the cause, but get some work she could live with and a real place to live.

But she couldn't let go of the need on the streets. Sometimes the cause takes you over, gets to be a hideout as bad as the booze and the road. Maybe she was afraid to give it up, think about a future. The past is pretty damn powerful. You can be awful scared it'll grab you again, take you back."

"Was she that fragile?"

"We're all fragile out there. We've lost or abandoned or been thrown out of the castle, the nice safe walls."

Kay had left the kitchen, walked around upstairs. In her office or our bedroom.

"She had a credit card and money. Cash money she carried around with her?"

"She carried maybe a couple of weeks' cash. She didn't want anyone to see her going to the bank."

"Spoil the image?"

"On the streets we have a hard time trusting the good people in regular houses and regular jobs. It's the world we couldn't make work or that didn't want us." He opened his eyes. "She didn't carry all that much. The rest was in a passbook account. It wasn't all that much neither."

.A passbook and a credit card. A ring, some cash and a ghetto blaster. Anyone could have spotted the radio and the ring, hoped for the cash. But who could have wanted the credit card and passbook? Someone who knew her signature, had some identification of hers that might pass in a place known not to be too fussy? A female who could look and act like her?

"Did Jerry know she had an account, a credit card?"

"It stands to reason he'd have spotted them sometime."

"You have the name of the bank? The kind of credit card?"

The bank was the lower State Street branch of the Bank of America. The credit card was a Chase Visa.

"Anything else you didn't tell me, Benton?"

"I don't know what you need to know, what's important."

Neither did I.

4

When you eat breakfast alone in a house with a sleeping woman, you're not eating alone. Man or woman. Sometimes I think that is a secret a lot of people don't know.

Kay had still been asleep next morning when I got up. Her breasts against my back, her arm over my left shoulder maybe to replace my lost arm, one leg between mine. It wasn't easy to get up, leave her. It never is. That's why, in the end, I came to California from New York. A city you've lived in off and on all your life is one thing, the right woman is another.

I wondered if Cassandra Reilly had learned both of those facts on the road, on the dark streets of her wanderings. And they had killed her.

Who would steal a credit card? Someone who knew her well enough to try to impersonate her, sign her name. Or an organized gang.

The woman looked out the window of Gus Chavalas's office on Figueroa Street at the sergeant's favorite jacaranda tree bare in mid-January. The man looked straight ahead. A short man with a bullet head, hair cut so close it looked almost shaved, a nasty V-shaped scar on his scalp. Neat in a cheap brown suit, brown tie, white shirt, brown oxfords, brown socks held up by garters. A wedding ring and an analog watch.

The woman was thin. Shorter than the man, but not more than an inch or so, and the same age. Late fifties at most, both of them. She wore a plain blue print dress, low-heeled blue shoes, had her hair pulled back in a bun. Chavalas waved me in.

"Mr. and Mrs. Reilly. Dan Fortune."

Cassandra Reilly's father sat firmly in a straight chair. The mother had her legs crossed, smiled at me.

Chavalas said. "Miller found their address and phone number on a welfare application she'd made."

"Cassandra on welfare," Mr. Reilly said, the disapproval in his voice.

"You didn't know she was living on the streets, Mr. Reilly?" Chavalas said.

"Call us John and Helen, please," Helen Reilly smiled. The smile was automatic. "We knew Cassie had troubles, Sergeant, but we didn't know the details. She rarely called. Or even wrote."

"She avoided us," John Reilly said. "She didn't want to talk to us about her life, what she was doing, where she was going, or anything else. Not since she walked out on Harold."

Helen Reilly said. "He should be along soon. He couldn't get away for our flight, booked on a later plane out."

Chavalas said, "Harold is her ex-husband? How long ago did she leave him?"

Helen Reilly said. "Harold never did accept that Nevada divorce. He's a lawyer, says it had to be based on fraud, but he won't do anything about it. He is a nice man, Harold. We were sad when she left him, her dad and me. I don't remember exactly when it happened, but—"

"Harold Flood," John Reilly said. "Ten years come February the tenth. Harold's a lawyer, but that's not what he does. Took over his father's old cabinet-making shop and built it into a big furniture manufacturing business. Fine pine furniture from the Adirondacks. Had his own house even before he married Cassandra. Nothing fancy, he doesn't overreach himself." John Reilly thought about overreaching. "We always had a house, since she was very little anyway. I thought she understood the advantage of owning your own house instead of throwing all that money away on rent. She was always smart, top of her class every year. Except for that last year at the university before she married Harold. She didn't do so well that year. Never did know why."

He looked around the office like a man who wasn't sure where he was. His lips continued to work, but no sound came out. He was a man not used to talking. He talked now to ease the pain, to hide from his own unwanted thoughts. The thoughts finally caught up to the words and he fell silent.

"She wanted something else," Helen Reilly said. "I'm not really sure what it was, but it wasn't what we have."

John Reilly turned his eyes toward her. He said nothing, but looked at her as if asking what else there was, what else there could be. Neither said anything more. They both waited. It was something they'd done all their lives and did well.

"Do either of you know who might have killed her? Anything she could have been involved in?"

"No, Sergeant," Helen said. "After she went away to the university she pretty much lost touch with her old friends in town. Then she married Harold and went to live in Utica."

"Where is town?"

"We live in Schenectady. John works for GE."

"Cassandra have any brothers or sisters?"

"No," Helen Reilly said. "I couldn't after Cassie."

"What university did she go to?"

"Syracuse."

"How long did she live in Utica?"

"Eight years." Helen Reilly sighed. "I don't think she made a single friend. I've got acquaintances, not friends, she said. She said Harold had friends, she helped him entertain his friends. That was a year or so before she ran off."

"Why did she run off?"

John Reilly said, "We have no idea."

He had not moved in the chair since I'd come in. Looked now at Chavalas and at me with a kind of defiance and an implacable certainty.

Helen Reilly said, "We never have known exactly why."

"They had no children?"

"No," Helen Reilly said. It was the voice of a woman who had wanted to be a grandmother.

"Did she run off with anything? Money? Another man?"

"Harold never mentioned anything like that. We . . . heard she had men while she was . . . away, but that was after she left."

"Did Harold try to get her back? Is he a violent man? Is he capable of killing her?"

John Reilly turned his bullet head to stare as if Chavalas were insane. Insane or incompetent. Not at all sure this policeman was smart enough to find his way home much less find Cassandra's killer.

"Harold still adores . . . adored Cassie," Helen Reilly said. "Harold would never have harmed her, Sergeant. No one from home would have."

"You said you knew very little about her life in Utica after she married. You don't even know what made her leave."

John Reilly continued to stare at Chavalas, then at me, an expression on his face that could only be called incredulous. Helen Reilly gave a small shrug, looked up at both of us.

"I suppose it's possible, Sergeant."

Chavalas said, "She left him and she left you. Avoided you. Did you have some conflict?"

John Reilly got up. "Don't all parents and children have conflicts? That doesn't lead to murder, for God's sake. Harold Flood is a good, solid man. It seems to me you're reaching for straws, Sergeant, looking everywhere but where you obviously should look—at those street people Cassandra was with. God only knows why." He made a short, abrupt upward slash with his arms that had to be his version of throwing up his hands. "Mother says she didn't want what we have, wanted something else. I haven't any idea what that might have been, and that limits me in what I can do to help find who killed her or why. But even I know that the place to look is among those street people or whoever else she's been with in the ten years since she walked out on a good, productive life with Harold."

I said, "Productive how, Mr. Reilly? Productive for whom?"

"For her, and for the country, Mr. . . . . Fortune, is it?"

"Fortune," I said. "Do the names Al Benton or Jerry mean anything to either of you?"

"Not a thing. Who are they?"

Helen Reilly shook her head. "No, I don't think I ever heard those names, Mr. Fortune."

"Jerry's the boyfriend, Dan?" Chavalas said.

I nodded, told him what Benton had said. John Reilly was still on his feet, listened with the concentration and intensity of a man hearing about an alien culture, a distant planet.

"Those two sound like you're on the right track at least, Fortune. These people make no contribution, always end up in a kind of anarchy. Those are the people who murdered Cassandra."

"We'll look at all the tracks, Mr. Reilly," Chavalas said, and to me, "We're checking into Jerry. If you pick up anything let me know right away, you understand?" He took a breath. "I think we better get the official identification over with. I want to warn you it won't be pretty. The killer was either very scared or very crazy or very angry or all three."

John Reilly gave his incredulous look. "It has to be done, Sergeant, doesn't it?"

"Yes."

"My daughter is dead. I think I can stand whatever has to be done, Sergeant."

Chavalas picked up the telephone, told Detective Max Miller to come to his office. Helen Reilly recrossed her legs. "I think I'll wait here, John. Is that all right?"

He gave her the same stare. I realized it was his way of responding to any action or idea that wasn't what he would do or think. I also realized he wasn't a man who thought about other people's reasons and motives. It made him vulnerable to being conned or fooled, but that didn't matter because he would never be aware of being conned or fooled. He would always be sure that whatever he did was what he wanted to do at that moment.

"It might be best."

Max Miller came in and took John Reilly out. Helen Reilly swung her foot, look down at the floor. "He's a good husband and a good father."

Chavalas said, "You want to tell us something, Mrs. Reilly?"

"His and Cassie's views on things weren't always the same," she said. "John believes in his views. He lives by them. He's done well. We're not rich, but we're comfortable and secure. He knows what he knows. That was all he wanted to do, teach Cassie what he knew."

5

John has the car packed for the trip to the new hospital in Albany. He alerts his secretary at GE, informs his department head, arranges with Ed Simmons to take his calls, continues to go to the office until the last moment. He impresses on Helen the need to be certain before she calls him to leave the office.

There are complications, Helen is in labor a long time. When the new baby is presented to John, he checks her limbs and configurations. He does not touch her, tells Helen when she wakes up that she has had a fine little girl. He has to return to the office but will visit her each night. Helen must remain in the hospital an extra five days.

John drives down from Schenectady every evening after work. Helen's mother, who has come to take care of John and the house, help Helen, cooks his dinner and he drives to Albany. After the five extra days he brings Helen and the baby home. It is a Saturday, John has missed only two hours of work the entire time. He finishes that year, as he always does, with the fewest missed hours of work in the company.

They are not rich, the Reillys. They are, in fact, poor for members of the white-collar middle-class in mid-twentieth century America. Both come from working-class backgrounds, both were Depression children. John's grandfather emigrated from Ireland in the last great famine, was a day laborer in America all his life. John's father became a fireman, retired early, failed in many business ventures, and died young at the start of the Great Depression. Before his father died, John left school to work at a local electric company after his father's final business disaster. He always tells his daughter that going to work for the small company was the most important event in his life.

"I learned about the electric business from the ground up, and that kept me employed when others were laid off. Whatever you decide to do, Cassandra, learn everything there is to know about it. You'll be far ahead of others who waste their time."

The local electric company is bought by a larger regional company that has a union. John refuses to join the union, rises slowly to be a second-level manager. His paycheck rises even more slowly, but he saves, invests in municipal bonds, and by the time he meets and marries Helen he has a second-hand car and has bought the small house his father could only rent. The regional company merges with a larger corporation that could cover the nation. This merger is reversed by President Franklin Roosevelt. John never forgives the Democrats for such stupid meddling.

"It's all to curry to the weak. It harms the strong who make the country a better place for everyone."

Unlike most of her friends and relatives, Cassandra grows up in her own house with a father who never misses a day of work, and a mother who is a good mother and who very much misses her days of work. John and Helen have talked, decided that through Cassandra's college years the bottom line is that the family will be better off concentrating on John's career while Helen cares for Cassie. They all will have a much better chance, especially Cassandra, of rising out of poverty that way.

The house has only two bedrooms, and the rooms are small, but they are all there—parlor, kitchen, dining room, cellar, an attic, a detached garage, and an acre of land. The attic can be expanded, the cellar improved, and rooms added on. The attic is never expanded, the cellar is not improved, no rooms are added. John puts his money into making the house free and clear of debt. It is his fortress, a castle for three against the marauding of the *others*—the rich and grasping, the poor and desperate.

Inside the fortress of the small house the celebrations, ceremonies and rituals are few and fixed. Church each Sunday, with instruction for Cassandra before mass. Not the church John's parents had gone to, not the church all his relatives go to, but one where the priest is an older, more reserved man, and where some people from John's department at GE go. (John has moved to General Electric soon after the war. With the meddling of Roosevelt, opportunities closed up at the regional electric company. He stays through the war because the regional company is essential for the war effort, but then accepts an offer at giant GE on the same level of middle man-

agement. John is not ambitious, his schooling is unusually meager
for his work, so he does not advance much at all.)

Holiday visits to and from their relatives where Cassandra runs
wild with her cousins, Helen cooks and gossips in the kitchen with
the women, and John sits with the men in the living room. They talk
about sports and politics, the other men. John is silent. He knows
little about sports, and he does not speak when he does not know.
The other men are firemen, union workers, farm hands, fools who
vote the democratic ticket, and John doesn't argue with fools. Birthday parties for Cassandra and her cousins and school friends are
held after school before John arrives home, or on Saturdays when
he does his household repairs, comes in for the cake, his tools in his
hand. Saturday evenings at the movies, and John treats at the soda
fountain afterwards.

"The three of us," John says. "That's all we need."

Cassandra needs something else. She does not know what.

"A baseball glove?" Helen says. "Do girls play baseball now,
honey?"

"I'm playing with the boys. It's fun."

She plays shortstop in the sandlot games with only five or six
players on a side, fields well but her hitting is weak. That's fine for
the pickup games, she is smart and uses her wits and gets on base
enough. But when the boys start to play in real games, with nine on
a side against opponents from other schools and neighborhoods,
she is not able to keep up.

"What in heaven's name is Motocross, honey?" Helen wonders.

Motocross is Cassandra's first fight with her father. He is a doting
father, helpful with her schoolwork, patient in explaining the world
and its questions, indulgent of her intense childhood needs and
desires. But there are limits he cannot go beyond, principles he
must uphold.

"I won't waste money, Cassandra. Those bicycles are too expensive for something you won't be able to do. I've watched those
'meets' at the park, and there aren't any races for girls. You'd have to
race against boys, it would be a waste of money."

He is not a cold man, John, it is simply that he has such a strong
sense of the limits of their money. There is only so much money for
them each year, no one but themselves to keep them from poverty,
and so many dangers, so many potential attacks from both others
and nature. Helen wants to tell John that Cassandra does not need

to win, only to be part of the races, but she can't. She knows that is not something John could understand.

"I hate you! I hate you!"

Cassandra cries for days, but she is young, John and Helen know she will get over it. They continue their Saturday evenings at the movies, the holidays with relatives, Cassandra's birthday parties, church. John never misses a day of work, Cassandra goes to junior high school and high school, meets new friends.

In her second year of high school, with two of her new friends, she gets a part-time job at an expensive restaurant. John is pleased. He sees that his talk of the need to work hard, save her money, build a secure position is bearing fruit. A year later he is not pleased. Cassie has saved her money, so have her friends. They have worked after school and all one summer at the restaurant, learned a great deal, and decide to start an after-school catering business for teen-age parties. One friend's dad will lend them some extra money, "And we can use our own kitchens to cook and all that!" They even have a name: Teen-For-Teen Party Gourmets. All three have decided this will be their life's work. They will find the best college restaurant programs. They will work, study, open their own restaurant.

John congratulates them on their enterprise, then considers the problems. "I don't think you can use your home kitchens, too much conflict when you have to fill an order at the same time as your mothers cook dinner, and the state will want to regulate and inspect your kitchens. You'll have to lease facilities, deal with inspectors. At least a year's lease. Are you sure there's enough market? Have you estimated what sales you can actually expect? What about competition? And who will your suppliers be? You'll have to line them up, find out what their terms of payment are. You'll need credit at a local bank, and insurance. Fire and business insurance are very important."

"Sure, Dad, but isn't it the greatest idea you ever heard?"

"I'm not sure the restaurant business is a good risk. Seems I've heard most fail the first year, and a mighty low percentage succeed over all. It seems a risky business. Too risky I'd say for someone just starting. You better study all the statistics."

The girls plan and research until the first excitement wears off. The other girls become nervous, talk to the other parents. They give up the idea of Teen-For-Teen Party Gourmets. Everyone still thinks it a great name, maybe they'll do it when they're older, if they decide to go to restaurant school in college. There are other exciting subjects to study. The parents of one of the girls really want her to study medicine.

"Couldn't you have encouraged us, Dad? Or just said nothing, you know? Let us try?"

"I'm sorry, Cassandra. I can't stand by and let you make that kind of mistake. If you don't understand the pitfalls and dangers of whatever you want to do, you'll always fail."

"We'd have learned the pitfalls and dangers ourselves, Dad! We'd have tried. Maybe we'd have succeeded!"

"You'd simply lose money."

"It was our money. So we lost it, big deal. What's a little money?"

"Money is nothing," John says, "unless you don't have it."

Cassandra cries. "You could have helped us try, Dad."

"No," John says, "I couldn't."

The time comes for Cassie to go to college. She has done well in high school, but knows she has no special talents or aptitudes. Except working with people. She decides she wants to study sociology and political science and be a social worker.

"Social work is a very low-paying field, Cassandra. It's all government as near as I can tell, local government at that. On that level government pay is ridiculous."

"I want to do something useful, add a little to the world."

"Wasting your time wet-nursing the lazy, drunk and useless I wouldn't call useful for anybody. Not even them. It only takes away whatever hope they have of climbing out of their misery."

"Maybe just a little less misery would be adding something," Cassandra says.

"What is this 'adding something' you talk about? The world is the world. You give to one, you have to take from another. That's science. The law of conservation of matter and energy. If you want to add, add to yourself and the family. I won't be here forever. Women are doing very well in many fields these days. If you want me to pay for Syracuse, you'll have to study something practical, something with a good future. Accounting, perhaps, you always liked math. Business Administration would be good. Even the Humanities. A good base for a wife and mother, helps the children later."

Cassandra says, "You know about *entropy,* Dad? You talked about science, you know? I mean, entropy says everything gets less, disappears. Mostly into heat. We don't add anything we won't stay the same, we'll disappear, Dad. We have to add—"

"All the more reason to make sure you keep everything you have. What other people have, you can't have. That's the only real law of the world, never mind your *entropy.*"

"All the more reason to add anything new you can."

"Do that then. But do it on your own. Not at my expense."

Cassie is too young. John stands firm, talks to her all that senior year. She doesn't want to go anywhere except Syracuse. Her friends are all going there. She likes reading, literature, so she majors in the Humanities. At Syracuse. Harold is there doing research on old furniture. They meet at a party when she is a junior. Her senior year she spends more time with Harold than she does on her classes, has her worst year in school. They marry as soon as she graduates, move to Utica where Harold is expanding his dad's old woodworking shop into a furniture company. John and Harold get along fine.

The new Santa Barbara Rescue Mission was on Salsipuedes Street near the freeway overpass. Nurse Janet Steiner wasn't there. She was looking for a pregnant woman who hadn't checked in with her, might be at the old Rescue Mission off lower State. When I got there, the usual line of ragged men leaned against the wall.

"Saw Nurse down to the harbor beach," someone said.

It's the least-used beach, the harbor. Two homeless men rummaged in the trash baskets. Nurse Steiner had given one of them antibiotic for an infected toe. He showed me the toe.

"She maybe go down East Beach."

Far down East Beach a woman in slacks with a large case at her feet talked to a group sprawled where the sand met a patch of coarse grass. As I arrived, she reached up to touch the neck of a big man who stood alone at the edge of the group. He leaped back and erupted into a violent whirlwind.

"Shit . . . shit . . . shit . . ." Arms waving, he backed across the sand to a sleeping bag and overstuffed backpack. "Get away! Get away! All of you! Don't none of you touch my stuff! Get off the goddamn beach. It's my beach, you all get off!"

The nurse followed him. "Bill, all I want to do is—"

"Goddamn shit! Goddamn!"

One of the group called, "Hey Bill, she only want to fix your fucking neck."

"Fuck you! Fuck you! Get the fuck off my beach! Go on!"

The group laughed. The nurse turned on them. The rage in her eyes silenced them. They stared sullen out to sea in the winter morning sunlight. A solitary fishing trawler threw white water from its bow out on the swell beyond an oil platform. Far out, the Channel Islands were clear. The nurse turned back to the big man. He brushed at his eyes, walked away to the trees along Cabrillo Boulevard. The nurse walked with him, talked.

The group on the grass noticed me and my empty sleeve.

"You want somethin'?"

"Only the nurse."

"She ain't here," a woman said.

Privacy and suspicion. On the streets no one knows, no one talks. At the trees along Cabrillo the bearish man hugged the nurse, but shook his head. She went on talking. The man went on shaking his head. The nurse came back to her carrying case. If she had seen me she gave no sign that I was anything unusual among the homeless. No one talks, no one sees.

"Nurse Steiner?"

She bent down to her case, removed bandages and a bottle of disinfectant, closed the case.

"My name's Dan Fortune. I'm looking for a man named Jerry. Cassandra Reilly's Jerry. They sent me to you."

She stood. "The police?"

"Mostly Al Benton."

She started back to the trees along Cabrillo Boulevard, the bandage and bottle in one hand, the case in the other.

"I'm a private investigator. I've been hired to help find out what happened to Cassandra Reilly."

"Who hired you? Her parents? The husband?"

"Benton."

We had reached Bill among the trees. "He's got an infected spider bite on his neck, but he's spooked this morning, won't let me treat him. I'll leave the bandage and disinfectant, hope some of his friends will tend him. Keep quiet until I'm finished."

Bill leaned against a tree trunk and stared at the traffic on Cabrillo. She talked to him. He didn't look at her, then grabbed the medicines and stalked away across the sand to his sleeping bag and pack. Nurse Steiner picked up her case.

"My car's over in the lot. Why would Al Benton hire you? Doesn't he trust the police?"

"Probably not," I said. "He thinks the killer could be out to get other street leaders, too."

At her five-year-old Dodge, she said, "What do you think?"

"I don't know enough about Cassandra or her world to think anything yet."

She opened the Dodge trunk, loaded her case, held her keys. "Transient and fragile, that's Cassandra's world. I treat patients, never see them again. I find someone a room, the public aid is cut off, they leave town. I nurse a recovering alcoholic, find him work. He's arrested for sleeping or fighting, goes to jail. He comes out, heads for the nearest bar for some comfort. He's arrested, the cycle starts again."

"They don't have rehabilitation programs for alcoholics?"

"Not enough and too much jail. Most of my patients are suspicious of the whole system. The street people are those the system has failed. Many of them can't handle walls, enclosures, demands. I have too many clients who've been institutionalized. I've had them ask me on the way to the clinic if I was taking them to jail." She closed the car trunk, looked out to sea.

"What started you on this job? Who pays you?"

"The county pays me. Traveling public health nurse. In a way Cassie Reilly started me. She went to the county director of health services and showed him the need for homeless health care. There's plenty of medical care for those who can afford it. Not so much for those who can't." She watched the lone trawler offshore. "I don't know who could have killed Cassandra."

"You know what broke up her marriage?"

"I sensed it was discontent and drinking. That's how a lot of them start and finish. A river of men to forget the days, and a sea of booze to drown the men."

"She said that?"

Nurse Steiner nodded. "She worked well with Benton, but she was the smarter. I'm almost sure she came up with that quotation from Anatole France they used in the fight against the sleeping ban, the one the newspapers all picked up."

"The law, in its majestic equality, forbids the rich as well as the poor to sleep under bridges, to beg in the streets and to steal bread."

"Yes, that one." She walked to the driver's side door. "I remember two things Cassie said always stuck in my mind. What counted wasn't where you slept at night, or what you did to survive, but how you treated other people. She always shared what she had, from a sandwich to her sleeping bag if someone needed it more. No one on the streets killed her, Dan."

"People can hate those who help them," I said. "What was the second thing she said?"

"If you want to change a country you have to first play the game of that country. Most people have accepted the game and its rules. They won't change until they're deconditioned."

"Confrontation won't work."

"That was part of what she was talking about."

"Benton says she had a fight with Jerry."

"Jerry's one of the crippled. Inside. He's younger than Cassie and immature. A child in a lot of ways. Cassie used to say she didn't think he wanted to grow up and that she didn't blame him. I never knew exactly what that meant."

"You know what they fought about?"

"Her independence. He wanted her with him all the time. He's basically gentle, Jerry, but confused and afraid. About a week ago Cassie was at the fig tree when Jerry made a scene. Apparently because she'd been sleeping somewhere else and not with him at 'their place.' She told him he'd been in one of his spells, stolen something, and she couldn't stay with him when he was like that. He was sullen but pleading too, swore he'd be okay. He went away, I haven't seen him since. I was concerned even before Cassie . . . was killed. He's gone from everywhere."

"Does he have a last name?"

"Kohnen." She spelled it for me.

"His 'spells'? What did she mean?"

"Something about his past, being violent. Apparently with her. Angry and stealing things."

"Was she afraid of him, Janet?"

"No. She was worried about him."

"Was she afraid of anyone or anything you know?"

She got into the Dodge. "Only that she was always running from her parents, her former husband."

When I arrived at the tree there was a wedding.

With a trunk circumference over thirty-five feet, branches that spread more than twenty-one thousand square feet, the largest Moreton Bay Fig tree in the northern hemisphere stands on a wedge-shaped plot between the railroad and the freeway near the harbor. Brought as a seedling from Australia in 1876, planted on Southern Pacific land when the SP ran the state, those halcyon days for industrial freebooters with the corporate version of the six-shooter at their hips (and too often killers with real six-shooters to discourage those who couldn't be beaten with money), the tree now spreads its mammoth branches over the domain of the homeless. Here is where they first arrive, where they meet, argue and plan the days. Once the Homeless Coalition tried to force the city to deliver mail to the tree, to accept it as their address for voter registration. Here they are mourned and married.

The wedding party, twenty-five or thirty people scattered on the grass and huge surface roots, had the tree to themselves except for a tourist family. The tourists were nervous, soon left for more understandable surroundings. The street people, long-haired and bearded, some barefoot, one shirtless with massive tattooed arms, were quiet and solemn. Two guitarists played barely loud enough above the constant noise of traffic on the freeway. A bottle of champagne went around, the minister read a poem he had written for the occasion.

In grimy jeans, flannel shirt, and stained suit jacket too small for him, the groom was a smiling man in his forties with a neatly trimmed mustache and a worn face. Younger, the bride held his hand. She had two roses in her disheveled dark blonde hair and a third in the hand not holding his. He slipped a ring on her finger and a beaded necklace over her head. They kissed, smiled, the crowd applauded. The ceremony took ten minutes. There were congratulations and hugs for the bride, the couple left to spend their wedding night in the weeds.

None of the men fitted the description of the vanished Jerry Kohnen. The minister shook his head. "I haven't seen Jerry in a week. Are you police?"

"Private investigator." I said. "Dan Fortune."

He sat down on a giant root. One of the two women in the wedding party offered him the champagne bottle. He smiled, declined. Under thirty, he wore the same clothes as everyone else: jeans, plaid shirt, sandals. He had a beard, needed a bath.

"Is that wedding legal?"

He nodded. "I'm the real thing. Matthew Perkins, doctor of divinity and duly ordained reverend. Found my true calling on the streets. Purgatory to salvation."

"Alcohol?"

He glanced to where the woman still passed the champagne bottle. "Yes, the immediate cause. The real causes run deeper. In my case call it loss of purpose, no one needed or wanted what I was doing. I found us to be a nation with little real belief in the words of our God, only in what He had to offer as the hereafter. It can cause a young man to have doubts, anguish, and a thirst for anesthetic. Here they hear the words."

"Did Cassandra Reilly hear the words?"

"In her own way. She didn't need God or me to tell her."

"How about Jerry Kohnen?"

Perkins looked to where the two guitarists had slung their guitars and the wedding party was drifting away. Four of the men didn't leave, talked to some newcomers who watched me and the minister. The shirtless man with tattoos on his thick arms was one of them. Others arrived as if some signal had been sent out.

"Not everyone hears the words even on the streets. Some hear nothing at all. That's Jerry Kohnen. Some hear a voice with a different message."

"Just like in normal life."

The group under the tree had grown to ten. Most of them wore parts of military uniforms. Army shirts, navy jackets, Marine Corps pants, camouflage shirts and floppy fatigue hats of the style worn now. Gear from Vietnam on men too young to have been there. Real or fake, uniforms were a good angle. People give more to veterans. There was no reason to expect street people to be any better than the rest of the country. They walked toward us.

"I think you'd better leave, Mr. Fortune."

"I haven't found Jerry Kohnen," I said.

I wondered if Cassie Reilly had believed in the redemption of the road, the purification of the streets, the insight of denial and the revelation of refusal. Rejection and suffering produce torturers as well as healers, tyrants as much as saints.

"What's this cop want, Perkins?"

He was the shirtless one with the thick arms who had been at the wedding. The tattoos were the Marine Corps emblem and a Nazi swastika. He would not have taken well to discipline.

"Fortune's not the police, Temple."

The big man saw my empty sleeve. "Where you lose the wing?"

One of the others said, "You a vet, mister?"

"World War Two. Any of you know where Jerry Kohnen is?"

"He ain't a cop, why's he askin' questions?" A fierce-eyed black in a Vietnam fieldjacket with an 82nd Airborne patch said. In his mid-twenties. Twelve when Vietnam ended.

"You lose it in combat?" the big man, Temple, said.

"He ain't a cop, what the hell is he?"

Perkins said, "A private investigator looking for the man who murdered Cassie Reilly. He needs all the help we can give."

Temple stared only at my empty sleeve. They related to my missing arm, maybe to my old clothes, but not to my questions.

"Fuck Cassie Reilly."

"He a private cop, who the shit hired him?"

I said, "Al Benton hired me to find Cassandra Reilly's killer before he kills again, kills more street people."

"Benton," the fake 82nd Airborne black spat in the dirt.

The shirtless Temple looked up from my missing arm. "Al Benton's a fucking ass-kisser."

"Go slow, go nowhere."

"Talk gets you damn all shit."

They were all relatively sober. Only the shirtless Temple seemed to have been drinking. They became silent. Not a friendly silence. Matthew Perkins stood close to me. A police cruiser came across the tracks on Montecito Street. Someone pulled the shirtless Temple away toward the railroad tracks and the dry ditch of Mission

Creek. The others scattered. Only the oldest, who could have been in Korea, still faced me, and a young one with a twitching mouth who had said nothing, only stared at my missing arm.

"You really lose it in the war? I mean, you get it blown off or something? I was in the Army. I didn't like it."

The older man said, "You lookin' for Jerry Kohnen?"

"To talk to him," I said. "Your friends didn't like Cassie Reilly."

"They're mostly talk."

The young one still twitched, still stared at my missing arm. "Temple got kicked out of the Marines. He don't let people tell him what he got to do. Everyone tells you what to do. You don't do what they want they hurt you. I don't like bein' hurt. It must of hurt. Your arm, I mean."

I said, "Is Jerry violent?"

"Who Jerry?" the young one said, looked up at me.

"Kohnen."

"He's a goddamn fag," the young one said.

The older man said, "Jerry's kind of a con artist, you know? Too young for the Reilly woman. Got to of been conning her."

The young man said, "I'm gonna have my own business. I had a store, my brother stole it. I'm gonna get another store. You got to work for yourself. Help everybody like President Reagan says. You like President Reagan? I'm sure gonna vote for him."

The older one said, "Reagan ain't president no more."

"He is so president. You think I don't know who's the goddamn president? I'm gonna vote for him."

I left them still arguing about who was president.

7

There are three pawnshops on lower State Street, and one of them isn't really a pawnshop anymore. Two had big ghetto blaster radios, but none of the portables had been pawned anytime in the last year. None of them had had a wedding ring pawned in the last few days.

I thought about Cassandra Reilly and a man who had to have her with him, a man who couldn't be alone. A man who wasn't ready to rejoin any world, who she would have known she couldn't take back in with her if she came off the streets. A man who had "spells" and was violent toward her when he had one. I would have moved, even temporarily, to a new hideout of my own, told no one. I would have had to face the fact that I would have to leave him behind on the streets. But I wasn't Cassandra Reilly, a woman who, according to Al Benton, had found life among the people of the streets hard to leave behind even if she went on working for them.

At the Bank of America branch on lower State the manager told me it was utterly impossible for anyone to withdraw money from someone else's passbook account even with the passbook. He was pretty upset about the whole idea, didn't much like the cut of my credentials.

"Your tellers know all depositors by name and on sight? Would recognize them all?"

"No, of course not, but—"

"So if a woman came in, had the passbook, and her signature matched your card?"

"That's forgery! I—"

"That's what it would be," I agreed. "Say it was a good forgery, the woman even looked and acted like the depositor, she didn't try to take too much out at any one time?"

"Well, I suppose a professional criminal might—"

"So maybe you could check the account? Maybe I could talk to your tellers? Or I could bring Sergeant Chavalas and make it all official."

He agreed to check Cassandra Reilly's account, let me talk to all the tellers. None of them remembered Cassandra coming in to make a withdrawal recently. None of them remembered anyone named Cassandra Reilly at all, and they said my description could fit half their customers. It was a busy branch with many small accounts. Cassandra Reilly's was a very small account. The last withdrawal had been over three weeks ago. One of the tellers did remember something odd.

"There was a man came in and said his girlfriend was sick, could he maybe make a withdrawal for her if he took a slip and got it signed by her."

"When was this?"

"Yesterday morning, or maybe it was Tuesday, I'm not sure. It was early, I'm sure of that. After noon it gets so crowded I don't remember individuals at all, you know?"

"What did you tell him?"

"I told him no way, of course. I mean, not without he had a power of attorney and all that."

"What did he look like?"

"Gee, I don't remember, you know? We get a hundred a day comes through the line."

The liquor store managers didn't want to look all through their recent credit card receipt slips. I explained pleasantly that I could go to Sergeant Chavalas and get him to come down and ask but I didn't want to bother the police and, besides, having the cops around was bad for business in this neighborhood, didn't they think? After a certain amount of discussion, some of it heated on their part, and agreement that, yes, they did keep the slips for a while even though most posted the information back to the credit institution electronically now, all but one of them saw my point and agreed to look for a slip from the last two days in the name of Cassandra Reilly.

There are a lot of liquor stores below Anapamu from Milpas to De La Vina. It took me the rest of the morning. It would have taken me all day and into tomorrow but Jerry Kohnen turned out to be a man who didn't risk himself far from home. The slip I wanted was in the first liquor store on Haley Street.

"Four bottles of white port. I remember, 'cause it was four bottles, and 'cause they'd been in here before. I mean, I kind of recognized the guy."

"Guy?"

"Yeh. The woman looked the same too, had the right I.D. and all. What's the problem?"

"The problem is the woman was dead at the time."

"Oh, yeah? Gee, I'm sorry."

"Can you describe the man?"

"Sure. A nice lookin' guy if you like the kid type. Maybe thirty, maybe older but sure don't look no older. I mean, the woman she looked thirty-five, forty, so maybe the guy is older, you know, but he sure don't look it. Small, kind of heavy, but pretty strong lookin'. Funny eyes, looks all around all the time. Kind of blond, wearin' a baseball cap. Jacket, cord pants kind of old and beatup. Work boots but don't look much like he works. I mean, you know, he looks like a guy needs white port."

"No name?"

The clerk thought. "The woman called him by somethin'. Joe or . . . Jimmy . . . Jerry! Yeah, Jerry. I mean, I think it was Jerry, you know? Like that anyway."

Alone in his office, Gus Chavalas rubbed his eyes. He'd been leaning back at his desk, turned to look out at the bare branches of his jacaranda in the winter afternoon sunlight. He listened as if half asleep, continued to watch the jacaranda while I told him what I'd found in Alameda Park and on lower State Street.

"Kohnen, yeah, we got the name this morning too, and we found her wedding ring."

I sat and looked out at his tree. "That mean you found Jerry already? Like the parents and husband?"

He smiled. "Nurse Steiner called after you'd talked to her, gave us the name." A bird hopped in the bare branches of the tree out in the sun. A small bird with a red crown patch. "We picked up a drunk trying to sell the ring for booze out in Isla Vista. It has her name engraved inside, Miller thought he'd struck gold. The drunk said he'd bought it from a drifter in Santa Maria last night, the drifter had bought it from a guy down here. The drunk proved he hadn't even been in Santa Barbara the night of the murder. Miller's still working to find the drifter who sold it in Santa Maria, find out who he got the ring from."

"But you figure it has to be Kohnen?"

"The missing boyfriend's always a prime." He finally turned from his jacaranda, faced me with his forearms on his desk and hands tented. "If the nurse hadn't called, because she figured if you needed the name we did too, it would have taken us a week to dig out Kohnen's name. The street people mostly won't talk to us unless we really corner them. Not even Benton. Especially Benton. We're the enemy."

"That's what experience has taught them, Sergeant. The police bring most of their trouble. And they're scared by what they don't know. They don't know who killed Cassandra Reilly or why and any cop they see could be trying to pin it on them. Benton's afraid she was killed because of her activism, and I've got a hunch he thinks a cop could have killed her. A lot of them probably do."

Chavalas watched the small bird in his tree. "It's happened, I won't deny it. Give anyone power and a gun and you never know for sure how he's going to turn out. You just keep on trying." He swung back to me again. "Anyway, Jerry Kohnen looks like our man. Now all we got to do is find him. We'll have to dig what we can get out of them, you can maybe do better, help out. If he isn't already a thousand miles away. Miller figures he is."

"You don't think he's left town?"

"From what you say about the bank account and the credit card, it would have to have been today, and we've been watching and stopping everyone who looks like a street person trying to leave town since yesterday. If he did slip out, he sure didn't go home."

"Home?"

Chavalas nodded. "Up north around King City. Wife and a couple of kids. They haven't seen him in almost a year. They miss him."

"A year? That recent?"

"He comes and goes, the wife says. Sometimes stays a year, sometimes a week. She never knows when he'll come, how long he'll stay, or why he goes. She doesn't know much about him at all. He never told her."

I heard it in his voice.

"But you do know something about him."

"Yeah, we got the report from Sacramento maybe an hour ago. We know a lot about Jerry Kohnen now."

8

At the time they decide the kid is screwing up everything and has to go, Reena Murphy and Candy Lou Montoya have opened an upscale dress shop in Fresno, and Candy Lou works on the side in a local restaurant to help pay the bills. Their long-range plan is for Reena to marry her live-in boyfriend and tap into the equity in his house and body-shop business to make the dress store go, so Reena has to work on the boyfriend and doesn't have time to take an outside job.

"I know the shop's going to make it big, honey. I mean, let's get married and go for it, okay?"

"I dunno, Reen," Steve, the boyfriend, says. "I mean, not the dress place, that's gonna be a winner sure. It's Joey, you know? I mean, I guess he still misses his mother and all."

"Maybe you miss his mother too. Maybe I should just walk away."

"Aw, Reen, come on. Joey'll come around. You just got to give him time, you know? I mean, what's the big rush?"

Reena sits on his lap in the big living room of the house his first wife's Uncle Mack had given them when Joey was born. Luckily, the uncle died before Joey's mother got sick, so when she died Steve got to keep the house.

"You ever think maybe I just want to be with you like all the time?" Reena says, runs her tongue around his ear.

"Hell, you're with me all the time now."

"That ain't the same thing. I mean, I ain't sure you really want me, just livin' here like maybe I don't belong or something. Like you don't trust me enough to marry me."

"Just give Joey some more time, honey. Okay?"

It isn't okay. Not for Reena and Candy Lou. And it gets worse when the dress shop doesn't catch on right away, doesn't start to build as fast as they'd hoped. Part of the problem is location, and part is name recognition, and they don't have money to move or to advertise enough where it counts.

"Why don't you just talk to Steve?" Candy Lou says. "Tell him we need the money right now."

"I can't do that, for Christ sake. He'd get the idea I was just after his cash. You know guys. They start thinking you maybe don't love 'em for their great bods and wavy brown hair an' they're long gone."

"So how's it different after you get married?"

"After, half of everything's yours. You're a team, right? In it together. He got to help out, right? He can't let the shop go belly up, not his wife's business, right? Besides, after, if he don't give you what you got to have, you don't give him what he got to have, and he can't just walk out like he can now, right? Not in California, anyway."

"So marry him."

"I'm working on it."

"Work fast, honey, we're gettin' out of time. What I drag down at the diner ain't goin' to cut it."

The truth is, Joey doesn't like Reena, not one damn, and she doesn't think a lot of the lousy kid either. A nasty little brat always making dirty remarks about her, putting her down, and whining about his goddamned mother. Always in the way, hanging around the house to keep her and Steve apart, banging on the door when they're right in the middle. Steve just won't stand up to the kid, lets him run the whole damned show, and Reena doesn't see it changing when she and Steve get married.

"He's nine, for God's sake, Reen. He only lost his mother two years ago. I mean, with me gone all day workin' overtime to build the shop, Joey was real close to Lise. He'll get close to you too, you'll see."

"She was closer to the kid than she was to you, if you ask me. That's kind of sick, you know? I ain't like that."

"It'll be okay. He just needs to get over Lise."

"He needs to get over ownin' you, Steve. What happens when we have kids? What's he gonna do then? I want us to have kids together, honey. Your kids and mine. I'm scared what Joey'll do to a new kid."

"That's crazy! He won't do nothing, you'll see. I'll talk to him. Give it a couple or six months, okay?"

"Sure, honey. I just want what's good for you."

Reena smiles, but she doesn't smile inside or when she talks to Candy Lou. "He won't do diddly shit, Cand. The kid got to go."

Steve is plain too goddamn weak to tell Joey to shape up and make it stick, and Reena doesn't want to put in the time to find another guy. She's worked too goddamned hard on Steve.

"It's him or us," Candy Lou says. "You grab for what you want in this world or you don't get nothing."

Jerry Kohnen's mother works in the same restaurant with Candy Lou. Roseanne Kohnen is only a few years older than Reena and Candy Lou, is divorced from Jerry's no-account trucker father, sometimes double-dates with Candy Lou and even triple-dates when Reena and Steve come along. A tall redhead, she has a lot of dates, so works mostly afternoons and evenings and Jerry sort of takes care of himself before and after school.

"He's a good kid," she tells the other women. "Maybe he's not so smart, but he's big for his age, takes care of himself."

Jerry isn't really a big boy, but he is muscular from working out with weights alone in the house after school, and he is advanced socially. Sexually, anyway. Not exactly streetwise, more like bedroom and backroom wise. Way-of-the-world wise. How to fool teachers and principals and storekeepers and make a fast buck. What a real man wants. Sex and money.

"Never gets into trouble like a lot of boys is alone a lot," Roseanne tells Reena and Candy Lou. "I mean, like I always know where Jerry is, and he keeps himself in shape."

Where Jerry is a lot of the time is alone and awake in his narrow bedroom when Roseanne comes home with her men. When the men leave in the morning. When Roseanne whispers and giggles on the other side of the thin wall and the men laugh. When the men hit her with the flat of their hands to her flesh and she moans and whimpers and then the sounds of lips and tongues. The sound of breathing, long and hard, short and quick. The moans and the sharp cries and the heavy grunts. The creak of the bed, the shaking of the thin walls themselves when the bodies roll against it. The final gasps and hoarse delights. The grateful whispers of Roseanne and the deep-voice victory of the man.

"That's some mother you got, boy. You treat her right now. I come back, she better say you been treatin' her right, hear?"

Where Jerry is, sometimes, is talking to the men Roseanne brings home early, or who don't leave until after Roseanne has gone to work. The special men. The men who come more than once. Who come sometimes for a year or more.

"You sayin' you got no woman, Jerry? Big boy like you?"

"Hell, thirteen ain't too young to get started, boy. Me, I was twelve first time. She was older 'n real nice to me."

"Fifteen and you don't have a girl? That's too bad, Jerry. Doesn't your mother know any girls your age?"

Jerry's mother doesn't know any girls or boys his age. Only her dates and her friends. There are no girls in the rundown bungalow court where they live, and when Jerry tries to talk to girls in school they laugh at him. He is weird. He is slow and dumb. He is too serious, creepy. Only his mother's dates and friends talk to him, and it is Reena who sees Jerry's muscles and silences, sees the look in Jerry's eyes, and gets the idea.

"He's big as a man, Cand."

"I dunno." Candy Lou studies Jerry when they all go over to Roseanne's house one night. "The more people the more chance of trouble. We can handle it ourselves."

"I ain't so sure the two of us can handle the goddamn kid at all. It got to look accidental, right? We got to be somewhere else, so we got to have help. Jerry's perfect. Dumb enough and hot as hell to trot."

"I dunno, Reen."

"You see those eyes look at us? All we got to do is tell him how much fun we'll all have soon as we get rid of the kid."

A Friday when Roseanne works the afternoon and evening shift at the restaurant, and Candy Lou knows she has a heavy date after and won't be home until late, they pick Jerry up on his way home from school. They tell him Joey is ruining everything for Reena, just like the smartass girls in school ruin everything for Jerry, how they'll all have fun once they're rid of the snotty kid.

Jerry isn't so sure. He likes Reena and Candy Lou, but he isn't sure about what they want him to do.

"It ain't like we're askin' you to really do anything much, Jerry. We'll handle most of it. We just need a man for some muscle, you know? A strong man like you, Jerry."

"Gee, I don't know, Reena," Jerry says.

Reena says to Candy Lou, "You're gonna have to show the dumb kid what it's all about, Cand."

"Why me?"

"You're younger, you ain't got Steve to worry he'll blab to. Hey, he's a big kid, you teach him how to do it you'll have more of a ball than he will."

Candy Lou decides the idea is a kick, she's never done it with a kid don't know which end is up.

"Christ, Reen, he really don't know which way to turn me!"

The two women have a real laugh over that, but Candy Lou gets to like making Jerry do anything she wants with her and for her, goes over and crawls into bed with him after school almost every afternoon that fall. At first, she tells Reena, she not only has to show him where to put it, she even has to put it in herself! She scares Jerry, both the women do. Scare him and please him too. Reena tells him all the stuff he'll have after they get rid of Joey. Like a VCR and a stereo and all the great records he likes to listen to on his radio when he's home alone after school before Candy Lou comes over and they go to bed and do all the stuff Candy Lou shows him she likes him to do. Even the first scary time it feels great, being inside Candy Lou like that, her playing with him and showing him what she likes him to do to her before she lets him go inside her. It gets better all the time, and Jerry tries to tell the kids at school but most of them don't listen, especially the girls who call him weird. Then he gets so he doesn't care. He feels bigger than all of them. He has a real girl, and he really wants to help Reena and Candy Lou get what they want and give him all the great stuff and make him feel good the way Candy Lou does.

It is right after Thanksgiving when Reena and Candy Lou figure out the plan to get rid of Joey. Steve is extra busy at the body shop with all the accidents around the holidays. He has to work overtime when business is good. So Reena takes Joey the places he has to go, the snotty kid is real smug about ordering her around. They go Christmas shopping over at the Mall by the river that Saturday. They've had some heavy rains and a good early snowfall in the mountains, the river is running high and hard. Reena parks in a remote corner of the parking area under the Mall. Joey likes to do anything Reena tells him not to, so after they finish shopping and are back at the car, she says she's forgotten something and tells Joey to wait in the car and be sure to stay away from the high river.

After Reena has gone back to the Mall, where she makes sure a lot of people she knows see her, Joey gets out of the car and runs from the garage down to the river. The river bank is rocky and steep, Candy Lou and Jerry are waiting. Halfway down the slippery bank Joey sees Candy Lou, realizes instantly and in terror what she is there for, tries to scramble back up.

"Grab him, Jerry!"

Jerry tackles the smaller boy, drags him struggling back down the bank. Candy Lou smashes a rock against Joey's head. Together they hold the boy under water until he stops breathing. They push his body out into the fast-moving river where it vanishes instantly in the surging white water. They scramble back up the bank, run hard to Candy Lou's car, and drive home completely forgetting to go to Reena's car and tell her everything is okay. At home, Jerry shakes so much Candy Lou can't even make him get it up until she holds him like a baby and tells him everything is going to be fine. Everything will be great now. Reena will marry Steve, the dress shop will be a smash, they'll get rich and give Jerry what they promised, everyone will get everything they want.

Everything, of course, is far from fine.

Reena has to call Candy Lou's place from the Mall. Once she gets the good news, she hurries in tears to Mall security and reports Joey missing. She tells the security men, and later the police, that when she returned to her car Joey was gone. She couldn't find him in the Mall anywhere. She is so distraught they have to call Steve to come and get her and bring a man to drive her car. She tells the police how guilty she feels for leaving Joey alone in the car. It is all her fault. If only she had taken Joey with her.

The police and Steve listen. Steve is sympathetic. The police are wary. They have searched the Mall area and already found the suspicious signs of the struggle on the river bank, the bloody stone that is not where it is supposed to be, some torn cloth that later proves to be from Jerry's sweatshirt. Candy Lou, who was supposed to have been in San Francisco, has been seen leaving her car near the Mall by someone who knows her. Jerry has been seen with her. Reena has been seen calling Candy Lou from the pay telephone only moments before she reported Joey missing, making it almost impossible that she went back to her car to find Joey missing.

When the body is found over a week later floating in San Francisco Bay, the wound on its head is inconsistent with a fall. In Joey's shirt pocket is a business card from the restaurant where Candy Lou and Roseanne work. No one ever finds out why Joey had the card, but it leads the police to Roseanne. She is stunned, tells the police that Jerry has been acting scared and coming to the restaurant to talk to Candy Lou ever since the night of Joey's disappearance. The police talk to Jerry who, with both him and Roseanne crying, soon tells the whole story.

Reena and Candy Lou are arrested, Candy Lou at San Francisco International where she had run the instant she heard that the police were at the restaurant to talk to Roseanne. Steve stands behind Reena, hires a lawyer. Candy Lou's parents hire a lawyer. The public defender represents Jerry, calls on the assistant D.A. handling the case and points out Jerry's age, family background and environment, isolation from the mainstream of his high school, and Candy Lou's initiation of the psychologically damaged boy into the delights of the bed.

A plea bargain is made. Jerry pleads guilty to second-degree murder, testifies against Reena and Candy Lou. He breaks down many times on the stand, crying and looking at Candy Lou who screams at him. The two women are convicted, get life without possibility of parole because it was a murder for gain. Jerry is committed to a California Youth Authority facility until he is twenty-three. He cries when the bus takes him away, looks out the bus window at Roseanne and all the other mothers, but it is Candy Lou he is searching for.

The first liquor store on Haley was doing its usual brisk business. Most of it was cheap white port, beer and muscatel, but they overcharged the street winos and it all adds up at the bottom line. The same clerk was behind the counter.

"They ain't been in since I talked to you."

It helps to have a good memory in a slum business where you run under-the-counter tabs to keep the poor on the hook. What you lose on the few who disappear into the wide blue, you up tenfold on those who are forced to come back because you're the only one who'll sell to them when the desperation is on.

"I been watching. Must of been a good forgery, sailed right through the company."

"It won't when they send the monthly bill to a dead woman."

He grinned. "That'll be a kick."

Outside I sat in my Tempo. Odds were if Jerry Kohnen hadn't slipped out of town yesterday he was still here. The police knew how to cover the exits, especially for a man without a car. He'd made his wine score in this store close to his home territory, which wasn't smart in the first place, but people are creatures of habit and the easiest path. It was odds-on he'd stick with what had been a success.

Waiting and watching is one thing that still makes me miss a cigarette. The other is nerves, tension. Boredom and anxiety, the twin poles of the twentieth century. Work is the best cure. If it fails, you can think. I thought about Jerry Kohnen, and about Gus Chavalas. *Who really got life without parole in the murder of that kid, Dan?* That was what Chavalas had said when he finished his story of Jerry Kohnen. Reena and Candy Lou, despite the sentence, would get out some day or die in prison violence. Roseanne Kohnen would have more dates. Steve would have more kids. But Jerry Kohnen? *There were two victims in that killing,* Chavalas said, *but only one of them got mourned.*

"You the guy askin' 'bout Jerry Kohnen?"

The fierce-eyed young black in the surplus Nam fieldjacket and 82nd Airborne patch leaned in my open window. He had a short memory, or all whites looked alike to him.

"You know where he is?"

"How much you pay?"

"How much do you know?"

His attention span was too short to negotiate.

"You got twenty?"

I gave him a twenty.

"He sittin' out back o' the Cantina right now." He grinned and hurried away clutching the twenty as if he'd pulled the coup of the decade.

The Cantina was a shabby saloon half a block away where street people hung out. It should have been the first place someone trying to find a street regular would look. The ersatz Viet vet had stumbled over Jerry Kohnen, then stumbled over me, seen a golden opportunity to sell me what he was sure I'd learn on my own any second. Except that the Cantina was about the last place I would look for a street person hiding from the police.

There was a parking area behind the row of buildings that included the Cantina. The man who looked like the description I had of Jerry Kohnen sat in the winter sun like someone who hasn't seen the light for weeks. The other drifters around him were in a heated discussion, but Jerry, if it was him, had his eyes closed, his face up to the sun. Totally at his ease, not a worry in the world. I had to decide whether to call Chavalas, or talk to him first myself. While I thought about it, he stood, said something to the other three, and went inside the Cantina.

I got out to follow him, when he came back out with a woman in black slacks, low black boots and a black high-necked designer top trimmed in silver. Dark-haired and full-faced, she looked a lot like Cassandra Reilly. She wasn't dressed like Cassandra Reilly, and I realized that Jerry Kohnen didn't look like a street person either. Gaudy in beige slacks, a blue blazer that accentuated his flabbiness, yellow shirt too bright for his pale face, tasseled brown shoes. A weak face, almost smug as he and the woman walked to a late model Pontiac with a rental sticker on the rear bumper.

They drove out of the parking area. I followed across to Santa Barbara Street. The Pontiac made no attempt to evade anyone who might be following, turned north. To Micheltorena, St. Francis Hospital and up California Street, Santa Barbara's version of the streets of San Francisco. I had to shift down to keep close. The Pontiac went to the top of California, made the Z-turn and on up to Alameda Padre Serra. Doubled back on APS to Moreno, made a right turn up toward the summit of the Riviera. Twisted past the old Brooks School and the Riviera Theater into the parking lot of the El Encanto Hotel.

The El Encanto has one of the best french-style restaurants in Santa Barbara, especially at lunch when you sit on the terrace and enjoy the view of the town and harbor and ocean through the towering eucalyptus trees. An expensive restaurant. Jerry Kohnen and the woman went in the front entrance past the outdoor concierge desk. From where I parked I could watch the entrance and the parking lot. Unless they jumped off the terrace, they couldn't get past me.

They came back out almost at once. I reached to start my engine, stopped. They didn't head for their car, they headed along the path past the pool toward the cottages where the hotel rooms are at El Encanto. I got out and followed. They strolled past some frame cottages under renovation to the small stucco buildings beyond the pool and a lawn. They didn't look back, wouldn't have known me if they had. They went up the steps of one of the stucco two-unit buildings and in the door of 328. They had a room key.

I had traded in my old revolver for a 9mm Sig-Sauer P230 small enough to hold between my knees to load, light enough to operate with my lone hand, and a lot easier to carry in holster or pocket. There is a time to move on in everything, we all have to change. This time I had it in my pocket, put my hand on it and looked in the window of 328. They were seated on a couch eating soft white bread and slabs of yellow cheese washed down with Coors light and watching television.

I knocked on the door with the pistol. "Hotel management survey. May we ask you some questions concerning your stay?"

"Come back later." The woman had a thick voice.

"I'm sorry, Madam, it must be completed this afternoon. We offer a complimentary split of champagne for your inconvenience and cooperation."

A scrape of furniture on carpet and light footsteps.

"Where's the bubbly, and how many quest—"

Gun out, I pushed in past the woman in the open doorway. Jerry Kohnen, if it was him, sat and stared at me with blank incomprehension. Not like someone who didn't understand what I was doing, but someone not sure of what he was seeing. As if I, and the gun, weren't in focus. The woman knew what she saw.

"He's gonna rob us, Jerry!"

Jerry Kohnen blinked. "What we got to rob?"

He continued to stare at me without moving. A large ghetto blaster stood on the floor in a corner of the room next to an opened back pack. A wallet, passbook, some bills and coins, and a credit card lay on the bare bureau where they'd been dropped. An old suitcase was open on the floor. It was full of stacked *Independents*. I crossed to the bureau and picked up the wallet. It was empty except for two pictures and a driver's license. Cassandra Reilly's license and parents. No matter how bad, we all need a past. If only to run away from.

"She must do a pretty good imitation of Cassie," I said.

The woman said, "He's a cop, Jerry! I told you it wasn't gonna work. It was all his damn idea, mister. He made me do it! Christ, you and your crazy ideas, Jerry. So easy, you said, live high on the hog, you said. Well I ain't gonna—"

"He ain't no cop," Jerry Kohnen said. "Cops got two arms."

He still hadn't moved, and his speech was slow, deliberate. His soft face wasn't alarmed or scared, only confused. Trying to understand what I wanted. I understood why he was still in town. Why he'd been sitting out in the sun behind the Cantina. Why he was dressed the way he was and in the room at the El Encanto. He didn't know the police were looking for him. He didn't know anyone was looking for him. He wasn't hiding, he was pulling a small scam, having a good time on Cassie Reilly's credit card.

"Why'd you kill her, Jerry?"

He lost what color he had in his face. "Kill?"

"Kill?" the woman said. "Kill who? He don't tell me nothin' about no kill! Jerry, you never said nothin'—"

Jerry Kohnen stumbled up from the couch, banged into the low coffee table, almost fell as he faced me with one hand on the low table to steady himself. He talked as he tried to straighten up. "I found her she was already dead! In that park, hiding from me, running out on me. All that blood. She was just lying there under that building. I was scared. Maybe whoever done it was gonna kill me. I ran outside, but they was gone. I didn't see nothing outside. I—"

"Who was gone?"

The woman across the room, her hand over her mouth, edged toward the door without really knowing what she was doing.

"Them. Like they was sort of shadows, you know? Black. I almost didn't—"

I waved the woman back from the door with my new Sig-Sauer. "Sit down, both of you. Start from the beginning. When did you see these shadows in the park?"

The woman got back up. "I don't know a damn thing—"

I waved the pistol. She sat down again. Jerry Kohnen stared at the floor. "She left me alone. I need her, you know? She walks away, leaves me on my own. All we was going to do, her and me, and she walks off. Like we got it all, but she walks away. I can't find her. I tell her, hey, come on, Cass, it's you and me. She says no way José, your screw's loose, I'm out of here. You get your head straight then come find me. I needs her but she walks off."

"That made you mad? You went looking for her?"

The woman said, "His screws're all loose you ask me. I—"

"I took the stuff back I swiped, you know? What was left, you know?" Jerry Kohnen watched his own feet in the elegant brown shoes with the stylish tassels. "She walks out so I go to the mountains a while. I got to eat so I sell some stuff. Alone I'm scared up in the mountains, so I takes back the stuff I ain't sold or eat and I look for her, you know? I look all over. She ain't nowhere she and me goes. I remember that park where that school with the good lunches is. She likes that park 'cause it got juice she can play her blaster. She goes there sometimes when she's mad at me, when she got to be alone a while, you know? I don't know if I should go up there. I say, hey, she walked on me, you know, I don't care she wants to be alone. I got to find her. So I go up there. What can she do me? She'll come back."

His tone and voice had shifted into speaking of Cassie Reilly as if she were still alive. Maybe she still was to him, that was why he hadn't run, didn't know anyone was looking for him. Part of the "spells" Cassie had talked about. Aware of reality, and unaware. The life sentence for Joey's murder, the legacy of Reena and Candy Lou.

He raised his face. His dark, distant eyes were there in the park, looked through the night for Cassie Reilly. "It's real late, you know, but I hear voices. One's Cassie. She's talking to someone inside that platform thing. Then I see them. Maybe two, three. All black. Like they's part of the goddamn night, you know. I think I see them, I ain't sure. Maybe they're shadows, you know? But I ain't taking no chances, I dives under a bush and hides. I listen, but I don't hear nothing. I waits a long time. I crawl where I can see, and they're gone. I didn't hear them go, I didn't hear nothing. I mean, no cars, no more voices, no running. Maybe they was never there."

The woman said, "Maybe you ain't all there. Jesus, what the hell am I doing here? Look, mister, it was all his stupid—"

"What did you do when they were gone, Jerry?"

"Nothing." He looked down at his expensive shoes again. They had to have been bought with Cassie Reilly's cash or credit card.

"I'm too scared. It got to be Cassie in there. But I watch for them shadows to come back. I don't see nothing, so I gets up and goes in to talk to Cassie." His head came up once more, mouth open, eyes terrified. "She's all blood. Blood all over. Everything's knocked around. I mean, she's dead, you know? I talk to her. 'Cassie, it's me, Jerry. Hey, I'm sorry I had a spell. I'm okay now. I'm back.' She don't say nothing. She's dead, you know. I shake her, push her. She's all soft, like she got no bones, like she's nothing."

His hands reached out, shook the air like a rag doll. I watched him. He was still there in the room under the bandstand. Or in his denial, in the illusion of the room his mind had invented and believed. Or in the lie he had invented and almost believed. Or in the lie he didn't believe but acted.

"She's dead, you know? She don't need no radio or wallet or that ring. Money and credit card and the passbook. She'd of wanted me to take them before the cops or someone got them. I grab the wallet, pick up the blaster, and get out of there. I ain't lettin' the cops find me."

"And decided to have a ball on Cassie's money and card."

He nodded, almost eager. "I was gonna sell the blaster, you know? Only no one wanted it. I sold the ring to a guy. I was gonna toss the card and the passbook. I asked the bank I could use the book. They said no way. I couldn't figure no way to use the card, then I remembered Dorrie." He grinned at the woman.

"I should of had my head examined." She whined to me. "He made me do it all, you know? Buy the clothes, get this here room, rent the car. I mean, after we got away with buyin' the wine an' all. So how about you let me walk out of here. I can make it worth your while?" She smiled the open invitation.

"Jerry's going to have to tell his story to the police. They'll want to talk to you too."

"Police?" Jerry said, blinked up at me the way he had when I first came in. It was as if some part of his brain didn't quite function. Not damaged, but somehow wounded, atrophied.

"They've been after you ever since Cassie was murdered. So far you're the only one with a motive to kill—"

The woman, Dorrie, bolted off the couch for the door. The pistol still in my hand, I hooked my arm around her waist. She fought like a wild animal.

The smashing of glass and wood came from behind me. I let the woman go, ran to the smashed window. Jerry Kohnen, his new clothes torn, bleeding from somewhere, was already down the cottage steps, across the grass and vanishing up the paths.

10

The only way to go through a closed window fast is first. After that, it's suicide. I took the door out. Or I tried to take the door. Dorrie had it open for her own getaway, grabbed me as I went past her. We rolled in a heap on the narrow porch and steps outside. When I pushed her off, she grabbed my leg and hung on. Down again, I sat and looked at her. There was no way I was going to catch Jerry Kohnen. The sound of more than one car starting off in the parking lot and fading away told me that.

"I thought you hated his guts for talking you into the credit card scam."

"That don't mean I'm gonna let the cops take him in on a murder."

"He has his story."

"Cops don't listen to stories from street people."

"Some cops do."

"You believe what he told?"

"They'll check it out, look for other suspects."

"Sure they will. You told it yourself, they ain't found no one else got any motive."

"When they find him he'll be in a lot more danger and trouble than if he'd gone in with me."

"There ain't no more trouble than the cops got you for the murder of your old lady."

I stood up on the cottage step. She didn't try to stop me.

"I hope he appreciates what you did for him. Credit card fraud, maybe accessory to murder, is trouble enough."

She shrugged, got up on her own. Inside the lobby I called Chavalas. She was the only connection I had to where Jerry Kohnen might go.

A connection that was no connection. She couldn't, or wouldn't, tell us anything.

"Hey, me an' Jerry we got nothin' goin'. We talk by the tree an' on the street. He got Cassie, right? So we all get a kick I looks like her. When he grabs that card he remembers me, we make the deal. He shows me her name on her license to copy, you know, it works like a charm. Who looks at what you sign long as the name's the same on card an' license an' you look like your picture. So we has a ball a couple days. That's all the hell I know about Jerry."

"You know he got you into a lot of trouble," Detective Max Miller said.

"I got born I'm in trouble. It was all Jerry's idea. He made me do it."

Chavalas decided to let her cool in a cell for a few days to think it over. I gave him the license of the Pontiac, a full description of what Jerry had been wearing.

"I don't know how bad the cuts from the window were, better check the emergencies."

There were only two in town, Max Miller checked them both. Neither had treated anyone who fit Jerry Kohnen's description. Chavalas sent word up and down the coast to pick up Jerry and hold him on suspicion of murder.

"Shouldn't take long," Miller said. "Kohnen's not the brightest guy in the world."

"Bright enough to know you weren't going to buy his story without a lot more proof."

"That don't take much bright. You caught him redhanded with everything she'd had on her when she was killed. Motive, opportunity, and he killed before. What more do we need?"

I watched the bare jacaranda outside in the late afternoon winter light. "He wasn't hiding from the police or anyone. He didn't act like he thought he had any reason to hide. He didn't even try to leave town after he rented wheels, used her money and credit card as long as he could get away with it."

"That's a way of hiding," Chavalas said.

"Not a very good way. They were bound to get spotted and have to run for it sooner or later."

"That's tomorrow, Fortune. Those street bums don't think about tomorrow," Miller said.

"Or maybe remember yesterday," Chavalas said.

I remembered how Jerry Kohnen had talked about Cassie Reilly as if she were still alive, aware of reality and unaware. Maybe unaware of the difference between reality and illusion, truth or denial, a lie and memory.

"What about the shadows he saw? The voices he heard?"

"Hell, I lay money he sees shadows and hears voices every goddamn day," Miller said. "Most of the time they're too stoned or drunk to know what the hell they do see and hear, what they did and didn't do. We pick him up, we even find the knife."

"The voices could have been on her radio, Dan," Chavalas said. "Alone in that park, the shadows maybe imagination."

"What about the men who attacked me?"

"Kohnen's street buddies," Miller said. "Maybe Jerry himself."

"We don't know that attack had anything to do with Cassandra Reilly's murder, Dan," Chavalas said.

"The boot prints, cigarette butts, military feel to the murder?"

"Same thing. Maybe nothing to do with the murder," Chavalas said. "Maybe some of it was Jerry watching that bandstand."

"Or he had buddies with him then too," Miller said.

Dumb enough to murder her, stay in town, sell her ring, use her credit card, make up a story, and still think the police wouldn't look for him? Or innocent enough to not be worried? To not even think about who had killed Cassie Reilly until I came along and told him the police were looking for him?

"The bare breast? The spit?"

Miller said, "You seen many lover killings, Fortune? I've seen a hell of a lot too many. Believe me, spit on a tit doesn't even count to how bad it can get."

I'd seen lover killings. I'd seen hate killings too.

*   *   *

After West and East beaches, the forbidden hobo jungle by the tracks, both Rescue Missions and both hospitals, I found Janet Steiner doctoring a sullen latino in the small, half-hidden Vera Cruz Park. The latino was drunk, had a nasty cut on his arm that had gotten infected.

"I told you to go to the emergency, Ernesto. Now it's infected, I have to clean it and give you a shot."

With swabs and alcohol she scrubbed the wound maybe harder than she had to.

"*Ayyyyy!* Jesus! You killin' me!"

"You are killing yourself, and doing a good job of it too. Get drunk if you have to, but show some brains and stay healthy enough to enjoy it."

"Chihuahua! Maybe I wanna kill me. You don' think about that? Anglos wants me stay alive so I work good, eh?"

"Hold still."

She jabbed the hypodermic into his arm, he swore loud and long, then slumped to the evening grass, sucked on an empty beer can. Nurse Steiner reached into her bag, brought out a can of Coors. Ernesto grabbed it with a big grin, and passed out clutching the beer to his chest like a teddy bear.

"I hope you're having more success than I am," Janet Steiner said to me as she repacked her bag.

"You look like you're doing pretty good."

"Ernesto's one of the easy ones. He even works sometimes. Hard work for small pay. That gets him down, so he drinks. The work breaks his back, so he drinks. Sometimes he feels really good, so he drinks."

"And doesn't take care of himself."

"He takes care of himself, he just doesn't go to doctors or hospitals. He hates to spend the money."

We walked to her Dodge on Haley Street. She strode out in her thin print dress with a down jacket over it, flat shoes. There was an anger to everything she did, from her walk to the way she gripped her bag. A sad anger, soft but determined.

"Have you seen Jerry Kohnen?"

"No. Should I have?"

I told her about Jerry and Dorrie, the credit card scam, and Jerry's dive through the window. "He was cut, how badly I don't know. He didn't come to you for treatment?"

"No. You think he could have been seriously hurt?"

I said, "Would you tell me if he had come to you?"

She loaded her bag into the passenger seat of the car, looked up toward where the glow of the evening sun was behind the Mesa at the far end of Haley. "Do you think he killed her?"

"The police do."

"I'd have to tell the police." She shook her head. "He didn't come to me, Dan. There's no reason he would. We weren't especially friendly."

"Who was he friendly with?"

"Almost no one. I think that was all part of that past of his Cassandra wouldn't talk about."

"No buddies among the street soldiers?"

"Jerry lived in a different world."

"A world of women?"

She got into the Dodge, looked out at me. "You must know something I don't. Jerry seemed to be closer to women, yes."

"Love and hate?"

She watched the darkness that had settled over the mountains to the east. "You could say that."

"Did he carry a weapon? A hunting knife? A combat knife?"

"I never saw him touch a knife or any other weapon. I think he's afraid of weapons."

We both watched the purple settle over the Riviera at the other end of Haley and the mountains behind it. She seemed in no hurry to finish her day. Or maybe her day wasn't finished, she needed a moment away from the wounds and sickness.

"Have you heard anything about anyone stalking street people? Vigilantes. Safety committees. Punks."

She started her engine, shifted into gear, sat without letting up the clutch. "There's the skinheads, of course. Neo-Nazis. The Clean-Streets people." Her foot gunned the engine a few times. A reflex. "There's been some talk among the younger men of latino gangs in some of the parks."

"Any names, places, times?"

"I don't even know if there's any truth to it."

She sat there as if contemplating skinheads and neo-Nazis, clean-street vigilantes, latino gangs and safety committees. Force and violence. Then she smiled up at me and drove away.

* * *

After dinner I called Sergeant Chavalas. There was no news. Jerry Kohnen had simply disappeared. By eleven I knew there would be nothing until morning.

In bed, Kay lay propped on her elbow. Her auburn hair hung long to the pillow.

I studied our ceiling. "If he didn't do it, why run, right? The perennial question of all the good people who've never had a question." It's an interesting ceiling, dark beams and cracked plaster. It looks old but isn't. "Because it's the instinct of any trapped animal. Because it's the first instinct of anyone in a hostile world where they see nothing for them. A world they reject, or that's rejected them, but where they have to live anyway. People like that run from any hint of confrontation, of contact. Their whole lives exist on never being noticed."

She touched where my arm was missing. "Then he had to run, didn't he?"

"And I don't know if he killed her or not."

"Harold would like to talk to you, Mr. Fortune."

Helen Reilly's hesitant voice was gray on the other end of the phone. Our bedside clock-radio read seven A.M. People must get up early in upstate New York. Or maybe only people married to men like John Reilly.

"Let me have breakfast, then come to my office. Say about nine?"

"Harold wants to take us to breakfast."

"Where?"

"Harold's staying at the Biltmore."

Some people, especially business people, don't like to talk on your home ground. It makes them insecure. They live their lives in their offices, in hotel and motel rooms, in coffee shops and restaurants eating while they talk. They feel comfortable in those places, safer.

"Nice for him."

"Harold is a good businessman, Mr. Fortune."

"Eight o'clock," I said.

Kay still slept when I left. I took my new Sig-Sauer in its fancy belt holster that didn't show a ripple under my old tweed jacket, wondered if the trouble with Cassandra Reilly had been that Harold was too good a businessman.

They serve a fancy breakfast menu at the Biltmore, that's what our comfortable middle class expects when traveling on business or pleasure or, most often, a combination of both. It's one of the reasons this ruling minority tends to be both overweight and committed to the exercise cult. Harold Flood didn't look like he was either of those things, money or no money.

"I appreciate your coming so early, Mr. Fortune. I simply had to know what you've learned about Cassie's . . . death."

He smiled, but his heart wasn't in it. Harold Flood didn't look like what Helen and John Reilly had led me to expect when they spoke about him. He was tall, graying, and almost youthful for his forty-five-plus years. The youthfulness of an inner peace. As thin and gaunt and out of place in his impeccable but off-the-rack three-button and three-piece brown tweed suit that didn't quite fit as an old time backwoodsman from the Adirondack region where he lived. Hawkeye from *The Last of the Mohicans*. The rustic Deerslayer from a more savage time. A younger and simpler time. More basic and direct and maybe more honest. Cruder and crueler, but with less hot air and hypocrisy.

"Not very much," I said.

"It has to be one of those street people," Helen Reilly said in that gray voice. It wasn't her I heard behind the words, it was John Reilly's certainty and decision.

"Mr. Reilly isn't with you?"

"John's arranging to take the . . . take Cassie back to Schenectady.

"Or perhaps Utica," Harold Flood said. "We haven't agreed on
that yet."

He said it quietly. When John Reilly made a decision, to Helen
Reilly that was the way it would be done. Not to Harold Flood. But
Helen did not object or protest or even smile. There was a quiet iron
in Harold Flood. He could and would stand up to Cassie's father, and
maybe that had been enough for her to marry him in the first place.
But not enough for him to keep her.

"What can you tell me about your marriage, Mr. Flood? What
went wrong? What happened to break it up?"

"Nothing happened. I think that's what went wrong."

The waiter brought our breakfasts. Bran muffins and milk for
Flood. Waffles, sausage, butter and syrup for Helen Reilly. Healthy
oatmeal for me. With real cream and raisins and good Assam black
tea. When it's free I eat richer. Rules of the game. Harold Flood
waited while it was set before us: real silverware, teapots, creamers,
plentiful butter swirls, cloth napkins. He waited neither nervous nor
impatient, radiated the same certainty as John Reilly but not the
same rigidity. A softness to the control that was all hard edges with
Reilly.

The waiter left. Flood went on as if he'd never stopped speaking.
"Nothing happened. Not a specific disappointment, you know. She
didn't marry me for anything specific. She married me to get away
from home, I knew that even then. I'm sorry, Helen, it's nothing
against you or even John, exactly. It's probably the reason most
young girls marry, especially an older man."

He looked at the other diners and out the windows of the fine old
hotel restaurant with its view of the sea and islands in the clear
winter distance. "She married for change, a different life. But not
too much change, not too different. Most of us like to think we want
the new, but not the too new. Most of we lucky comfortable. The
poor probably don't mind change, a world turned upside down. I
don't know that, I've never been really poor, but it seems logical."

In the off-season winter morning only a few of the local comfortable were walking and jogging in their designer sweat suits along
the beachfront esplanade across Channel Drive, and no boats were
on the water.

"I was different from John, younger and in love and ready to do almost anything for her, and yet I was a lot like John too. The same man in an entirely different position. She could escape from John and their conflicts, but not too far. A revolt against failing herself and going to Syracuse instead of standing up to her father. Pretty standard."

"Pretty standard," I said. "When did she change for real?"

Helen Reilly said, "You're too hard on yourself, Harold. She loved you. I think she really always did."

"I know she did, Helen. I never doubted that. She loved you and John too, but it wasn't enough to build a life on. Not for Cassie." He turned his gaunt, oddly serene face to look at me. He was orderly, thorough. A man who answered everyone in turn when asked more than one question. "That was when she changed, Mr. Fortune. When she realized that I wasn't enough. Our life wasn't enough." He watched a young woman who looked vaguely like Cassandra Reilly must have fifteen years ago come into the dining room with an older man. She was dressed all in white to show off a deep winter tan acquired somewhere farther south than Santa Barbara. "When I married Cassie, I used to think of her as blue. Do you believe people have colors, Mr. Fortune? I do. An aura of color around all of us. Maybe it's working with furniture, the colors of woods. I'm sort of brown, a walnut without any red in it. John is a hard gray, a steel gray. You're a combination of black and gold, an optimist but without a lot of real hope. Cassandra back then was blue. Floating through the Utica house in an aura of distant blue."

I said, "What was enough for her to build a life on?"

"I never have known." For the first time he seemed tense, and I did see him as the color of walnut. Solid brown walnut with the soft shine of centuries of hand rubbing. I saw him as a craftsman of the old kind. A man who made what he made for the love of what he made. But an American, a practical Yankee, so he had to sell what he made or he couldn't go on making it. Not for the glory of God, man, or art. For cash. For more than a glass of wine, a night in the cantina or the wood and paint and polish to make another. Had to be a businessman, and that is something else. "I know it wasn't what we had."

Helen Reilly objected. "You gave her a fine life, Harold. A beautiful home, an important place in the community."

"It wasn't her life, Helen." He waved to the waiter for coffee. "It wasn't mine, either, but I didn't know that then. I don't live that way anymore. Cassie leaving did that for me. I was immune to it all while we were together. I had my work, my business. The rest was all she had, she couldn't be immune."

"What did she find when she left?" Helen Reilly said. "What life did she have the last ten years? A life that killed her."

"At least it was her life. Not mine or yours or John's."

"A gypsy, a straw in the wind, a whore!"

Flood shook his head. "That's not you talking. It's John. And he doesn't believe it. He doesn't really know what he thinks about how she lived. He won't let himself. It might change what he thinks about himself."

"How do any of you know how she lived?" I asked.

"Because Cassie and I kept in touch, Mr. Fortune." He drank his coffee. "Does that surprise you?"

"It surprises me. How did you keep in touch?"

"She'd call, send a postcard. We'd talk, I'd write if I had an address. Sometimes I'd go to see her."

"When did she call or write last? When did you go to see her last?"

"She called less than two weeks ago. I haven't seen her in some years."

Nowadays anyone could fly in and out of Santa Barbara from upstate New York in a matter of hours. Unseen and unknown until long after and, with care and some luck, not even then.

"Were you in the military, Mr. Flood?"

He nodded. "And Cassie was a protestor at Syracuse. We didn't talk about it much. Maybe we should have."

"Vietnam?"

"That time, but not there. Germany. I was lucky."

"Trained but never used it?"

"More or less. Why?"

"Can you prove where you were when Cassandra was murdered?"

"Mr. Fortune!" Helen Reilly was horrified.

Flood only nodded again. "I suppose so. Will I have to?"

"Possibly," I said. "Tell me about Cassandra's life after she left you? What color was that?"

"Even bluer for a long time. Then red, an angry red. Anger not just at me and Utica, but at John and Helen and her whole life until then. She went to New York, got a job. Not much of a job—sales clerk, I think. What could she do? She'd married me right out of college. She drank even more than she had in Utica. There were men. Three or four years went by with John and Helen hearing from her only a few times, me not at all." He stirred his coffee, but didn't drink. "One day she called me. To tell me she was sorry for her silence. She'd been angry not at me but at what she was, what she'd been made into. I didn't understand, kept saying she was a perfectly good person, always had been."

The coffee had grown cold, he pushed it aside. "She said everyone was good until the world got to them. She said she was going to find out who she was before the world got to her. She'd traded one empty life for another empty life. She was leaving New York. She didn't know where she was going or what she would be doing. She was just going. On the road. Until she found the road that would take her where she belonged."

"All she found," Helen Reilly said, "was the gutter. Alone in a public park."

I said, "The redemption of the open road. As old as America and about as false a myth as Mr. Reilly's power struggle."

Harold Flood nodded. "For a long time it seemed like that was all it was. Never in one place longer than a few months, drinking even more than in Utica or New York, losing job after job, more men. Until one last man abandoned her in one last unknown town." He looked at his cold coffee, looked vaguely for the waiter, but we were among the last few in the morning dining room, no waiter was in sight. "She called me from Los Angeles. She'd lost everything, even her car, had nothing and no one. Except the other people on the streets. That was the answer Uncle Warren had tried to tell her. She'd finally realized what Uncle Warren had been saying."

"Who was Uncle Warren?"

Helen Reilly said, "My brother. The youngest. She'd loved him, he was wonderful with children. John detested Warren, said he was an arrogant fool. Warren said exactly what he thought. He laughed at John. I tried to keep peace between them, but John threw Warren out of our house and he died soon after."

Harold Flood said, "When we talked a few weeks ago, Cassie told me something Warren had told her: Most people want to dream of being king, so they need a king to know that it's possible. It's harder to dream of being a free person with other free people all doing what they can for each other, of using your skill and talent and work to serve not rule."

12

Uncle Warren is a slender man with a big smile who rarely laughs. When Cassie is still in grade school, Warren comes to the small, neat house a few times a year. He will appear suddenly and unexpectedly. He wears strange clothes and carries even stranger gifts. Cassie knows he is unexpected because her father is stiff and silent. Her father does not like the unexpected.

"What do you like to do most in the whole world?"

That is the first thing Uncle Warren ever says to Cassie. Before she even knows who he is.

"Stay home from school," Cassie says without thinking, is afraid when she looks at her father who is not smiling.

"No way," Warren says. "How about a ride on an elephant?"

He takes her to Albany and a carnival where there is an elephant you can ride. She is as amazed by how Uncle Warren knew there would be an elephant as by the ride itself, which is slow and swaying and the elephant smells bad. Only years later does she realize that he has seen and even stopped for a time at the carnival as he hitchhiked his way through Albany. Warren sees everything, stops wherever and whenever he decides he wants to, moves slowly through life.

After that first time, now that she knows he is her Uncle Warren, he always squats down to smile at her when he comes in the front door on one of his surprise visits.

"Cassie, my love! You've grown. I'm jealous."

Before he stands to kiss her mother, shake hands with her father, drop his backpack in the guest bedroom, and bring out the presents.

The first present, the visit of the elephant ride, is a painted wooden doll with the face of a wolf, a skirt, boots, fur and feathers.

"It's magic," Uncle Warren says. "From the Indians."

For her mother there is a bright, multicolored blouse with a design that is not always exactly the same, and for her father a squat brown clay figure with an ugly fat face. The figure goes into the back of her father's workshop, her mother is embarrassed to wear the badly made blouse that is too loud. Over the years Cassie gets a walrus tusk with a drawing on it, colored rocks from many places, a fossil leaf millions of years old, seashells, posters from peace marches, plastic monsters, wooden animals and birds carved all over the world. She keeps them all on a special shelf in her room, and her friends laugh, say they are weird, but they are envious, too. None of them has an Uncle Warren.

Sometime between Cassie's Motocross fight with her father, and the Teen-For-Teen Party Gourmets, Uncle Warren comes on one of his unannounced visits and stays longer than usual. He does not go out much, sleeps a lot. He is always there when Cassie comes home from school: reading in the living room, or outside lying under the big old maple that stands in the center of the front lawn, or in the backyard seated on one of the redwood benches around the barbecue and looking to the northwest where the peaks of the high Adirondacks are visible on clear days.

"When I was a boy we all went to the Adirondacks for two weeks in the summer. None of them climbed the high peaks except Helen and me. I did most of them, Helen only got to do a few before Dad stopped her. It was a waste of her time, Mother needed help around the cabin. My brothers and my dad preferred to fish, have something real to show for their time, but I climbed the mountains."

"Why do people always want you to do what they do, Uncle Warren?"

He looks up through the branches of the maple, or lays his book in his lap. "They're afraid, Cassie. Afraid they might be wrong."

It is on the visit when Uncle Warren stays so long that Cassie realizes that her father doesn't like Uncle Warren. She hears her mother and father arguing late at night when she and Uncle Warren are supposed to be asleep. Her father's voice is angry. It is one of the few times Cassie ever hears him lose his temper. Her mother's voice is angrier, something Cassie has never heard. Her mother's voice shakes, her father's is rigid. Uncle Warren's name is clear through the thin walls. It is the only word she can hear, but it is enough. Her father does not like Uncle Warren

"You make the assumption, John," Uncle Warren smiles, "that if informed people anywhere in the world are given free choice they'll always choose capitalism. So if they *don't* choose capitalism they

have to be ignorant, or the election can't have been free, right?"
Warren waits, but her father doesn't answer. Warren shrugs. "The
trouble with that is it's self-fulfilling. No one can win except you."

Her father says, "Everyone wants to destroy freedom and America. Well, no one will."

Warren looks off at the distant high Adirondacks when Cassie
comes home. "Force is the whole game. Force first for *me* and
second for *us*. All the way back to the *Iliad*."

"We read the *Iliad*. It was scary. That Greek, what was his name?
He dragged someone's body around the whole city. *Ugh*."

"Achilles. A great hero."

John's violent voice through the wall, "He never did a good day's
work his whole goddamn life, Helen! He's a bum! He'll always be a
bum and I've had enough!"

Helen's rage, "He's *my* brother, John Reilly! He's honest and free.
He doesn't want to be here anymore than you want him. He'll leave
when he feels better."

Cassie lies under the maple with Uncle Warren. "Why doesn't my
dad like you, Uncle Warren?"

"He's afraid of losing what he has. That kind of fear's the worst,
Cassie."

"You said force was the worst."

"They're the same thing."

One day she comes home and Uncle Warren isn't under the tree
or out back or reading in the living room. He isn't in bed. His
backpack is gone.

"He had to leave, honey," her mother says. "It was time."

Uncle Warren never comes back. He dies a few years later in
some kind of accident in another country. Cassie cries and so does
her mother. Helen doesn't blame John. She remembers thinking
angry thoughts, but it isn't John's fault.

"Warren was everything John had given up. The forces of darkness, John used to say. John worked hard for all of us, and it was my
job to stand with him. I think Warren knew that. He didn't leave
bitterly. I think he left too soon, never did really recover from that
fever he'd picked up somewhere in Central America, but that wasn't
John's fault."

Cassie is less forgiving, accuses her father of killing Uncle Warren, but really knows even then it isn't her father or even Uncle
Warren himself but something that has happened to both of them.

She goes into high school, and there is the Teen-For-Teen Party Gourmets failure, the fight over college, Syracuse and Harold Flood.

Harold takes her out to good restaurants and concerts and the theater and all the expensive places her father considers a waste of money. He is older than the boys in her classes who never want to do anything except drink too much beer and go to bed. He doesn't intimidate her like the student radicals with their loud voices as strong as her father's when she marches in protests with them. He thinks she is smart and beautiful and fun and sexy and exciting. He dotes on her the way her mother does, respects her the way her father never has. He is so different, so exciting. He owns his own company, has his own car and house in Utica. He takes her to parties in Utica, at the country clubs and the houses of successful people he knows, and he gets along fine with her parents but doesn't let her dad intimidate him.

In Utica the successful people turn out to be narrow and isolated. At the country club everyone is the same. They look the same and think the same and do the same. Cassie misses Syracuse, the mind of the university. She misses the radicals and even the beer-swilling louts. Everyone is too old, but that isn't it. Not their age but their certainty. They all know what has to be done, what is right. Like her father. She misses the Harold of Syracuse. The Harold of Utica has his life and his work. His ambition. In Utica she comes to realize that she has nothing of what she wants. She doesn't know what she wants, but Utica and Harold isn't it anymore than what her parents are.

That is when she sits in her darkened afternoon living room, watches television and drinks and thinks again of Uncle Warren.

"They're afraid, Cassie."

She has married her parents.

"The force and the advantage," Uncle Warren says. "That's the same thing."

The people in Utica are as afraid as her father. Harold is afraid. What she doesn't know, what Uncle Warren never really told her, is what they are all afraid of. Maybe he didn't know either. That is what she thinks about in the afternoon living room with the television and her vodka. In the morning kitchen with her cigarettes and brandy. After dinner with her Scotch.

Cassie likes Harold, he still dotes on her, gives her all he can within his limits, tries always to please her. She has even come to love him the way she loves her parents, but she has to find out what they are all afraid of. She has to find out why Uncle Warren wasn't afraid, and why fear and force are the same thing. She has to find out why she isn't alive in Utica. Not life as she means life but doesn't know what she does mean. She can't put it into words, what she means by life, but she will know it when she finds it.

In New York she finds a job in a small bookstore and Manuel. Learns to type, gets a better job and Mark. Mark and Manuel are not the answer. Their idea of life is drinking beer and going to bed. The jobs have even less to offer. There are better jobs, other men. One, Edgar, lasts two years. Another, assistant editor on a literary magazine, lasts three. None of them answer the questions she asks alone in her apartments in the early mornings and late nights. The vodka, whisky, wine, beer don't give the answers either, but they dull the questions.

She leaves the assistant editor, quits the literary magazine, drives west.

Sometimes there is a man, sometimes not. Sometimes she, Cassie, knows the man's name, sometimes not. Sometimes she knows which city it is, sometimes not. She always knows where she works and what she does there. Or she says she does. She never drinks on the job. Not until the end. That comes, the end, or as she says later when she calls Harold the day after she stops drinking, the beginning, in Beverly Hills.

She meets the studio publicity man in Tucson where the movie company is on location. He is older than the men she had in New York or on the road. He doesn't intimidate her the way some of the physical men in the small towns did. He thinks she is smart and beautiful and fun and sexy and exciting. He is short, and heavy, and not exciting. But he is rich, has his own Rolls-Royce and a house in Beverly Hills. He takes her to Hollywood parties and ski resorts and Pacific islands and cinema festivals. In Beverly Hills the successful people turn out to be narrow and comfortable and everyone is the same. They look the same and think the same and do the same. Cassie misses the road, the wind as she drives, the unknown and new from day to week to year. She drinks from day to week to year. He is too old, but that isn't it. He knows what has to be done, what is right.

She drinks too much, cheats, makes scenes. He throws her out. On the road once more she is too old, the men are too young. There are no jobs. She has been with the studio man too long. She returns to Beverly Hills where she knows what to do and lives in her car. There she discovers all the other women alone in cars on the streets of Beverly Hills. Invisible women. Only when she is with them does she see them. Because they are all from Beverly Hills, or Bel Air. They have all lost their place in the comfortable world by losing their men. Or their jobs. Or both. They sleep in their cars, bathe at the Beverly Hills Public Library or in the ladies rooms of the best shops. They know where there is free food, cast-off clothing as good as new, even friends who don't know what has happened and still invite them to lunch.

Cassie wants to talk to them, be friends with them, know them. They are all the same together. They do not want to know her, talk to her. They are hiding. They are waiting for their sons to graduate from college and rescue them, their daughters to marry and ask them to come and live. For their husbands to take them back. For a career job to arrive, for money to put them on their feet. They do not want an answer, they want to have no questions. The comfortable certainty has cast them out, but they don't want to change it, they only want to return to it.

Then she knows what Uncle Warren could not tell her, and she could not see. Why the fear and force were the same thing. Why, now that she had nothing, she could, at last, live.

13

"Nothing," Harold Flood said. "That was the answer. Everyone with nothing. Nothing and nowhere. She had a community to work with. She'd stopped drinking, stopped running." He glanced around the almost empty morning dining room of the elite hotel. "She had to strip everything away before she could find herself, build her own order, her own life."

"How long ago was that?"

"A few years. She called more regularly after that. Never took another drink. Went around helping the street people worse off than she was. The sick and the wounded, she said, the scared and the hopeless. Then she found Benton and his movement up in San Francisco, and they eventually came here because it was a key town to confront the problems of the homeless in the so-called normal community."

"She tried to help once too often," Helen Reilly said.

Flood said, "Is that what you think, Mr. Fortune?"

"It's possible."

"But there are other possibilities?"

"There are others."

"What others?"

"There may be an anti-female slant, a military angle."

"That's why you asked about my military career."

"Can you think of any military connection that might have ended in her death?"

They shook their heads.

"Woman-haters?"

"No," Flood said.

Helen Reilly didn't answer. It wasn't a question she wanted to think about.

The black with the 82nd Airborne patch on his surplus outlet fieldjacket sat against the fence of our rented hacienda in the mid-morning sun.

"You remembers the old Dago used to ride a bike 'round here, play guitar, sing down on the bluff? Got hisself killed maybe las' year, year before?"

"Rocky," I said.

"Yeh, Rocky." His angry eyes stared out over Summerland and the sea. "Old mother never hurt no one."

"Neither did Cassandra Reilly."

He went on staring out, scowling. When he did turn, his battered face had that same shrewd, cunning grin when, for twenty dollars, he'd told me Jerry Kohnen was behind the Cantina bar.

"You find that Jerry guy yet?"

"Not yet."

The grin widened, unable to hide his glee. "Now where you figure he be? I mean, you figure he in town?"

If I had the patience to wait he would eventually tell me whatever he had come to sell this time. Booze, drugs, minimal brain damage or just the slow mind of a poor and useless and wasted education, he could not hide whatever thought went through his head at any instant, could not hold a thought or purpose for more than a few minutes. Not without constantly reminding himself of what that purpose was.

"You don't think he's in Santa Barbara, Mr. . . . What the hell is your name?"

"McGee. You calls me McGee, 'cause I's so Irish." Laughed aloud. Scowled. "I ain't say he ain't in Santa Barbara."

I didn't have the patience or the time.

"Look, McGee, the police'll find him sooner or later. So if you know where he is, you better name what you want and tell me."

Sullen. "It worth more'n before."

"Okay, make it fifty."

"Fifty?" McGee licked his lips. "You got it?"

I gave him fifty. He stared at the bills in his scarred hand as if they frightened him. "He up north. Got a wife, kids. Him an' them they up north."

"King City? The cops would have checked that, have it staked out."

"San Leandro."

"His wife and kids live in King City, McGee."

He shrugged against the fence, looked past me at the distant ocean. "Don't know 'bout that. This guy say he know Kohnen. He come down here las' night, say he see Jerry an' his wife an' kids up San Leandro. Jerry he run off when he see the guy. The guy say Jerry's a goddamn nut. Says he figured he see him here, then spots him up San Leandro. The nut runs like a fuckin' rabbit."

In my office, a note told me Kay had gone to Los Angeles with a model on her first assignment. I called Gus Chavalas.

"They found the car in Atascadero," Chavalas said. "Maybe he's visiting friends."

Atascadero has a state mental hospital.

"How'd he get that far?"

"Switched plates. Stole one from a car in the K-Mart lot out in Goleta, the guy didn't notice until this morning."

Jerry Kohnen might be slow, but not that slow.

"You watching King City? The wife and kids?"

"Watching the house twenty-four hours. The wife and kids aren't there. House was empty when the cops up there got to it."

"No sign of Jerry?"

"Not a smell."

"He called her from Goleta, had her meet him in Atascadero."

"That's how I read it too."

"You have a line on her car?"

"We do now. A blue Toyota Corona. It took the King City cops a while to get it out of DMV. We didn't get the picture until they found the stolen car this morning."

"Plenty of time for them to go to ground."

"Tell me more."

"Let me know when you get him," I said.

I hung up. We all make mistakes. Maybe because I didn't think Jerry Kohnen had killed Cassandra. Maybe because I knew he would run again, and didn't trust the police in a strange city.

I drove north.

After a call to the Department of Correction Archives in Sacramento, and a stop at the public library. My contact up in Sacramento went to Inmate Finder, told me that Jerry Kohnen had been released from the Juvenile Authority to the probation office in Sacramento, was off probation years ago. The only address listed was one in Sacramento with a Mrs. Roseanne Cannio. The San Leandro telephone book at the library listed a Mrs. Roseanne Cannio at an address on Santa Rosa Street.

It's a long drive from Santa Barbara to the bay area, I had plenty of time to think about what I was doing. The police must act on what they see, what fits the facts, what experience and precedent tell them. All of that pointed to Jerry Kohnen as Cassandra Reilly's killer. Everything except the savagery of the act, the evidence of possible military-style action, Jerry's lack of worry after the murder, and the attack on me in the same park. But that was all judgment. My judgment. The police used their judgment too, but it had to be second until supported by factual evidence. The police in Santa Barbara had the same situation to judge that I did, it would modify their actions. The police in San Leandro didn't have the same situation. What they would have were the bare facts of the case from Santa Barbara.

I stopped for lunch at The Black Oak in Paso Robles.

My judgment told me Jerry Kohnen had not killed Cassandra Reilly. He was too dependent, too wounded by the past, too lost to kill for anything but fear—extreme, violent, unreasoning fear. Not physical fear, mental fear. Panic. Jerry would panic and run, or resist and maybe kill then. Kill a policeman. It happened too many times. I wanted to reach him first, talk, get him to trust me and come back to Santa Barbara with me. Trust was the key word. I was half way there—he knew me. It didn't matter how he knew me, or why, but simply that he did. It was strangers who would scare him. My judgment told me that would be enough to get me close. Once I was with him, he would do what I told him. That was my judgment. Or maybe just a hope.

The freeways fork around the bay after San Jose. What used to be 17, and is now I-880, goes up the less affluent east side of the bay through a series of towns that are really one large town all the way to Oakland. San Leandro is the community just before Oakland itself, and it was dark when I pulled off the freeway into the evening streets. The major avenues looked the same as in any of the contiguous towns up the eastern shore of the bay: traffic, fast-food places, small shops, pedestrians doing their last shopping on their way home. But San Leandro is an older town with neat, quiet side streets of apartments and houses that reminded me of the blue collar middle-class sections of Brooklyn and Queens when I was a boy. Only everything seemed smaller than my memories of Brooklyn and Queens, but maybe that was just me and time.

It was a two-story house that needed paint, set behind a yard of brown grass and wilted shrubs. I had the feeling the grass and shrubs would have been brown and wilted without the years of drought. The windows downstairs and upstairs had light behind them, the blue Toyota Corona was parked in front. I saw no sign of the police as I cruised by, parked up the dark street. There was a damp winter chill in the January air that came up from the bay.

On the other side, along the ocean and bay neighborhoods of San Francisco, there would be a fog tonight. Here it was only a wet cold. The water influence is not that strong on the east side of the bay. San Leandro has a marina with a fancy motel, but the rich live up in the hills to the east where it is warmer on the days when the wind blows from the west. But it was cold enough, and I was glad I'd had the sense to bring my duffel coat. I pulled it from the back seat, struggled into it, slipped my new Sig-Sauer into the pocket, and walked back to Jerry Kohnen's mother's house. I kept my hand in the pocket with the gun.

The blue Toyota in front of the house had seen better days. Rusted and dingy, at least ten years old, it was empty except for the books, comics and food wrappers of older children traveling. The light from the house reached all the way to the car and me. If anyone looked out I'd be as visible as a black cat in a spotlight. But no one seemed to look out. No one walked on the street either, even though it was only a few minutes after seven. Maybe the cold kept everyone in San Leandro off the streets and away from the windows.

I went up the broken concrete walk. When I rang the bell I heard no ring inside, either close or distant. I knocked. And again. Maybe there was another reason no one looked out the house windows. It had more light showing than any other house on the street, yet no shadows crossed the light. No one and nothing moved inside Rose-anne Kohnen Cannio's house. Where there should have been two pre-teen kids. Damn.

Tried the door. It was locked.

The concrete path led on around the house. A small backyard ended at the rear of a garage that opened onto an alley. The garage was empty, its outer doors closed. The light from the house was as bright in the backyard. Two low steps led up to a back door. It wasn't closed, as if they'd left in a hurry. Double damn. Jerry Kohnen could have seen me, recognized my Tempo, or been scared off by something else before I got here.

I pushed into the kitchen, slipped and fell on the wet floor, looked up into the staring eyes and gaping mouth of a dead woman.

14

A woman with two mouths. Her throat cut. Oozing blood and plasma. An older woman.

I got up. My hand, knees, duffel coat were covered in blood. The woman's blood that had flowed from her throat like water from a break in a dam. The blood I had slipped in as I walked through the open kitchen door.

I took deep breaths. The urge was to wash. To tear off my bloodied clothes and rush into the shower and wash and wash under the hottest water. Long, deep breaths, and after a time control returns. Like a soldier, trouble and pain and blood and death were my stock in trade. Trouble and pain every day. Blood and death not that often for a private investigator, but always there somewhere in the background.

It's amazing how we can become inured, how easily the dead cease to be human beings like us. How quickly the victims aren't people at all. For soldier and policeman, and, today, for all of us who watch the news on television.

Control returns, it has to, and I looked down at the dead woman with my professional eye. In her fifties, not all that old. A wedding ring. Slacks and high heels. Black slacks and silver high heels. A blouse that might have been yellow but was only blood now. Hair in an old-fashioned upswept of the kind worn by some waitresses to keep their hair out of the food. Reddish-blonde hair. Like Mary Queen of Scots whose head had been cut off.

Roseanne Kohnen Cannio's head had only been half cut off.

Squatted down in the blood, I saw that Jerry Kohnen's mother had not had her throat cut, she had been almost decapitated. Not a sudden, cold-blooded attack from behind, but the hot, violent slashing of some large, heavy knife. Her left arm and hand had also been slashed, and her shoulder. Deep, to the bone. A wild and uncontrolled attack with a large, sharp weapon.

The younger woman was in an upstairs bedroom.

She had been small and as reddish-blonde as Roseanne Kohnen, if that's who the dead woman in the kitchen was, and I had no real doubt of that. The younger woman wore a dowdy print dress that had probably come from K-Mart. Her hair was cut neck length and had no style as if she cut it herself. If she was Jerry Kohnen's wife, she probably had. She lay on the bed in her own blood, had died from what looked like a single knife wound in the heart.

One child, a boy eight or ten years old, sprawled at the far end of the upstairs hall. A girl, maybe a year or so older, was still under the covers of one of the narrow beds in the bedroom at that end of the hall. They had both been stabbed. The girl's face was peaceful, as if she at least had never known what had happened to her.

I knew. Jerry Kohnen from fear or despair or rage or panic or psychotic episode, all different stages of the same thing, had massacred his family. Or that was how it looked.

Only one thing was missing.

I walked through every room on both floors. I looked in the closets, under the beds, in both bathrooms.

Jerry Kohnen was nowhere.

The normal psychotic episode script called for four murders and a final suicide. I thought about the open back door, the empty garage. I thought about the knife. A large, very sharp knife. It was not in the house either.

The noise was in the house.

Small, light and quick. A movement, or an object struck by movement. Maybe near the kitchen. One small, sharp sound, then silence again. Not even a car or a footstep out on the street to break the silence as I listened in the house with all its lights and death.

Hand on the pistol in my pocket, I went back to the kitchen, stopped in the doorway. No one was in the kitchen. The dead woman hadn't moved. The rear door was open a few more inches. Maybe a foot. Outside I stood in the backyard and heard the voices in nearby houses, back in the alley behind the garage, but nothing and no one moved in the yard clear in the light from the house.

The switch for the garage light was outside its rear access door. I turned the knob on the door with my gun in hand, used the barrel of the Sig-Sauer on the light switch, kicked the door open all the way.

The garage was still empty. No cars inside and the main door closed. There was no blood on the bare concrete floor, no signs of a large, sharp knife.

Back in the kitchen I stood above the dead woman and the darkened pool of blood, looked at a door in the side wall. Most new houses in California didn't bother with basements, but the older ones often did. Again I turned the knob with my gun still in my lone hand, stepped back and kicked the door open.

Wooden stairs led straight down into what appeared to be a clean basement. A well-lighted basement.

The small noise came again.

I went down.

Jerry Kohnen wore the beige slacks, blue blazer, yellow shirt and tasseled brown shoes he had in the room of the El Encanto Hotel. He lay in the far corner near an old gravity furnace. On his side, his hands on the hilt of the long *samurai* sword that went into his belly and protruded from his back. In a pool of his own darkened blood, the gaudy clothes stained with blood, dirt and grime.

I went upstairs, called the San Leandro police, and sat in the bright living room to wait for them. I needed the lights on as much as Jerry Kohnen had. If I hadn't found him at the El Encanto, told him the police wanted him, he might not have broken under the pressure. If I had taken Chavalas with me to El Encanto, he might not have escaped to come up here and kill them all. If I'd told Chavalas my hunch, let the police handle it, they might have reached him in time. When we make choices we change events, bear some of the responsibility.

I never did find what had made the small noises.

Three days later, Monday, I sat in Sergeant Chavalas's office, looked out at the bare branches of his favorite jacaranda.

"That's it? Case closed?"

The San Leandro police had taken my statement, questioned me for a couple of hours, called the Santa Barbara police. Chavalas confirmed my story, told them he'd be up in the morning to check out the house, car and bodies for any possible evidence in the Cassandra Reilly murder. No one wanted me around. I drove home.

"He was a borderline case for years, finally flipped, killed Cassandra Reilly, ran when he knew we were after him and cracked all the way."

"Did you find any evidence up there? About Cassie Reilly?"

Chavalas shrugged. "You found all we need, Dan. He had her

stuff, he was unstable. He killed before. He ran when you confronted him. He killed Cassandra Reilly, knew we were after him, panicked and ran, cracked completely, massacred them and killed himself."

"It'll hold up in court," I said. "All true except I don't believe he murdered Cassandra Reilly. He was afraid of the police, of prison, of being hunted. When he was recognized by the street person up in San Leandro he knew the police would find him, they wouldn't believe him, he'd go to prison, maybe the gas chamber. Probably wasn't even that rational. The police were hunting him, they would find him. Life was pain and horror. His whole life was pain and horror. He couldn't face it anymore. He would save his children, his wife, the pain and horror of living. Psychotic and berserk. But it was pressure, not guilt. A breakdown, not a confession."

"He even used a knife both times, Dan."

"Not the same knife."

Chavalas looked out at the bare jacaranda. "Because those guys jumped you in the park? Because Kohnen wasn't hiding, never tried to leave town? Because he said he saw some shadows, heard voices?"

"Because you sensed a military angle. Because someone spat on her bare breast after she was dead. Because Jerry had no reason to kill her. Because he wasn't a killer."

"Kohnen was sick, irrational, had spells. The voices were her radio. The military angle wasn't part of the murder. He wanted Reilly back, she wouldn't come. Inside, he hated women. From his mother on down. The guys who attacked you were muggers or Kohnen's friends."

"He had no friends."

But it would hold up in court. The police had no evidence of anyone or anything else. Jerry Kohnen had confessed in such a shocking way anyone would believe it.

Except me. And all we have in the end is our own judgment.

The police's story didn't sound right. Jerry Kohnen's story did. Jerry Kohnen had found her dead, had taken all her stuff. She hadn't needed it anymore. I'd found him and scared him. He'd panicked, cracked under the pain and the pressure, released his family and himself from any more pain. But someone else had killed Cassandra Reilly.

15

Harold Flood packed his bag on the bed of the Biltmore hotel room. A careful packer, meticulous in folding and arranging his clothes.

"It was this Jerry Kohnen person?" He shook his head. "What did you say Cassie said he was—one of the wounded?"

"One of the wounded who needed help. He killed them all, that's what the police and District Attorney's office seem to have decided."

He made slow trips between the bed and the closet. A man who hung his clothes in a hotel room, even when he had tragedy and sorrow on his mind and no idea how long he would stay. If tragedy and sorrow was what he had on his mind.

"You haven't decided the same?"

A man who emptied his suitcase into careful rows in the hotel bureau drawers. John Reilly would do that too in a hotel room, even for a one-day stay.

"I don't think Jerry Kohnen killed her."

"Do you know who did?"

"No."

"Do you have someone who could have? Who had a reason?"

"No."

He checked the closets and drawers one last time. Snapped his suitcase closed, set it on the floor near the door, went to stand at the window that overlooked Channel Drive, the beach and the sea, with the islands clear in the winter distance.

"We're taking her home today. John and Helen are with the funeral people now. We decided she should be buried with her family in Schenectady. I'll put a memorial in my family plot in Utica. I'm not sure I care who killed her. I don't think I care if the police are right or not. I don't think it makes much difference." He continued to look out toward the islands so close on clear winter days. "If a man and a woman don't delight in each other, there's no point to a marriage or any other relationship. That's what really happened. To John and Helen too, and that affected her. Too busy doing what we were supposed to. John and Helen and me. In one way we all killed her."

"I've thought about that," I said. "And not metaphorically. I guess you wouldn't want to hire me to continue investigating?"

He turned to look at me, but said nothing. He picked up his bag. "The police know where to find me, Mr. Fortune."

When I came into my office, Al Benton waited in the easy chair.

"He wanted to pay you," Kay said. "I told him to wait."

"Jerry Kohnen," Benton said. "Who the hell would've thought he had the nerve."

"He didn't," I said.

Benton looked at Kay, then back at me.

"Anyone want coffee? Tea?" Kay said.

There was a chill in the air, a possibility of rain. "I'll have some Lapsang if you want to make some, honey."

Benton still looked at me. Kay closed the door when she went out into the hall.

"He killed his family and himself," Benton said.

"And a boy a long time ago," I said. "But not Cassandra."

Al Benton wanted to get out of the office. Go somewhere. Anywhere he wouldn't hear what I had said. His crossed leg swung where it balanced on his knee. He had thought it was over. He wanted it over. The unknown and the danger. He wanted to know there never had been any real danger to him. A personal murder that would not be repeated. An aberration.

"You got some kind of proof, Fortune?"

I told him what I had. He wasn't happy with it.

"None of that says who did kill her, if Jerry didn't. It's guessing. Maybe you're wrong, the cops're right."

"You really believe Jerry Kohnen would have killed her?"

He wanted to, needed to, but couldn't. Not really. He had known Jerry Kohnen and Cassandra too well.

I said, "The ones who jumped me. The military feel to what happened that night in the park. The shadows Jerry saw, the voices he heard. I see more than one killer. Maybe those macho veteran hardcases, real and imaginary, on the streets. Hatcher's Protective Association vigilantes. Latino gangs. Someone we haven't even seen yet."

"Latino?" His leg went on swinging. "There was this guy. Old Sid.

Sid hangs out alone, sees things, doesn't always remember where he is or where the hell he was."

"Old Sid?" I said.

Benton nodded in the easy chair. "He run into me last Friday, wanted to know if Cassie maybe spoke Spanish."

"Did she?"

"He'd just heard about the murder. Like I said, old Sid walks in his own world. He said he thought maybe he was in that park that night and heard people talking around the bandstand. They were talking Spanish."

Out on the street a car passed. The steady hum of the freeway seemed to come out of the silence. The door opened and Kay came in with the teapot, sugar, milk and cups on a tray. She set it on the coffee table between Benton in the chair and me on the couch, gave me a kiss, and went out.

"I mean," Benton said, "Old Sid couldn't say when he was in the park, if it was even the right park. Hell, I'm not sure he knew the right day. I forgot about it. No one said anything about latinos."

"Did she speak Spanish?"

He nodded. "Both of us. You need it sometimes. I learned up in the vineyards, the lemon orchards."

"Where'd she learn?"

"In school. On the road. Some boyfriend. I don't know. She wasn't good at it, but she could get by and understand."

"You know of any trouble with latinos?"

He shook his head. "Not Cassandra."

"How about you? Any of the homeless?"

"Some. Run-ins down in the *barrio* sometimes. Nothing to speak of. We don't have a lot of latinos on the streets here."

"You better tell the police."

"Not me, hell no. They don't listen to me. They don't want any part of me except to get me out of town, me and all the street people. Sweep us under the rug. We don't fit into the image of the top dogs of the planet."

I poured the tea. Lapsang souchong is black tea with the flavor of tarred rope from long ago when it traveled in sailing ships from China to England. The English ritual isn't as formal as the Japanese, but it has its precise rules: warm the pot with boiling water, put in the tea, bring the pot to the kettle so the water doesn't go off the boil, put the milk into the bone china cup first, pour the tea through a silver strainer, cover the teapot with a cosy to keep the tea hot, add sugar to taste.

Benton drank the smoky tea. "It's a free country, right? We're free to say anything we want, even do anything as long as it ain't any real danger. Only no one listens to us because no one can hear what we're saying except other dissidents. The smoothest system ever invented to make dissent unimportant."

"I thought what you wanted was back into the system."

"The system drove us where we are. It got to be different or we can't get back in it."

"Is that what Cassandra found? A different system?"

He nodded. "We don't fit in the power world. We can't live with it. We break, fall apart." He emptied his cup, held it out to me. "You got to believe nothing counts except you. It got to be for *me,* for *us.* The rest, everyone else, they don't count."

"What was Cassie Reilly's different system?"

He emptied the second cup, set it on the coffee table, looked down into it as if reading the few tea leaves that had escaped the strainer. "You got to get rid of all the bullshit, strip right down to being human. Then you see what Cassie saw. We're all in this to-gether. Everyone, everywhere."

"Cassie and you?"

"And me," he nodded, looked up from the teacup. "Only you got to take it a step at a time, start small fightin' the power world for the rights of the invisible."

"And somebody didn't like that," I said. "Maybe someone who spoke Spanish."

Benton looked down again at the teacup. The answer wasn't going to be found there.

On Figueroa Street, Sergeant Chavalas wasn't in his office. Detective Max Miller was. At Chavalas's desk, Miller thumbed through a file with his thick hands. It looked like slow work.

"Tell me about latino gangs," I said.

"In L.A.?"

"Here."

"We've got 'em. Not many but they're growing."

"I know we've got them. Do any of them operate in Alameda Park?"

He looked up. "That's upper eastside, for Christ sake."

"I know where it is, Miller. I've heard that some gangs have been in the parks."

"Where'd you hear that?"

"Is it true?"

He went back to his thumbing through the file. "It's a small city. People go a lot of places."

"Have you heard of any signs of latino gangs in Alameda Park?"

He shrugged without looking up. "Maybe we've had some reports. Individuals. Some graffiti tags, colors."

"Trouble?"

"Nothing serious." He looked up again. "Some hassling, we've got it under control, okay?"

"Were there any gang members in the park the night Cassandra Reilly was killed?"

He closed the file. "Jesus Christ, Fortune, I don't believe you. You know who killed the Reilly woman, you just about solved it yourself."

"Were there any signs of a gang in the park that night?"

He went back to his paperwork again. "Not that I know."

"But gang members have been seen in that park?"

He thumbed a page. "We've had some reports."

"I want to talk to Dorrie Cooke. Can you arrange it?"

"D.A. dropped the charges. She swore she was scared Kohnen would kill her if she didn't go along with his scheme. After San Leandro, I guess they figured that was a pretty good defense."

Miller shrugged. He wouldn't have let her off.

Dorrie Cooke wasn't hard to find. Choices of where to go, where to be, are limited for the homeless.

"What the hell do you want?"

We were out behind the Cantina where I'd first seen her with Jerry Kohnen. In the winter sun with four others. The tattooed hulk, Temple, was one of them. He stared at my empty sleeve again, but had his mind on something else now.

"He botherin' you, Dorrie?"

People give their true minds away when they act under stress without thinking. After the recent liberation of Kuwait, the worst insult a Kuwaiti male could think to inflict on Iraqi dictator Saddam

Hussein was to redraw his face on a propaganda poster to make him look like a woman. Cassandra Reilly hadn't escaped male arrogance on the streets. If anything, females had less power among the homeless, needed the physical protection of males all too often, and that was the instant reaction of the tattooed Temple to anger in Dorrie's voice. And on the streets, as anywhere else in modern America, females still prospered by manipulating men. Dorrie didn't think she needed protection from me at the moment, and I could be useful in the future.

"It's okay," she said to the massive man. "He just wants to talk."

"Talk is all the son-of-a-bitch does," Temple said as he walked away.

"What do you want?" Dorrie said. "The cops got nothin' to hold me on."

"Talk you said, talk is what I want."

"I got nothin' to talk about."

"I don't think Jerry Kohnen killed Cassandra Reilly."

The streets strip away veneer, leave a Cassandra Reilly with the self-knowledge she sought, leave others with nothing but the need to survive. Jerry Kohnen's rampage of murder was Dorrie's only safe defense for her own involvement in his little credit card scam.

"What the hell you talking about? Didn't he kill his whole family up north? He even threatened to kill me."

The tone of her voice changed, became belligerent with the last sentence. She was a bad liar. Jerry Kohnen hadn't made any threat against her.

I was a better liar. "But he didn't kill Cassie, only I'm pretty sure he knew who did. You could be in a lot of danger if the real killer thinks Jerry might have told you while you were enjoying your scam."

"He didn't tell me nothing!"

"Maybe not, but it would help catch the real killer if we knew everything he said those days after the murder."

"I told the cops everything!"

"Anything you can think of you forgot, or didn't think was important. Maybe about those voices he said he heard before he found Cassie's body. Were they just ordinary voices? Like you and me?"

She was uneasy now. "I didn't forget nothin'. Someone talking around that bandstand. Spanish, hey, that's it. The talk was Spanish, yeah. That's all he said."

* * *

Kay, her face propped on her hand, watched me in bed.

"Spanish?"

"Two witnesses heard Spanish voices. Cassandra spoke some Spanish. There have been reports of latino gangs in that park."

"What does Chavalas say?"

"I haven't talked to him. Miller thinks I'm crazy. As far as the police are concerned, the case is closed."

She watched me for a time, then turned on her back and studied the fake old beams on the ceiling of our bedroom. The winter surf was loud on the beach across the freeway and the railroad. The moon was bright and high outside.

"So what are you going to do?"

"Talk to latino gangs."

II
THE BARRIO

The lighted window is on the second floor.

"Jesus, he's only a fucking P.I., Wolf. What the hell can he do?"

Crouched in the shadows of tall palm trees across the dark street from the two-story hacienda, its white walls and red-tile roof ghostly in the moonlight, two of them face the silent house with the single light in its upstairs window. Two face east and west, their backs to each other. The fifth faces south, his back to all the others. A defensive perimeter ready for any attack. Alert, they watch the night, shadows in black. Only the one on the east, the one who spoke, looks back at the two who face the house. The others talk without taking their eyes from the night.

"He kick your balls off in that park, Roach?"

"His big gun scare you, Roach?"

"The bastard got one lousy arm, Roach, what the fuck's to worry?"

"He kicked all our asses in the park."

"Hold it down."

Wolf's voice is quiet, calm. They all become silent. Only the one on the east, Roach, continues to look back at Wolf. Wolf does not look at Roach.

"Everyone sacrifices," Wolf says, "takes risks."

"The police got the street psycho, Wolf. Why take the chance?"

"You want to hide underground all your life, Roach?"

"The bastard's still snooping around."

"We rag this guy, Spider, the police know the street psycho didn't waste the one on the park."

They are silent in the night, all look at Wolf. Wolf looks only up at the window of the ghostly hacienda across the silent street.

16

His mustache is thick, black and droops at each end against his Aztec skin and cheekbones, Castilian nose and eyes. He looks like Emiliano Zapata. He knows that, works on the image. Only his eyes don't fit. They're blue and cold, not hot like those of the tiger of Morelos. They were immobile above his smile in the nice, comfortable office at the university. I'd met him first at political rallies and militant parties. We'd come to respect each other. At least, I respect him. Officially, he's a liberal Democrat, but he's a lot more radical than that. The FBI keeps an eye on him. He uses his Freedom of Information Act rights to check their file on him from time to time. It's a chess game. They both enjoy it.

"What can I help you with, Dan? Another latino act of violence that's completely unexplainable? No rhyme or reason? The anglos just can't understand it?"

He looks more like a Zapatista revolutionary than a full professor of History and Chicano Studies at a university in the California system. Outside the school he acts like a revolutionary. Maybe inside too. I told him what he could help me with.

"And you think this Cassandra Reilly, militant street advocate, was killed by latino gang members?"

"I don't know who she was killed by, Luis. I'm just pretty sure it wasn't Jerry Kohnen. I'm trying to find out who did kill her, if the voices witnesses heard speaking Spanish that night have any significance or not."

"What other significance could they have?"

"Maybe witnesses. Maybe they saw something in the park that night, or know something about Cassandra Reilly."

"You have any evidence of a connection between this woman and a gang?"

"No."

"Between latino gangs and the street homeless?"

"No, but they've got to bump into each other on the lower west-side, on lower State, on Haley and Milpas."

"You mean bums and slums, Dan?"

That's his way. Confront. Give no quarter until he's made his point that the American latino, chicano, Mexican, is part of here, of us, of today, always has been in this land that was once his ances-tor's, and needs to be seen, heard, faced.

"I mean poor and poor, Luis. Outside and outside."

"Latino and homeless, brothers under the skin? Those without a home in their own land, and those without a land in their own home? You think your Cassandra Reilly knew that the wretched of the earth are that way because Europeans made them that way? That our society institutionalizes injustice and corrupts human potential to keep itself in power?"

"I don't think she read either Fannon or Marcuse," I said.

"You never know," he grinned.

"But she would probably have agreed with them anyway."

"You think so?"

"What can you tell me about Alameda Park, Luis? What gang might use it?"

He rocked in his high-backed desk chair and looked at me the way Emiliano Zapata himself must have looked at Francisco Madero when that honest, educated, but hopelessly ignorant man spoke of freeing Mexico. Ignorant of the real Mexico. Of the life and hopes and needs of ordinary Mexicans. Of the world he lived in.

"Alameda Park is anglo. No gang uses it."

The words had finality. His voice didn't.

"But?"

"What do you really know about Santa Barbara gangs? Any minor-ity gangs?"

"We have them. They grow in poverty, slums, exclusion, lack of opportunity and even hope."

"Words and theories. Right, but miss what it feels like. Talking about a battle but never being in one. If you've never been shot at, you can never know what it's like." He rocked again in the chair, ran his hands over the soft leather of the arms as if remembering when he hadn't had such a chair. "In L.A. the gangs are heavy metal. Drug-dealing, shootings, territorial wars, neighborhood ruling, the works. Armed, violent, vicious and dangerous. It's a war: gang to gang, gang to community, gang to cops. Pretty much out of control."

He rocked, stroked his fine leather. "That hasn't happened here. Not yet. It will if we don't stop cutting and eliminating every damn public service that gives minority kids something to do, jobs, education, housing for their families, a sense of belonging to the larger community so they don't have to make one of their own. Gang recruitment is on the upswing, but so far the streets aren't out of control."

"What does that mean for Alameda Park? For the night Cassandra Reilly died?"

"It means gangs here aren't all that territorial yet. It's a nice, small, clean city where fear isn't in control. Not yet. The gangs don't hunker down in their turf, fight off the world. They band together for community, support, somewhere to belong in an alien world they feel excluded from. Especially newcomers who don't speak enough English. But they move around the city pretty freely, get their safety from being together, in a group even in anglo areas like your Alameda Park."

"Sort of like soldiers in enemy territory?"

"Something like that."

I watched him rock in his professorial chair. "A lot of ex-soldiers in the gangs, Luis?"

"The older guys I expect. Probably the younger guys all have brothers in the services. Hey, you're a poor beaner, no jobs, not much education, and very little hope, you join the services just like the blacks. The gangs, the drug dealers, the thieves, the delivery boys and dishwashers, the unemployed or the services."

"Not a lot of choices,"

He shrugged. "The Latino-American lives in a culture as macho as the American. You're poor and excluded, you feel your *huevos* are cut off. You got to be an *hombre, muy hombre*. A uniform, a gun, it's always been a male way to show his balls, right?"

"So which gang goes into Alameda Park?"

He swiveled in the high-backed chair to look out his window. He's got a nice view of the heart of the campus, Storke Tower sticking up, even some water. Of the young, clean, bright, mostly scrubbed anglo students who poured across the sunny winter campus. "The Westside Rockers control Micheltorena a couple of blocks across town. They've been known to go over State from time to time, sweep the park, hassle some anglos. They also have ties to the lower eastside *barrio*—girls, family, friends. Alameda Park is on the way to the *barrio*."

I said. "What about street people? They hassle them too?"

"There's been some clashes. Being homeless doesn't always make people less bigoted, you've got a lot of macho types on the streets too." He turned back to me. "The Rockers have never been known to use firearms, kill anyone. They're an established, cohesive gang, militant but not violent. They'll fight, but they don't hassle individuals. They're assertive, not secretive. They protect their rights instead of trying to take from others."

"What weapons do they use?"

"The usual: knives, chains, pick handles. How was your Cassandra Reilly killed in the park?"

"Multiple stab wounds. Not robbed or raped."

Luis swung back to his window. "The Rockers don't kill, Dan."

"The voices spoke Spanish, Luis."

His back remained toward me for some time. Then the chair swung back. His mouth smiled under the fierce bandit mustache, but over it his eyes didn't smile. "Hey, maybe they did cut the woman. You know chicanos, the latin temperament. You never know. Maybe they'd had a bad enough week. Enough kicks and snubs and trouble with their *chiquitas.* Like the Greeks at Troy, right? Bad vibes at home, got to get it off with a little killing and looting and raping, pillaging and slaughtering. No way you can be Achilles if you don't have a war, a Hector to slay and drag around the walls."

"I'm just trying to solve a murder, Luis."

"I'm just trying to tell you the Rockers aren't bad violent. Not so far. Muscle and hassle, yes. War and killing, no. Most of them are in high school or already graduated. But a lack of justice, community, and worth to your fellow man makes violence. Given the right fuse, anyone can explode." He shook his head. "I don't know if some Rockers could have lost their heads that night. You could be too late anyway."

"Too late?"

"The Westside Rockers got into a messy raid at City College last week, most of them are in jail. Maybe they've found a war."

"A raid on who? Over what?"

"You'll have to talk to the cops."

I stood up. "Thanks, Luis. I hope I'm wrong."
He didn't smile. *"De nada."*

Joe Barry is an assistant public defender, Philip Anderson is the
chief investigator for the public defender. They sat at a table at the
rear of the brew pub on the ocean side of the freeway.

"Join the merry circle," Barry said. "We have just watched the
D.A. send an eighteen-year-old first offender who speaks no English
to the gray gates of Folsom for life for the slaying of the brutal
father who beat him senseless for most of those long eighteen
years. Have a beer, Fortune."

I had a pint of porter. Brew pubs and micro breweries may yet
save beer from Budweiser and Miller.

"You couldn't get it reduced?"

"Alas, he shot dear old dad nine times in the back, six of the times
while the poor man lay on his kitchen floor in the remains of his
own shattered six pack."

Anderson said, "I found more than enough to show the boy had
been battered and hounded almost psycho, needed help not prison,
but he'd turned eighteen a week before the murder and the D.A.
wanted blood."

Barry is a compact man with a disarming smile that lulls deputy
D.A.s into overconfidence, and an irreverent manner that infuriates
his boss. But he's a brilliant lawyer who more often than not gets his
poor, half-crazy, illiterate, hopeless, and guilty defendants lesser
charges, reduced sentences, plea bargains, psychiatric treatment,
and even an occasional not-guilty verdict. A great deal of his success
is built on the investigation work of Philip Anderson. A six-foot-four
giant of two-hundred-and-fifty pounds with a graying beard, Anderson's background included both CIA and Interpol as well as various
police forces. He prefers the job of keeping the police on their toes
and honest.

"It doesn't sound like murder one to me," I said.

"It wasn't," Anderson said. "But we had nothing to bargain with.
The boy confessed, couldn't speak English, was sullen and Asian.
He was full of guilt, wouldn't defend himself, and the jury was as
law-and-order as the D.A."

Barry drank his ale. "I doubt if Dan has come to help us drown our sorrow for the triumph of fear and retribution over justice. I sense a call for aid."

"Who's handling the Westside Rockers?"

"Ah, now, I'm not at all sure anyone can handle the Westside Rockers or would want to."

Anderson said, "It's not Joe's case, but it sure as hell's mine. What's your interest in it, Dan?"

"Not the case," I said. "Them."

Barry said, "As a gang that rumbles and graffitis, or individually as people with, presumably, private demons?"

"Both, I suppose."

"I don't know much about them as individuals," Anderson said.

"As a gang then."

He finished his porter, waved the empty glass at the waiter. "Probably the tightest, best organized of the gangs we have, but so far this isn't L.A. Not especially violent, there's not a lot of gang competition here yet. Sell some Mexican pot, nothing too heavy. They don't run the westside, but they protect their own interests, their rights. That, and a tendency to roam, to show anglos the flag, is what got them into trouble this time."

"What trouble?"

Barry peered into his half empty ale glass. "It appears that a number of City College students, always in haste to reach their appointed classes, struck upon the dandy idea of using the back streets between Carrillo and Cliff Drive as a shortcut. A number of fender benders caused confrontations with the Rockers and considerable animosity which culminated only last night in an invasion of the college by the Rockers that led to many injuries, some of them, alas, quite severe."

"The police took most of the gang," Anderson said. "Tossed them into the slammer on assault, riot, attempted murder, you name it."

"What about the college kids?"

"Bite your tongue," Barry said, waved for another ale. "We anglos are clearly the injured party. The Rockers, who left their proper domain to mount an unprovoked attack, are a menace to society."

"Aren't there a lot of latinos at City College?"

"A fact helpfully pointed out by the D.A." Barry savored his fresh ale. "I fear that logic has never been the hallmark of ethnic resentment, which, unfortunately, is unlikely to be held as mitigating the danger of the Rockers to law, order and social tranquillity."

"The Rockers," Anderson said, "are up shit creek."

"Can I get in to talk to them?"

"I doubt the D.A. will look with favor upon such a request," Barry said. "Why do you want to talk to them, Dan?"

I told them. They weren't happy. A killing would not aid the Rockers' cause. Another attack outside their own area could be used to establish a pattern of consistent and deadly violence, a calculated war against the anglo community. That Cassie Reilly had been farther outside the anglo power community than even the Westside Rockers would be conveniently overlooked. On the other hand, the truth was important to them.

"They're reading the information on them in the courthouse now," Anderson said. "Let's go."

17

The Moorish courthouse in Santa Barbara sits on a square city block surrounded by lush green lawn, palms, hibiscus, pines, bougainvillea and tourists. The fourteen Westside Rockers had been bussed in from Goleta for the reading of the information. Two assistant public defenders conferred with assorted juvenile authorities, social workers and psychologists at a table on the right of the courtroom. The young defendants all sat sullen and defiant on a long bench behind the crowded defense table.

Most of them were thin. With hollow cheeks, bony Indian faces and deep-set dark eyes. Three were short and squat, their eyes sleepy and hooded like pre-Columbian Aztec stone statues. Two were unusually tall, but my eyes were drawn to one on the very end of the bench. He had a girlish face with smooth brown skin that looked like it would feel silky to the touch. Thinner than even the thinnest of the others, and younger. A scrawny, almost delicate body. The face of a shy young girl on a body not developed enough to be a girl or anything else. His face was as defiant as the rest, but it wasn't sullen. Alert and nervous.

"Yeah," Anderson said beside me, "he's the one I'm after. Name's Edgardo Montez. I need something to work with, anything mitigating or extenuating. There's something missing, I feel it, but I've got nothing I can use. Montez is different, comes from over on the lower east, the other side of Milpas. Out of the Rockers' westside neighborhood, even goes to City College."

"You think he's innocent?"

Defense lawyers and investigators think all their clients are innocent. Or say they do. That's our system. If they do their job well, thieves, killers and psychos go back on the streets, and that's the risk we take to be sure no innocent man is found guilty. It doesn't always save the innocent or convict the guilty, but it's the best system so far. The last few years too many people seem to have forgotten how long and hard we had to fight to get this far, would prefer to execute an innocent man than turn a guilty one free to kill again.

"No, he's as guilty of the attack as the rest. But what's he doing in the gang? What drove him into a gang not even in his own neighborhood, made him go on a raid against his own college? He doesn't have any police record. The rest have sheets as long as their hair."

If Edgardo Montez was different, he was trying hard not to show it. As surly and defiant as the rest where they sat before the judge who seemed to see them and not see them while he read papers on his high bench, supposedly listened to what the deputy district attorney and the public defenders told him about the backgrounds of the boys and what had happened that night at City College.

Behind the fourteen boys on the hard seats of the courtroom in the fine Moorish courthouse, the older people sat wrapped in bright colors and black hair and quick, frightened Spanish words. The constant whispering and touching of people who understand little of what they are seeing and hearing, but who know what they are seeing and hearing is important to them. So they shift, and pluck at each other, and talk because they can only wait for someone to tell them what has happened, if it was a time to laugh or a time to cry.

The droning voice of the information, ". . . on this night, about the hour of six P.M., did wilfully attack with intent to commit murder and inflict severe bodily harm . . ."

"How do they plead?"

Each boy, standing now in front of the solemn judge and nudged by an assistant public defender mumbled his, "Not guilty."

One of the tall ones, the oldest, Raul Gonzales aged twenty-one, said, "Hey, they gonna send us back to Mexico, lawyer man?"

"Keep your clients quiet, Counsellor."

Fourteen surly young men remanded to county jail to await trial. The date set. No bail. And loud Spanish wailing that went slowly up the aisle of the courtroom and down the polished stone corridors into the city that was named in one language and owned in another.

Anderson sat in his car, tapped his fingers on the steering wheel as he looked out at the courthouse across Santa Barbara Street. I looked at the Sheriff's bus with the barred windows that would take the fourteen Westside Rockers back to jail.

"What's so important about Montez, Phil?"

His fingers continued to tap. He makes even a Volvo look like a small car. "None of the other thirteen are going to say one word to anyone, cooperate in any way. Name, rank and serial number is what the police, D.A., courts and we're going to get. Unless they're told by their leaders to cooperate, talk to us."

I watched the fourteen walk in a long, silent single line to the bus. Across Santa Barbara Street, on the same side we were, a small crowd of latinos watched as silent as the boys. "You can't get the leaders to tell them? Which ones are the leaders?"

"*El Cholo,* Esteban Gonzalez, Steve Gonzo. He's the only real leader they have. *El Jefé,* the boss."

It wasn't a name listed in the reading of the information. None of those names had been in the information.

"He wasn't arrested? Or wasn't he there last night?"

"He was there." We both watched the white Sheriff's bus drive away with the fourteen boys who looked out with stone faces at the city that celebrated *La Fiesta* at every first full moon in August. "He got away with four other members of the gang. Now they're all missing, vanished, flown the coop, gone underground."

"And you have to find him."

"So do you if you want to learn anything about the Westside Rockers."

"Or Edgardo Montez will tell us?"

"The youngest, the newest member. A different background. Maybe he's into more than he bargained for."

Thin and undeveloped even up close in the small interrogation room, the girlish shoulders bent, the glaring light harsh on his black hair. Hands so small and delicate it was hard to imagine them holding a knife or club. Impossible to imagine the smooth brown skin with blood on it, the thin arm feeling the shock of flesh and bone as the club struck another human in the dark of a college parking lot.

"They want to go for attempted murder on all of you," Anderson said in the interrogation room. "They say you were all laying for white students, out to kill them. You all planned it and a lot of students got hurt, some pretty bad. Only I don't believe you planned a damn thing. I don't believe you knew what was really going down."

His ankles in the jail pants were thinner than Philip Anderson's wrists. Chicken legs, a scrawny neck even I could break with my one arm, and a child's hands. But a club, a knife, a gun are wondrous magic that make a man out of a thin boy, cut giants down to size, grow a delicate kid ten feet tall. A kid who looked at both of us with blank black eyes and said nothing.

"They say you all went to that campus looking for trouble. Knocked over signs and benches, ripped up bushes, stomped flower beds. You wanted someone to kick butt on, you didn't care who or how bad they got hurt. I don't think you really wanted to hurt anyone, knew what was going to go down. I think you were scared and sorry you ever got into it."

"I think you're full of shit," Edgardo Montez said.

"I've talked to your father. He doesn't believe you could do such a thing. He doesn't believe you joined a gang. No good lazy bums."

He looked straight at Anderson, his dark eyes like mirrors in the glare of light. "My old man, he got a big black mustache, you know? He's a real little guy, but he got this big mustache. Down in Mexico a man always got a big mustache, right? He's real macho, my old man, a big shot in the *barrio*. Only he works all his life digging holes for the white man. The white man comes in the house, my old man with the big mustache he holds his hat in his hands." Black eyes that were anything but soft. "I never been to Mexico. Maybe I go sometime. Sit on the beaches. Not the good beaches, they're for the rich *gringos,* right? Go to the mountains and eat bananas. My aunt she goes once. She don't like it so good. She's got a white boyfriend, right? I mean, he's a dago, no whiter than me."

His tongue lived in three worlds. Whole sentences from the local high school where all boys are created equal. Words from the *barrio* slums where no one is equal. And the accent of *salsa* and *mariachis* and the past of Castilian cavaliers and slaughtered Indians and silent slaves both black and brown.

"Montez," Anderson said, "you joined the gang only a couple of weeks ago. You should never have been on that raid. Give me something I can use to help all of you. Tell me where I can find *El Cholo.* The other four. Not the police, me. I'm on your side, that's my job. Cholo's got to come back, tell your side of the story."

The black eyes that were not like the eyes of a child studied us. Then he laughed. A loud laugh. In the silence of the interrogation room the laugh echoed away.

"Hey, man, Cholo he got away."

"Hiding out won't help anyone or anything, Montez. Where is he? I have to talk to him."

His eyes became empty. *"No habla Ingles, señor."*

His thin shoulders moved. A delicate, almost imperceptible shrug, his eyes flat and empty, the girlish face expressionless.

Al Benton leaned against the parapet above Butterfly Beach. He had a protest going in Coast Village, the chances of him being seen here by anyone who knew him were slim. He leaned and looked across Channel Drive at the Biltmore Hotel.

"The husband was over there, right? Took her home. The husband and the parents. Everything she run from."

"They couldn't help what they are," I said. "They want to know what happened too."

"They always want to know what happened when it's too late."

I turned to look out to sea. "Anything from the streets about latino gang trouble?"

"Not a whisper. I been asking all over town. Some of the hardcase guys say they get run-ins, but no one got anything solid to tell. Why would Cassie have trouble with latinos?"

"That's what I'm asking. You don't want me to go on?"

He turned, looked down at the beach. "You figure the killer is still out there? Is maybe after more than just Cassie?"

"Killers," I said. "More than one, and I don't know what they're after."

He watched three overweight men come out of the gate from the Coral Casino onto the beach. "I guess you better find out."

18

This time Gus Chavalas was in his office working on papers. He waved me to a chair.

"Miller says you're not convinced. You think Jerry Kohnen killed five people and himself, but not number six."

"I'm not convinced."

"Tell me when you get your man. Or woman."

"You're convinced, Sergeant?"

"It's the way to bet."

"Totally?"

He leaned back, his hands behind his head. "I've never been totally convinced since the third grade when I found out the teachers, my father, and the President of the United States weren't always right."

"But enough to close the books."

"Enough to work on cases a lot wider open."

"I don't have a case wider open."

"It's Al Benton's money."

"If I find something?"

"Books can be opened."

I told him about the Spanish voices, the Westside Rockers in Alameda Park, the City College rumble. Chavalas thought for a time, his hands still behind his head where he leaned back.

"She knew Spanish?"

"That's what Benton says."

"She went to the bandstand because she could play her radio. She was in there listening to the radio. A Spanish station. The voices were the announcers."

It was an explanation.

"Do the Rockers have special enemies, allies?"

"Not my beat. You want the gang banger. That's Sergeant Abrahams."

Sergeant Abrahams was a burly and silent black who listened to my story with no expression whatsoever. When I'd finished he thought it over for some time. Then he nodded as if he'd entered all the facts into his interior computer, come up with a positive readout.

"The Westside Rockers move on Alameda Park sometimes. I wouldn't put it past them to hassle street people. Got no reports on that at this time. We'd like to pick up Gonzalez ourselves. We'll ask about your Reilly woman when we do."

"How about enemies or allies?"

"Got no allies up here. There's a smaller westside gang, the Hondos, who don't like the Rockers too much."

On the phone the secretary said Professor Rivera was at a meeting. I asked when Professor Rivera would be out of the meeting. She said no one ever knew when Professor Rivera would be out of a meeting. She said Professor Rivera did have a class immediately after lunch. I asked her where. She told me. I drove out to Isla Vista and had lunch in the Mexican restaurant on Embarcadero del Mar.

Luis was ten minutes late for his class, had no time for me until after. I took no chances, sat in on the class. It was a lecture. He was a good lecturer, knew exactly what he wanted the class to hear, moved easily between English and Spanish. Firm and blunt, with humor. All about how relentless invisibility over a long period of time, thorough and calculated, day to day and historically, can lead a people and culture to be, in the end, invisible to itself.

"How'd you do with the Westside Rockers?" He was breathing hard as we stood outside the class afterward, as if he'd run a marathon. In a way he had. Every time he told the young what he'd learned, what had really happened and still happened.

"Not too good." I told him about the City College raid, the missing five Rockers.

"Cholo himself? He won't be easy to find, Dan. Lost in L.A. or somewhere else by now."

"That a hint?"

"A guess. The Rockers have some ties down there. What do you want me to do?"

"There's another westside gang. The Hondos. I want to talk to them."

He shook his head. "It's a small gang. As tight and hard as we get up here. Ties with East Los Angeles too, and not the same ties. They don't talk to outsiders."

"Try."

Anderson was already inside the small, neat house of Edgardo Montez's family on the lower eastside when I got there.

They were lined up on a flowered couch. The three women and the small boy, stiff and prim, hands in their laps. The father sat apart in a high-backed carved wood chair. No taller than his jailed son but twice as thick. The long graying mustache Edgardo had sneered at bristled with anger. His black eyes were outraged under a wide-brimmed straw sombrero with a tassel hanging from the back.

"My son is good boy. He work hard, has respect. He does not do what they say. We all born here, Californios. Have respect."

The small boy was a miniature of his father and his brother. Thin and delicate, wearing a sombrero. The father traditional in the ways of an old country he had probably seen twice in his life on formal visits but claimed in his dress and manner as his own because everyone has to claim somewhere.

"Edgardo he go to college," the older woman said, "study, know all about America."

The women were between the country of their real language, and the country where they had been born and lived. The older woman, the mother, wore a loose print dress proper for a Mexican matron, but American too. The youngest, the sister, sat in a pink party dress with a big bow for company. The third was Edgardo's girlfriend, young and slender in a white sheath and low heels, her dark hair short. American clothes and hair, but in the father's house she wore a dress.

A dress and scared eyes. "Edgardo couldn't have done what they say, Mr. Anderson. He couldn't hurt anyone."

"What was he doing there then?" Anderson said. "Why was he in the Rockers? You don't have to join a gang, you do it because you want to. Was he glad he was in the gang, Miss—?"

"Rita Cardenas." She was very young, and she didn't look at us. "I don't know why he joined that gang. I never wanted him to."

The mother said, "He is not with those *cholos*. He is not where they say. He has good job, goes to the college. He is Americano."

The father jumped up, waved his short, muscular arms, his thick mustache bristling. The anger in the father made his jaw muscles stand out like cords. He was in a rage inside over what had happened to his son, against what was being done to his son. But he had spent his life suppressing that anger, hiding it, finding excuses and explanations that would allow him to go on living in the anglo world he had to live in or give up all he had done and start over. Deny his whole life.

"That is why he is in trouble! He listen to both of you. You make him want to be *gringo*. You see what is happen?"

Confusion in the Montez household, in the father himself. To stay apart in your own world—not of the country you were born in, not in the country you are part of—or to cross over into the bigger world? Which one, and what will it do to you? In the land of your ancestors, but a land that no longer belongs to the descendants of your ancestors. To hide, suppress and go on, or to challenge? Edgardo had stopped hiding. It was easier for him, he had nothing much to lose.

I said, "Did you ever talk to Edgardo about the gang, Rita?"

"Sometimes." She looked down at the floor.

"Tell us what you talked about. What Edgardo said."

She didn't want to talk about Edgardo. Especially not in front of his parents. She didn't want to talk to us anywhere. But she wanted Edgardo Montez to get out of jail and come home and be her boyfriend and go to the movies and have fun. She wanted to do something to make that happen. Something more than crying or listening to Edgardo's father say it had all happened because Edgardo wanted to be a gringo or Edgardo's mother deny it had ever happened.

I said, "Where did Edgardo work? He went to City College, right?"

She nodded. "He works at Able Instrument on Olive Street. He is studying to be an engineer, or he will when he graduates and transfers to the university."

Anderson said, "What does he do at Able Instrument?"

She still looked at the floor with its colorful rugs over cracked but scrubbed linoleum. "He is the office boy, runs errands, cleans the office."

"What did he say when you talked about the gang, Rita?"

She didn't want to tell us about Edgardo, her man, but she was scared. They were all scared. What was going to happen to Edgardo? Edgardo was in jail. In the *barrio,* people don't have many good experiences with police, D.A.s and jails. We were gringos, and close to being police, and she didn't want to tell us anything, but we *were* gringos and close to being police and maybe we could help.

"At work he pushes a broom, gets coffee, goes out to buy doughnuts and lunch for everyone else. He says at City College he walks around like he is the invisible man. He feels like he isn't even there the way the anglos and a lot of the professors look at him." She shrugged—the eloquent latin shrug combined with the sullen American teenager shrug—looked down at the hem of the skirt she wore because she was in the house of *Señor* Montez. "I like going out, you know? I work hard in school, help my mother at home, study so I get a good job after I graduate. On Friday, Saturday, I want to go to parties, you know, eat some nice place, go to the movies. Edgardo got a job all day, goes to college three nights, got to study the other nights. There ain't a lot of time to party or go to the movies. Edgardo, he takes me to the movies this Friday, you know?"

19

A Friday in mid-September. *El Grito De Dolores.* Back to school. A hot Indian summer in Santa Barbara.

There's this real good movie Rita wants to see. It's way out by Plaza Del Sol. But, hey, Edgardo says, his girl wants to see that movie, that's what she's gonna do. Friday they'll drive out to Plaza Del Sol for the movie Rita got to see, eat Italian at Marianne's, maybe find a party later.

Only on Thursday Edgardo's beat-up old Datsun won't start, has to be towed into Akira, needs some parts and is going to take at least until Monday to fix.

On Thursday, Edgardo has a bad day pushing his stinking broom on the job, fights with his boss over him getting a chance to help one of the engineers test a new instrument, does lousy at school, stops in a bar on Haley for a couple of beers and gets into a late-night crap game.

On Friday there's no car and all he has in his pocket is fifteen bucks.

Rita says, "Okay, we'll eat cheap at McDonald's and take the bus to the movie."

That's what they do. They have a great time. It's a good movie, and McDonald's isn't all that bad. Only at the movie they get carried away, or Rita does, eat too much popcorn and candy. They forget they have to take the bus home.

"We find someone gives us a ride," Edgardo says.

They look for someone in the audience when they go out who can give them a lift home. They don't find anyone. It is not a movie popular in the *barrio.*

"Okay," Rita says, "we walk home."

"All the way to the *barrio*? You're crazy."

"It's a nice night, 'Gardo. Come on, it'll be a kick. Something different."

Edgardo laughs. "Hey, so why not, you know? I walk that far before."

They start out like a couple of kids. It's a crazy ball walking all the way from Plaza Del Sol to past Milpas and way down almost to the ocean! They laugh a lot, hold hands as they walk, and Rita stops and looks in all the stores on State and De La Vina and Chapala. She loves to look into store windows at all the neat stuff there. Edgardo does too for a while, then he starts to get annoyed.

"Jesus Christ, Reet, you got to look in all the goddamn stores?"

"I like to look in stores. I like nice things."

"Why you chicks got to do that, for Christ sake? How you think it make a guy feel he ain't got money he can buy all the stuff in them stores?"

Rita hasn't walked so far before, she goes slower and slower, stops to look in more windows, and they both get tired. They're on lower Chapala, still have to walk across town on Haley Street all the way to Milpas, down Milpas to Carpinteria Street and then across and down to Cacique and Canada Streets where their families live.

Edgardo sees this second-hand store on Haley near lower State with chairs and tables and other second-hand stuff out in front. They are old wooden chairs battered and worn and in need of paint. Rita looks at the chairs, and at Edgardo. She is so tired her eyes say she has to rest.

"Go ahead, honey, take a seat. We sit a while, you feel better."

Rita sits on one of the battered old chairs on the sidewalk. So does Edgardo. It feels good just to sit after their long walk, and they begin to feel better. It's a bang after all, an adventure. All the people out on a Friday night visiting the bars and restaurants and rock clubs on lower State walk past and look at them. Even the homeless and winos look at them as they shuffle past. Not all the passersby smile at them, but they don't care. They sit for maybe ten minutes, talking and watching the night life of the city, when this guy comes out of the store yelling like all hell has broken loose.

"Hey! You *cholos* get outta those chairs! Get the hell out of those chairs! What the Christ you dumb beaners think you're doing?"

The crowds of people that walk past on the streets stare at the shouting store owner and at Edgardo and Rita. Many stop and watch the two young latinos on the old chairs and the angry store owner.

"You fucking greasers think you own the city? Lazy fucking bums! Get out of my chairs!"

Rita starts to cry. Some people in the throng around them laugh. Rita jumps up to run away. Edgardo stops her. He holds her arm in a hard grip that hurts her, the muscles of his arm as rigid as his face.

"She's tired, man," he says to the irate owner. "We ain't hurting your goddamn fucking junk chairs."

"You gonna pay me, *cholo?* You gonna buy those chairs, *pachuco?* Who buys them they see you beaners in them? No white man's gonna buy them you sit in 'em, *Pancho.*"

Everyone on the street is looking at the scene. Some of them call out in support of the store owner, swear at the damn beaners. Some are angry for Rita and Edgardo. Rita sits and cries and looks away along Haley Street. She's frightened. People are laughing. People are shouting. People are staring. Even those who haven't stopped to watch. Edgardo holds her in his hard grip.

"Sit down, honey. Don't let this anglo son-of-a-bitch—"

The store owner snarls, "Who the hell you callin' a son-of-a-bitch you stinkin' wetback greaser! You know what, you sit in those chairs, you bought 'em. You damaged 'em, you pays for 'em. Ten bucks. For you, *señor,* ten dollar American. Special. You got ten dollar, *señor?*"

Edgardo doesn't have ten dollars. He doesn't have a dollar. He wants to take ten dollars and shove it in the pale anglo face of the store owner. The fat, sweaty, sneering face of the pig of a store owner. But he doesn't have ten dollars. The owner knows he doesn't have ten dollars. Everyone in the crowd knows he doesn't have ten dollars on a Friday night.

"Ten dollar a chair, *señor wetback.* Whatsamatter, *señor?* You ain't got twenty American dollars? Bet you ain't got ten American dollars. Maybe you want to pay me in pesos? Yeah, you got a pocketful of pesos, *señor?*"

Rita can't control her crying. Her head is down where she sits in the chair and cries to the sidewalk. Edgardo tries to comfort her, unaware that he is hurting her, making her cry even more. Some in the crowd still laugh. Some drunks sneer, shout obscenities.

"Shit," the owner laughs. "I bet you ain't got a goddamn fucking peso, *cholo.* Okay, get the fuck out of those chairs right now."

The owner grabs Rita's other arm to pull her up out of the chair. Edgardo hits the man.

The owner is twice Edgardo's size, three times his weight. He lets

go of Rita and charges Edgardo. Edgardo dodges, the owner
sprawls over one of the chairs and crashes down on another breaking it. The owner staggers up, cursing.

"Fucking goddamn thief! You see him hit me? Goddamn thief!"

The owner charges Edgardo again. This time Edgardo picks up a
chair and hits the man. The owner goes down bleeding and howling.

"Police! Get the cops! I'm bleedin'. You all see—"

Edgardo and Rita run. Along Haley in the warm September night,
all the way to Garden Street before they slow, panting and trying to
get their breath. Rita is still crying. Edgardo is in a wild rage. The
fun and adventure of the night is gone. They walk, Rita still crying
softly no matter how much Edgardo tries to get her to stop. They
walk on to Milpas and finally turn down toward Carpinteria and
Canada and Cacique.

A police car cruises down Milpas behind them.

They both hide in a doorway.

The police car passes on along Milpas.

A block farther down Milpas they see another second-hand store
with chairs and tables out on the sidewalk. The same police car
comes back up Milpas toward them. It slows as it comes close to
Edgardo and Rita. The police stare out at them suspiciously.

Edgardo picks up one of the second-hand chairs on the sidewalk
in front of the second store, and throws it through the store window.
Inside the owner of this store starts to yell. The police car screeches
to a halt, the policemen bolt out toward them. Rita can't move. Edgardo doesn't move. He stands and waits for the police.

They throw Edgardo up against the building, search him. The
store owner is on the sidewalk, raging at Edgardo, demanding that
the police arrest him. The police ask what did he think he was
doing? Breaking windows, smashing property. Edgardo tells them.

The two policemen stare at him.

One says, "So you break the window at a different store?"

The other says, "It ain't the same store?"

Edgardo says nothing. Rita cries more.

They take Edgardo to jail, let Rita go with her parents when they
come for her. Eventually, they convict Edgardo, fine him, suspend a
sentence, and make him pay for the broken window. They also
make him pay for the first owner's chairs.

When it is finally over, Edgardo quits his office boy job and goes to work on construction to make more money so he can pay it all off. He quits City College, goes across town to join the Westside Rockers.

20

Montez would talk, Anderson was sure. Break down in his jail cell, think about what his anger had gotten him into, and tell all he knew about *El Cholo,* Esteban Gonzalez, the chief. Realize what a mistake he'd made and save himself.

"He's not used to a cell, had a taste before but got out fast and light and easy. This time won't be so easy, and he'll know it."

"What if he doesn't, Phil?"

"Then I'll have to try something else. We're looking for the other four Rockers, one of them might lead us to Gonzalez."

He drove off. I sat in my Tempo on the quiet *barrio* street in front of the Montez family's repaired, painted and well-kept cottage. Anderson was probably right about Edgardo Montez, but it could take time, and I didn't have time. With Jerry Kohnen dead and buried and convicted, the case would grow colder by the second.

I called Luis Rivera.

It's not as hard as a meet with a mafia don or Lieutenant Colonel North when he ran our Latin American policy—Santa Barbara isn't New York or L.A.—but it's hard enough. You have to pass word you want to meet, and maybe you get an answer, maybe you don't.

I was lucky, Luis got me the right answer. As it does in everything, it depends on what's in it for them. The Hondos wanted everyone to know they'd had nothing to do with the attack at City College, deplored it strongly. A bad scene. They would never do such a thing.

"You tell the man we don' make no noise like that there. The fuckin' Rockers are crazy. They's real dangerous, you know, man?"

We were at a table in the back of a *bodega* on San Andres Street. The owner sat behind his counter up front, his feet braced on the top, and watched the door without being too obvious about it. Some of the Hondos who'd come with their leader were outside, but in the store we were alone except for the owner.

"I'll tell them," I said. "How about Esteban Gonzalez? You have any ideas where he's hiding out?"

"What you think? Cholo's a fuckin' pig, man. We got no piece o' Cholo."

His name was Carlos. Just Carlos, and he was another skinny one. Skinny but a long way from girlish or delicate. Scars and beard stubble and hard leather. The same hot black eyes, but cold too, with an intensity close to the edge of sanity. He wore black jeans, a black sateen shirt open to the silver cross in his chest hair, and a black leather jacket like his troops, but he was an easy twenty-four.

"You know Cholo got away? Him and four other Rockers? They're all missing."

"Like, maybe we do, maybe we don't, you know? No way we gives out that information, right?"

"Where would he go, Carlos? The public defender wants to know, not the police. Philip Anderson. You know who Anderson is, you could need him sometime."

He was half lost in the interior shadows of the back room. A cigarette that glowed, smelled like it had more than tobacco in it. "Hey, you sees old movies? Foreign Legion an' all? We don' ask no questions, don' answer none."

"It's high profile trouble," I said. "The good citizens take a bad view of gang fights at their colleges, especially outside the *barrio*. The injured kids are mostly anglo. That's a race riot. The good citizens are mad as all hell."

I didn't have to draw pictures for him. He knew that heat on one latino gang was heat on all latino gangs. Angry anglo citizens didn't know one gang from another. They didn't know enemy gangs from allied gangs, and don't want to know. A *pachuco* was a *pachuco,* a gang was a gang. Hang them all. Anglo city governments listen to anglo citizens, especially rich and angry anglo citizens. He wouldn't have met me if he hadn't wanted to divert heat from the riot on the campus away from the Hondos. Maybe even use it for their benefit, take over Westside Rockers' territory and members. Increase recruiting for his gang at the expense of the Rockers. He wanted me to carry his message back to City Hall. *Quid pro quo.*

He tilted back against the wall. "Cholo got a chick down East L.A. He come around here day after it go down, tell Manny the Rockers is gonna play it real low a while, but they gonna be back, Manny he better don' forget that. He tell Manny he want the word every day. What go down on the westside, in the court. He tell Manny send word down to Luisa Bombal in L.A."

"Who's Manny?"

"Owner."

"This store?"

"You got it."

"You have an address on this Luisa Bombal? A phone number?"

"You crazy, man? Hey, we got the chick's name 'cause Manny got a sister goes with a Hondo an' she hears Manny tell his old lady what Cholo says to him."

"Can you ask her to get an address, phone number?"

"No way, man!" His chair legs hit the floor. He leaned across the table. "We give you Cholo's chick's name, okay? Them anglos at the college was lookin' for trouble too. The Rockers is assholes, Cholo's crazy, we got no eyes for crazies. The cops bust him, *bueno,* that's good. But we don' do no work for the cops. We's neutral like, right? We don' help no one."

It was his official position. A communiqué from the White House, 10 Downing Street, the Kremlin. The explanation of the Hondos noninvolvement in a regrettable but understandable incident.

"I'll tell the cops," I said. "You have anything more to tell me and Anderson about this Luisa Bombal? Off the record? Is she in some East L.A. gang?"

He tilted back again, blew smoke into the silence.

This time there were four and they were more efficient. Or more determined. Or more scared.

Two came out of the dark as I walked from the garage in the alley to the side entrance to my office.

Ahead of me.

Two were in the alley behind me. I saw the movement in the dim light over our garage door from the corner of my eye.

Part of the dark night that moved. As black as the night. The same black with flashing white. Ski masks. Black clothes. Rattle of bicycle chains. Flash of silver in the light that came from our house so far ahead.

Held out straight in the night in front of me. A pistol.

I charged into the flash. (The shot went somewhere. No burning of my flesh, no rush of air or whine too close. A wild shot. Surprise. Always surprise the enemy. The unexpected.) I hit an arm and the weight behind it. A chest and shoulder. A thin chest that fell away.

"Jesus Christ!"

The sudden voice in my ear that fell away to the black ground. Rolled over grass and rocks and . . .

"Hit him! Hit him!"

The metal wind of a bicycle chain. The chain like razors on my ear. Scramble and crawl and climb bushes.

"Hit him Scorpion!"

"Kick the bastard!"

"Where's the damned gun!"

"Cut him! Cut him! Jesus Christ—"

Shapes of the night that moved and whirled and grew and vanished and kicked and slashed and shined and breathed and kicked . . .

"You!"

An explosion as loud as the night.

"Get away from him!"

The second shot that exploded the night from our house slammed into the side of the garage.

Echoed through the night as lights and voices came from the surrounding distance. Echoed through a wide, empty night without shapes or shadows. Nothing that moved. A large night with soft air and the sound of surf somewhere above the near voices and lights and unintelligible questions floating on the light air. No frantic voices, no kicks or slash of chains or flash of silver or explosions of light and sound . . .

"Dan? I heard the shot, came out to look, and . . . Dan? Are you all right?"

In the dark yard Kay stood tall against the lighted windows of the house, my old cannon in her hands. Both hands. A cannon not a pistol. How had I carried it for so long?

"Dan?"

Hands on me. Kay and two neighbors. Up, I searched the night on all sides. There was only light from windows and open doors. The faces on the night street, the face around me, were eager, curious.

"Are you all right? I better call the doctor—"

I felt the ache and the wet. On my hand the blood from my right ear. Blood on my shirt. Sore ribs. A cut again on the back of my lone hand. I smiled at the helpful, eager, curious, excited neighbors. An adventure. In their own neighborhood. That detective again.

"I'm fine. Thank them, take me inside."

Thanks going all around. *It was nothing. We could see he was in trouble. Who were they? Should we call the police? Who the hell were they?*

"It's fine," I said. "I'll call the police. You were all great. Thanks again."

They all smiled, disappointed.

21

On the couch in my office I lay with the ice on my ribs and back where they'd kicked. A bandaged right ear where the black grease said the bicycle chain had slashed like a razor. Iodine on my hand where the knife had nicked.

"Philip Anderson called on your line, I was in your office when I heard the shot outside. I grabbed your old pistol from your desk drawer, ran out and saw them kicking at something on the ground. I knew it had to be you coming in from the garage so I shot into the air. That stopped them, but they didn't move away, so I shot toward the garage and they ran."

"What did they look like? Describe them."

"It was dark out there, Dan. Until the other people on the block put on lights and opened doors after I shot."

"How many?"

"Four or five."

I'd sensed four. More than the first time in the park.

"Tall, short? Old, young?"

Kay reconstructed in her memory what she had barely seen in the action of the moment. "Thin. Some not too tall, some tall. Dark clothes. Black faces and white eyeholes, sort of reverse KKK hoods. I—"

"Ski masks."

"I saw you on the ground and I shot in the air."

"They seemed jumpy to me, nervous and scared. Missed me a lot, weapons and feet. They never used the gun again."

"You didn't fire that first shot?"

"No, they did."

"I didn't see any gun, Dan."

I'd stopped only once on the way home from Carlos to call Anderson, got no answer at either his office or his apartment, left a message that I had news, call me. Not more than five minutes total. But Carlos had plenty of time to send men if he knew where I lived, and that was as hard to find as looking in the yellow pages. Or could Steve Gonzalez, *El Cholo,* and his four missing Westside Rockers not want me to find them or even look for them? Had the black shapes sounded latino?

"What did Anderson want?"

"He got your message, said he'd be here in an hour with some news of his own. Do you feel up to dinner?"

In the short run the small things are more important for each of us than the big. The short run is all each of us has.

"I always feel up to dinner."

Kay's a fine cook, if usually she has no more time to do it than I do. I can put food on the table, but she's a cook, and I take advantage of that any time I can. I sat in the kitchen and watched her make the crepes she would stuff with scallops and lobster mixed in her special sauce, then bake. I needed some time. To steady and think after the attack.

They read more and more as amateurs playing at soldier. A Los Angeles gang would be more deadly, but everyone agreed that Santa Barbara gangs were still kids, still amateurs. That amateur? And how would the Westside Rockers know what I was doing, thinking? Unless they'd been watching me all along?

"Melt the marge for the asparagus."

I melted the margarine, and we ate as always at the dining room table with the full china and silverware and good glasses.

Phil Anderson arrived in time for dessert. He didn't join us.

"Something's going on outside."

I got my new Sig-Sauer.

"At the far end of that alley behind your house. Four or five guys milling around in the bushes. A lot of noise."

"Are they in black? Masked?" I told him about the attack on me.

His PPK looked like a toy in a hand that size. "Didn't see them close, they sure blend into the dark except they're making so damn much noise."

We moved along the alley, me against the left garage doors, Anderson against the right side doors. I heard the noise ahead. A macabre combination of whispering, swearing and low laughter, with heavy feet tramping in the thick undergrowth of the open field at the far end of the alley. It was a vacant lot next to the first house on our side of the street. The owner of the house had planned to build on it before the water moratorium had struck and he'd been unable to get a water hookup ever since. In anger he let it grow as thick with weeds and brush as he could before the fire department came down on him and made him cut it.

On the east side of the alley the garages went all the way to the end. I had the cover of the building shadows. Anderson didn't. The last garage on the west ended at the edge of the vacant lot. He flattened his bulk against the corner of the last garage, motioned me to get on the other side of the five dark figures trampling the field in the night. They appeared to be searching for something, kicking at the brush.

Somehow furtive and surreptitious and making too much noise all at the same time. Whispering and stifling laughs. Shushing each other and talking too loud. Like drunks coming home late at night, elaborately attempting to be quiet and not giving a damn. Not paying a lot of attention to anything around them, growing louder and louder in both their giggling and laughing, and their whispering and shushing.

Damn.

Young kids. The thin voices, the obliviousness to anything and anyone around them. The rising level of wildness and the escalating scale of loudness. I stepped out of the shadows.

"You kids! What's going on over there?"

Anderson jumped out to back me up. "All of you hold it right where you are!"

Kids they were, and, like kids, changed in an instant. From strutting, big-time night prowlers out on a dark mission, to five scared juveniles caught in the act by adults. They scattered like a school of minnows with a predator pike among them. Zebra from a charging lion.

"Stop—!"

It was as far as Anderson got as they raced away under street lights. Early teenagers, all in dark sweaters and jeans, running and panicked and laughing all at once. Out on a weekday-night adventure when they were supposed to be at home studying.

"Shit." Anderson lowered his PPK.

We watched the kids vanish into the night in five different directions. We were alone with the dark alley and the empty lot.

"They were in that field for some reason. Searching for something. They weren't playing at random."

We spread out to go through the field.

"I saw them first close to the alley side," Anderson said.

That's where he was. On his back, arms flung out, his dead eyes up to the millions of stars of the night outside the city. Anderson bent, felt the dead man's wrist, stood up.

"I'll get my flashlight."

He went off to his car parked up the street in front of our hacienda. I waited over the dead man. All in black. A black ski mask. Black gloves. Legs sprawled, a bicycle chain in one outflung hand. In the black clothes, lying among the high weeds and thick brush, he was all but invisible from the alley and from the streets on both sides. Unless he was stumbled over by a gang of young teens out on a night of prowling fun.

"Christ."

Anderson held the flashlight on the fallen man. In the beam of light the multiple stab wounds were like lips in the black cloth of his turtleneck shirt and tight jeans. His mouth was like a stab wound, gaping open, the tongue protruding. I bent and pulled off the ski mask. The face was mottled, the neck and throat bruised.

"They did a job," Anderson said. "He was choked, maybe smothered as well as cut up."

He couldn't have been more than seventeen. Black hair cut short, and even shorter on the sides. Straight white teeth and a round face. A darkish skin color and large nose. The dead eyes brown. Anything from a tanned anglo to an Americanized Iranian. Sicilian or South American or a darker all-American boy.

"Rage or panic or both. The same as Cassandra Reilly."

"He's one of those who attacked you?"

"I'd say so. How long's he been dead?"

Anderson bent again, examined the sprawled body. "Maybe an hour or so. I'm no coroner."

An hour would be about right. "Identification?"

"Nothing on him. Zero."

"Remove all identification," I said. "Military raid."

"He's got a watch. Expensive one."

"You know him? Maybe one of the missing Rockers?"

"He could be a gang guy. But I don't know him."

We both stood in the night and looked down at the dead boy. It never really becomes routine.

"You want to be here when the Sheriff's people come?"

"I was never here," Anderson said. "They attacked you. If this is connected to the Westside Rockers I don't want to know it ever happened until someone tells me."

"What did you have to tell me?"

"Edgardo Montez. I got one name: Luisa Bombal. He doesn't like the future the D.A. has laid out for him, says it's a bad rap on all the Rockers, Cholo knows the real story. The Bombal girl is one of Cholo's chicks. She lives down in East L.A."

"I got the same name from Carlos." I told him about my visit to the chief of the Hondos.

"Call the Sheriff, we'll go down in the morning. As soon as I've made some calls, and if you want to come with me."

"I want."

When he had gone, I called the Sheriff's office. They arrived in under five minutes in the usual force and order: patrol deputy and sergeant, coroner's detail, major crime detectives, and crime scene investigation detectives. By now I'd been in California, and in their hair, long enough for them to know me. That didn't make them love me, and while the patrol officers taped off the field in their bright yellow tape, the detectives put me through the questions. I had nothing to hide, except the Westside Rockers and Hondos, and there was no way they would appear in the case unless I told about them.

"You're working on a case S.B.P.D. has closed?"

"Yes."

"They know that?"

"They know."

The Sheriff's detective grinned. "Nice. I'll talk to Chavalas. You think this killing is connected to that case?"

"That's what I think."

Now he laughed. "I'm going to talk to Gus myself. That's all you can tell us? These four guys jumped you, you didn't see any of them? Ski masks and black clothes. What about the gun?"

"I never saw it after I hit the one guy."

"Let's take a look."

They searched the night all around our house and the neighbors houses, found no gun or anything else.

"You don't even have a guess who he is? Any ident at all?"

"No."

They took my story, took the body, searched the field half the rest of the night while I watched. They came up totally empty, finally gave up and went home with a man left to watch the field until morning.

Kay was asleep, only mumbled pleasantly when I got into bed. I lay awake a long time, thought about the missing gun. I knew it had been knocked into the night when I hit the shooter. One of them had come back and retrieved it. More determined, or more worried.

22

"No ident, no missing person, no runaway, no known gang member. Not a Santa Barbara gang, anyway. A John Doe. I called Chavalas and the Sheriff's department this morning. The Sheriff has no information on the boy, Gus wonders which of my old cases the guys in black could be connected with. Did I ever go up against the Gestapo? The SS? Maybe their sons are getting even."

"Gus always wanted to be a comedian," Anderson said. He'd picked me up early in the Volvo, we were already over the Conejo grade. He knew where Luisa Bombal was. Or where his L.A. connections said she might be.

Before we left, I'd told Al Benton about the latest attack, suggested his money was being well spent after all. It didn't make him feel better. My description of the attackers and the dead boy meant nothing to him. He didn't know who they were or what they wanted and that scared him. It scared me.

Anderson had to make a stop in Northridge-Glendale to talk to a witness the police didn't know existed, but who didn't want to come back to Santa Barbara to testify.

I sat in the car in the quiet, middle-class neighborhood of small, flat-roofed houses, each with a tiny patio and an even tinier pool. They all had miniature corrals behind the houses that opened onto a fenced horse-way that led to trails up in the foothills around the valley. They were cheaply built little imitations of the homes of the wealthy, the estates of the horse set, had cost the owners so much work and struggle to own. Proud and happy owners, achievers of their dreams. Why did they make me feel depressed and frustrated, helpless and hopeless, these flimsy little mini-estates with their pet horses and narrow runs out into the brown and barren foothills?

Anderson got the woman to agree to return to Santa Barbara. We drove on south.

* * *

The *barrio* of East Los Angeles is one of those abandoned places where few dreams are achieved and too many of those that are end in sudden death. A cosmic brown hole from which little escapes.

Off the freeway we drove deeper into the world of graffiti, vacant lots where there had been buildings, boarded store fronts, debris and trash and bare windows with neither curtains nor signs of life. It wasn't wise to stand at the window and look out in East L.A. Some dying minor planet, a meteor-devastated world on the far side of the City of the Pueblo of Our Lady the Queen of the Angels, matched only by the distant South Bronx and Watts. A dying planet crowded with creatures who couldn't save it and didn't even really want to try. A different life form. Not the same as those who lived on the green and comfortable power planet so many light years away at the other ends of the freeway.

A life form that sat silent against the storefronts, in the abandoned doorways. Dark faces that stared at us from weed-grown empty lots as we passed, lounged against the walls and fences, milled around the littered sidewalks, wandered all along the bare streets. Saloons, *cantinas* all along the trashed boulevard among the boarded storefronts, littered doorways, bare windows. Inside, through open doors, dark-skinned men, old and young, big and small, sat in the morning and watched the television over the bar with its bright images of all they wanted but would never have.

Off the boulevards along the side streets there were still stubborn blue-collar neighborhoods where older residents tried to maintain the sense and appearance of pride, community, self-sufficiency and even standards of proper behavior their poor and immigrant parents had instilled into them. Paint on the small, maintained houses, flowers behind neat fences, swept driveways, sidewalks and gutters. Even some grass on tiny lawns brought by January rains and mowed. But for the most part the side streets were as bare and battered as the boulevards. Unpainted houses, bare yards, broken fences, graffiti and litter. The burned or abandoned shells of the empty buildings, the boarded or curtain-covered windows of the crack and heroin houses.

The address Anderson had for Luisa Bombal was not on one of the green side streets. Gray and sagging, the house had its windows boarded and its yard littered with the rusted remnants of what could have been cars or even appliances. An all but deserted street. Two chained dogs at a ramshackle house a half a block away. Three young children playing under a bare and dusty tree, a loud and belligerent game of knocking each other down and posturing. One old man taking the sun in a white wicker rocking chair set in the dirt of the next house.

"I'll go alone," Anderson said. "They don't expect you, it could spook them."

In the car I sat with my lone hand on the Sig-Sauer in my tweed jacket pocket, watched the street in back, front and on all sides, and thought about the dead boy last night. Alone and nameless in the county morgue. Why was he dead? Somehow, I knew the answer to that would tell me who had killed Cassandra Reilly. I suspected the Westside Rockers were part of that answer. The question was how, and that answer could be dangerous.

I watched up and down the gray street. We were in alien territory, and how could they know we were on their side? If we were. Alone, sweat on my hand that held the pistol.

The woman who came out of the front door of the house walked toward the next corner without a glance at the Volvo. A tall, slender latina with dark hair, her hands deep in the pockets of a red leather coat. High heels and a quick step that clicked and echoed on the deserted street. She turned the far corner.

The longer I sat in the Volvo on the gray street, the more dangerous it was. A Volvo parked on a street in East L.A. would be seen, reported, and, eventually, investigated.

No one appeared to join the old man in the wicker rocker. The kids were gone. Only me, the two dogs and the old man.

One of the men came from around the house where Anderson had gone. The other around the opposite corner of the gray cottage. Two short, heavy men in their twenties who looked like the pre-Columbian statues every tourist in Mexico brings home. *Monos,* all fake today. Real ones would not be allowed from the country. Not with a tourist. They disappeared around the far corner.

The old man up the street rocked in the noon sun.

No one else came from the gray cottage.

I walked up the cracked and weed-grown concrete driveway. Through spaces between the boards over the windows I peered into a bare room without furniture. No one answered my knocking. A path led around the house to the rear. The back door stood ajar. In the kitchen dishes soaked in the sink, the remnants of a meal littered a scarred wooden table. Three wooden chairs around the table and nothing else. In a tiny dining room there was a cot, an easy chair, a rug, an old bureau whose drawers wouldn't close, and a black and white television.

Anderson was in the living room.

"You took your goddamn time. Anybody else show outside?"

He sat in a heavy wooden chair with wide arms and a high back. The big chair was the only furniture in the living room. It was out of sight from the windows I had peered through. His arms were tied to the chair arms, his ankles to the chairs legs, his big body to the high back. They hadn't put a gag on him.

"Why didn't you call for help?"

"How the hell did I know who was out there besides you? You going to argue or cut me loose?"

I smiled, cut him loose with my pocket knife. He stood up, stamped around the dirty room raising dust and shaking the whole cottage, rubbed at his wrists.

"Where did they go? Did they meet anyone, get picked up?"

"The woman walked right, the two men left. No one picked them up, they met no one. What the hell happened?"

He continued to walk the room, swung his arms. "I knocked at the back door, the woman answered. I asked if she was Luisa Bombal. She said she didn't know any Luisa Bombal. I said I'd come to talk to her about Cholo and the Westside Rockers up in Santa Barbara. That's when she asked who I was and I told her and she took me into this room and into the two guys with guns."

"They threatened you?"

"They suggested I sit in the chair and the woman tied me up. She's good at it, had some practice. You see anything on your way in? In the kitchen?"

"An empty yard, dirty dishes and old furniture."

The only other rooms were two bedrooms, each set up like the dining room as a semi-separate apartment, and empty.

"What did you find out about Steve Gonzalez?"

"Nothing. They asked, I answered. They did the talking, especially the woman. Who sent me, why, what did I want, how did I know her name, what did I know about Cholo."

"What did you tell them?"

"Everything I could. She was pumping me to report to Cholo. I want him to know I'm working to defend the Rockers."

We found nothing that gave us a clue to where Cholo Gonzalez might be, or anything else about him or the other four Westside Rockers. Outside, Anderson went to the Volvo to get his backup gun. They'd taken his PPK. Never miss a chance to pick up another weapon in a war, from friend or enemy. Anderson saw the old man who still rocked in his white wicker chair.

"He looks like he's there every day."

"Neighborhood watchdog."

"Worth a try."

The old man watched as we approached him through the dust of street and yard, never stopped rocking his white rocker. He had the same thick, drooping mustache as Edgardo Montez's father. That was the only resemblance. Older, in his late seventies or even eighties. A light brown face with the hooded eyes and high cheekbones, a thin nose and lips as hard as the lips of a wolf. Eyes that calculated our value and our worth, what he could get from us, how he could use us.

"Hola, *señorés,* you got cigarette? I have no cigarette all day."

I didn't smoke. I knew Anderson didn't. But he produced a pack of some brand, shook three out into the old man's hand, held the almost full pack in front of the old man's eyes as we talked.

"We're looking for the people in that house where our car is parked. You know them?"

"Cabron!" The old man spat in the dirt, lit his cigarette with his own matches, grinned at us. "You cops? They got to send more cops. Those people, they come here, sell *coca,* sell shit. No good, you know? I live here fifty year, you know? I don' know no one no more."

"They have names?" Anderson said.

"Always they come from someplace else, you know? Sure hope you guys is real tough cops. They sells shit, trash everythin'. The woman's a *chingada.* Cops is all scared come in here."

"They sell dope, prostitution? They're a gang? What gang?"

"You cops dump all them trash people out here."

"You know their names? What gang? Where they went?"

All at once the old man's dark eyes went vacant and distant as if the brain inside had gone somewhere else. "Don' know no one no more. They's all gone, you know? They come back soon." The dark eyes were suddenly bright again. *"Ninos* all come back. All rich, *muy dinero.* They come back, bring money, I buy house, new car, big TV, everythin'. *El jefe."*

He grinned up at us, but his eyes were a million light years away in another universe. His sons would come back and make him rich. He rocked in his white rocker on the dirt of his broken-down house and dreamed of being rich, the boss. I thought of all the men in the morning *cantinas* along the boulevards watching the television over the bar. I thought of my grandfather.

23

Tadeusz Jan Fortunowski is born of Polish parents in a small town in Lithuania that is then part of the empire of the Tsar of all the Russias. The Polish and Lithuanian people and the Russian authorities do not like each other. The Polish and Lithuanian people, the Russian rulers, and the Jews, do not like each other. The Polish people, the Russians, the Jews, the Lithuanians who once owned Poland but are now owned by Russia, and the Ukrainians who want independence from the Tsar, do not like each other. The Cossacks like no one, not even each other, but are paid by the Tsar so serve him and do most of their fighting and killing for Mother Russia.

(He was my grandfather. I never knew him. He died before I was born, old Tadeusz, but that is how his widow, his second wife not my grandmother, described where he was born. In the front room of the six-story old-law tenement on Seventh Street in lower Manhattan where she lived on, she described to me the town and country and people where he was born and lived the first fifteen years of his life at the end of the nineteenth century. The same set of years I live in now, a hundred years apart, in a state and country seven thousand miles away to the west, but not that far away or apart in all the rest she had to tell me when I was a boy back in New York in a new world for old Tadeusz.)

It is a time of change, of turmoil, of industrialization in the empire of the Tsar, and there is little for an ambitious, impatient fifteen-year-old to do in a small village in Tsarist Poland. Ambition and change are in the cities, and to the city Tadeusz goes. To work in a factory and make money to send home to the farm and his sisters who wait for husbands. To work and join the workers. In the city he learns that the Tsars and Princes and Counts and landowners and industrialists and bosses live and survive on the work of the workers. That the workers produce the goods and the bosses get rich selling them. That, in the words of the great President of the United States of America, Abraham Lincoln, tyranny is where one man toils to produce the food and another man eats it, and that he, Tadeusz Jan, is not one of those who eat.

(She was Polish too, my step-grandmother. His first wife, my real grandmother, had been Russian, and my step-grandmother laughed over that, said, "When it came to women, your grandfather did not worry very much about ancient enemies, eh?" She talked to me about old Tadeusz in that front room of the railroad flat on sunny Sunday mornings when my mother and father would be in our fine uptown apartment sleeping off the Saturday night parties or celebrations or just a policeman's off-duty nights on the town when, in those days, the owners of all the local establishments would wine and dine their good police friend free of charge and everyone thought that was how it was supposed to be done because that was how it had been done in the old country and even in the new as long as anyone could remember. At the dinner table when my father was on duty and my mother sat alone in the front room after dinner and listened to the radio, or went out with other policemen's wives and sometimes by herself. On the edge of my bed when my father was on the night shift and my mother had her own life to lead and I was not to be left alone uptown.)

In the city Tadeusz joins the union. He has, by then, read Marx, Engels, Bakunin and even Nechayev. When the Tsar and the Princes and the Counts and the landowners and the industrialists send soldiers and police to stop the unions, he fights, and when he is beaten and jailed he becomes a socialist. A socialist in Tsarist Russia is liked even less by the Princes, etc., than a Pole or Jew. In the Polish part of Tsarist Russia the Polish Princes, etc., dislike socialists even more than they do the Russians. It is a difficult life for a man under twenty-one without land or money. There is persecution and unemployment and prison and hunger and when there are, finally, no jobs at all for him and no way they can help him at home in the village, and his time of service in the Tsar's army nears, Tadeusz emigrates to the distant United States of America.

He sails with the other thousands in the crowded steerages of jammed ships where they live like cattle, immediately organizes a committee that forces the ship's officers to give them better food and treatment, and arrives in the homeland of Honest Abe, the Railsplitter, at Ellis Island. The barracks, examinations and interrogations of Ellis Island are not exactly the welcome he or the thousands of others had expected, remind Tadeusz more of the methods of the Tsar of all the Russias and the Princes, etc., of Poland. But they are in the New World and everything will be good and safe and equal once they get off the island. That this is not what is to be in the clean new land comes as a great shock to Tadeusz. An angry awakening. A sadness.

(My step-grandmother looked out the high window of their tenement living room, and talked about my grandfather. At the ocean of black tar roofs and clothes blowing in the sun on clotheslines propped up by poles to keep the drying clothes from touching the tar. At the forest of buildings of the lower westside, ranks of identical brownstone tenements all the same height, fire escapes in front, with the skyscrapers of midtown in the distance behind them like peaks above the timberline.

"Such anger, Daniel, such sadness. That there were Princes in the free land too. Their shining words, their pious pictures, their pretty promises, meant no more than the ancient war cries and benevolent patronage of the old countries."

Now when I thought about the people who lived in that same living room, in those same tenements, the forest of brownstones, I knew they were not shocked and they were not sad. Only angry that they were not Princes. In the rows of run-down little houses in East Los Angeles or Watts. From sea to shining sea.)

Tadeusz Jan Fortunowski, in a strange land and not yet twenty-one, lives in the forest of tenements, rides the trolley cars and the subway to his job in a foundry, drinks and sings and dances in the Dom Polska halls of lower Manhattan. There are union struggles not so different from those of the Princes, etc., in the old country.

The troubles of politics and oppression and exploitation. He finds as much need for socialism in the new land as in the old. He marches, makes speeches, fights police, goes to jail, is beaten. Little has changed. What has changed is that in the new country he can work, there is much need for workers, and if all is not equal or fair there is at least a job.

A job does much to temper struggle, to make a man think of things other than equality and what is right and wrong. There are the Polska halls, the dances, the good drinking, and there are girls. Good Polish girls, lively and hardworking. But it is a Russian girl he marries. Ethnic hatreds are useful to Princes, etc., not to people. There is a child, and better apartments, and a place in the community. There are the conditions of life in the slums, and equality, and what is right and what is wrong. Tadeusz did not come to America to be silent. The people of the slums are his people, and when there is something that must be changed, an evil that must end or a good that must come, he talks and organizes, forms action groups and pressure groups, puts the screws on City Hall until there is change or new faces at City Hall. If neither of those happen the fight goes on.

("God did not decree that we live in poverty and slums, and the Princes live in wealth and castles. That is what Abraham Lincoln said, and what socialism means," Tadeusz Jan said.

That is what my second grandmother told me, and when I saw those same slums on television, drove by on the freeway, they were not even of the country I lived in. As alien from the comfortable minority that rules the country I lived in, and to which I belonged, as the jungles of the Amazon. There was no community in the slums, no neighborhoods. The faces came and went like a grainy movie. Each season there were new people to lean against the barren walls, sit in the chairs on dirt yards and sidewalks, sprawl drugged or drunk in the empty doorways. The dead man in the alley had no address, no one who knew him. Transient and irrational, a world of *us* and *them*. The floating rootless, disoriented and without a center beyond their own needs.)

As Tadeusz grows older, his wife dies and his son fails him. He marries again. A Polish woman this time who understands the fierce beliefs that are the core of his world, if perhaps she knows that world is already past. But his son moves out of the old neighborhood as soon as he graduates from high school and changes his name to Fortune because his new home is uptown among Americans and Irish. His son's friends are uptown among the Americans and Irish. His son's dreams are uptown far from the slums. His son turns his back on the slums and moves into another world and, eventually, into the world of the enemy. The son of Tadeusz Jan Fortunowski, working-class slum activist, union organizer and socialist street fighter, becomes a policeman. Joins the bosses. A servant and defender of the Princes, etc.

Tadeusz never speaks to his son again. He has no son. Where his son had been there is a great hole in his beliefs, his dreams of a fair and just world somewhere ahead if only men will see the truth and fight for what should belong to them not to the Tsars and Princes, etc. His son has become a Cossack, and Tadeusz Jan Fortunowski does not speak to Cossacks. He will die before he will speak to the son who, for the sake of living uptown and having a refrigerator and becoming one of those who prosper by serving the Princes, etc., like the turncoat Poles who served the Tsar of all the Russias so long ago, will deny who he is and turn his back on all those left behind in the slums.

So he dies. In the slums. A socialist. A working man. With his second wife beside him and no son.

(My second grandmother, at the dining table in Tadeusz's old railroad apartment alone with me—my father and mother somewhere else, together or apart—had no regrets that old Tadeusz had never again spoken to a man named Fortune, had never seen his namesake—Daniel Tadeusz Fortune—born. For her, accustomed to the stupidities of men, to be part of my father's family was possible if sometimes painful, but she could and did honor the white-hot principles of a man who had all his life believed that the people would overcome the pain and injustice and exploitation of poverty and neglect together, that there would be one fair and just and equal world without Princes or castles. Only the people together would escape, triumph, overcome.

She had no regrets that Tadeusz did not live to see my own painful path away from both his and my father's worlds into one of my own that, sometimes, comes close again to that of the old Pole born in Lithuania under Russian rulers. All she would say was that he, the old man, would have preferred my way to my father's way. "Times and places change, Daniel, it is only the heart that counts.")

I drive past the slums now, see them on television, even walk among them and see the black, brown, yellow and, sometimes, white men silent inside the saloons at midday, silent in the bare doorways, in rows of chairs along the littered sidewalks. I know who they are. They are my father who changed his name and moved uptown. They watch the comfortable aliens in the TV above the bar, those rich people in their expensive houses with their big cars and all that money can buy, and know they will be one of them someday.

Each man at the bar dreams of escape, of triumph. Not all together, but each alone. Each man, each woman, each child on these late twentieth-century slum streets, cries out alone: "Hey, man, don' gimme fair, gimme share."

And I hear the voice of my grandfather speak to me in the soft, gentle tones of my second grandmother, "That, Daniel, is why so few will ever escape or overcome or triumph or even share. Why they have been so easily handled by the Tsars and Princes over the last half of the century. Why there are so many more each year. Why the victims are in the slums and the enemy is somewhere else."

24

Gaudy in violent colors, the jungle bird rose up like the phoenix out of the debris and litter of the *barrio* street. Great yellow wings spread across the gray houses and rusted metal and barren yards. Thick red body and yellow feet, red head, hooked and cruel beak like a curved Aztec sword that flashed yellow in the sun. Screamed in the sun. Savage screams that flew and echoed among the low buildings and dusty streets. A mythical condor, an unknown bird of night and legend, a winged and feathered demon, Quetzalcoatl himself. He hovered in a shaft of sunlight, lord of the universe in his chariot that swept across the sky.

Settled to earth and became a man riding on yellow-and-red filigree. On the hood of a truck covered with iron filigree and painted. The bed of the truck full of a loud *mariachi* band with its horns blaring. Superman in red and yellow and gold. Masked and caped and booted. Superman with a belly, thick chest and short legs, portly with love handles in red tights and T-shirt. Gold lamé bikini shorts over the tights, S.B. emblazoned in yellow on the red chest of the T-shirt. Masked in red with black eyes behind the yellow eye holes, a smiling mouth framed in the yellow mouth of the red mask. Flying through the *barrio* on the hood of the filigreed truck, arms upraised, calling out in Spanish to anyone who stopped to look or even turned.

"What the hell's he saying?" I asked Anderson.

Anderson laughed. "That he's Super Barrio, the masked crusader for truth, justice and democracy on behalf of latinos everywhere. He brings a message of brotherhood from all Hispanic peoples to the *chicanos* of Los Angeles. Solidarity and hope. Stuff like that."

A gaudy hero in red, yellow and gold. The plumed serpent in his chariot that swept away the litter and the smog. Flying through the *barrio* at the head of a ragtag parade in chinos and jeans, running shoes and feathered hats, headbands and flattop hats, cheap wool shirts and windbreakers. A parade of pickups, motorcycles, ancient Cadillacs and broken Chryslers. Hordes of big-eyed brown-faced children too young to have disappeared yet into the graveyard of *barrio* children—the school system, the bars at noon, the empty lots and emptier doorways, the gangs. Adulthood.

"What is it? Some advertising gimmick?"

"I heard something about him," Anderson said, watched the gaudy figure at the head of the parade. "He's from Mexico City, represents some big slum coalition, speaks for the poor even to the Mexican Congress. I guess he's come north."

On the red-and-yellow painted iron lacework that covered the old pickup from hood to tailgate, the stocky masked man in his red tights and gold bikini and yellow cape and boots, spotted the old man in the white wicker rocker, us beside him in the barren yard. He flew off the hood toward us, the wings of the yellow cape billowing him across the street and yard.

"Buenas tardes, padre, these anglos giving you trouble?"

"They cops."

The masked man looked at us. "Why you bother this old man? Or maybe it is Super Barrio you come for, hey? Send Super Barrio back to Mexico, he nothing but trouble, cost bosses lots of money. Hey, you got bad luck. *La Migra* already pick up Super Barrio. The caped crusader he got all his papers, you know? The masked marvel of the latino people he got visa, permits. We gonna bring the word to all the *chicanos* everywhere. Got to fight the bosses the cops works for, hey?"

The voice of Tadeusz Jan Fortunowski echoed in my mind. In the third world it was still 1900, labor was still cheap, and the Princes, etc., wanted to keep it that way.

"We're not cops," Anderson said.

Behind the filigreed pickup, the old Cadillacs and low-riders, the children and the adults of the rag-tag parade watched and waited. As certain we were cops as Super Barrio.

"No INS," I said. "No landlords."

"My kids, they make plenty *dinero*," the old man told Super Barrio. "I will be *jefe, patrone*."

"So what are you?" Super Barrio said to us. "If you ain't in the *barrio* to watch Super Barrio, subversive caped crusader, what you doin' here?"

Anderson told him who we were and what we were doing in the *barrio*. The old man in the rocker was having none of it.

"They cops. Snoopin' on them *cabron* trash next door."

Super Barrio shook his head. "Gangs is bad. Only gangs is maybe how a young guy feel he got friends, belongs somewhere, has somethin' worth doin' with his life."

"I know, and you know," Anderson said. "I need something an anglo jury can appreciate. Make them realize that under the same circumstances they could have done the same thing."

While they talked, I watched the kids and cars of the parade who waited restlessly. Only a few minutes had passed, but the attention span of children is short, and *barrio* low-riders aren't known for patience. The fat man was in danger of losing all his followers, his whole parade, and didn't seem to care—his mission appeared to be to help the exploited wherever he found them, one at a time or an entire *barrio*. Whatever he ran into. The image of my grandfather appeared in my mind again. He would have understood Super Barrio.

I thought about Super Barrio and Tadeusz Jan Fortunowski as four more cars appeared on the street. Old cars, dented and worn and in need of paint. Two stopped at the curb, one in front and one behind our Volvo. Another had stopped beside the Volvo. Its driver slumped down behind the wheel with his head back against the seat as if asleep, a blue L.A. Dodger cap pulled down over his eyes. The fourth, a battered old Chevy Impala, idled in the middle of the street ahead of the yellow-and-red filigree of Super Barrio's pickup and directly opposite where the yellow-caped crusader talked to us and the old man in the rocker.

Expressionless faces looked out from the fourth car with its engine idling, looked at Super Barrio and the old man in the rocker and us. Some mustaches. Hats with broad brims, hats with feathers, more Los Angeles Dodger caps, red-and-green headbands.

"Anderson."

He looked. "Part of your team, Masked Marvel?"

"No mine."

The stone faces saw us notice them. The old Chevy pulled to the curb, one got out of each door. They came to us spread out. Even gang members go to the movies. The leader was a short, chunky *chicano* like Super Barrio himself. Black jeans too tight over the thighs, an L.A. Laker sweatshirt, black leather jacket, flattop hat with three feathers all tufted in green.

"You lookin' for Cholo?"

The other three—two skinny and another chunky—all wore something small and green: a wrist-band; an L.A. Dodger cap with a green pin button; the laces of running shoes dyed. It had to be the gang color.

Anderson said, "Is that what Luisa Bombal told you?"

"Why you lookin' for Cholo?"

Anderson said, "I'm chief investigator for the public defender in Santa Barbara. We're defending the fourteen Westside Rockers. They won't talk to us, give us a reason why they went up to City College. I need the story so we can defend them."

"What the hell you care about the Rockers, man?"

The skinny one with the green shoelaces said, "Don' need no goddamn reason. They was goddamn anglos."

I said, "They aren't all anglos at City College."

The spokesman didn't look at me. "Who the fuck's this guy, man?

Luisa said one guy. Big fucking guy come down from Santa Barbara. What's this guy want Cholo for, man?"

"He's a private investigator. He . . ."

I said, "I want to talk about Alameda Park. About the bandstand in Alameda Park. About a homeless woman someone murdered in the bandstand in Alameda Park."

All four turned to stone. Anderson and Super Barrio looked at me. Murder is a strong word. They thought I was crazy. Maybe I was, but I needed to get their attention, stir a reaction. Rock the boat. Get to Esteban Gonzalez, *El Cholo,* if he was the only one who could make them talk to me.

Some of them laughed. The leader didn't laugh. For a time he didn't do anything except look at me. Then he smiled.

"Hey, maybe you better come on an' talk to Cholo, you know? Both you guys better come an' talk, okay?" He looked over his shoulder at the other three cars, then back at us. Two more of them got out of each car. The leader still smiled. "Tell you what, you go get in the Volvo, we take you guys to Cholo. *Muy pronto.* Okay?"

His smile was all dazzling teeth. Friendly. Sincere. The three others moved around us, one on each side, one behind us. Three of those at the other cars walked toward us. We had guns, it was possible they didn't. Anderson shook his head. There were at least ten of them, we were in the heart of the *barrio* with a lot of other latinos around us. And we wanted to talk to Cholo. That was what we had come to do, and sometimes you have to take a risk.

"We take you to Cholo, okay?" the leader repeated. "All you got to do is follow the Chevy."

They herded us to our Volvo. At least in our own car we could change our minds. So could they. If they wanted to, they could lose us. It was another chance we had to take. But they had no intention of losing us. As we neared the Volvo, three of them grabbed each of us, held our arms. All three arms. My missing wing confused them, but the guy on that side grabbed my belt instead. The third had us around the throat. It wasn't easy to hold Anderson, but they hung onto both of us long enough for a fourth guy to get our guns.

"Hey, you don' need no guns. Cholo don' like guys got guns aroun' him. Maybe we take you in our cars, too, hey?"

He motioned with his head, and they hustled us to separate cars. We'd taken the risk, and we'd lost. The kids and adults in the waiting parade stood and watched. They did nothing. What could they do?

They lived with gangs, they knew there was little help to be had from the police, from the city. They had no reason to love or trust anglos with guns. They didn't trust gangs, either, but at least the gangs lived in the same slum.

Then the horn began to sound. The *mariachi* band started to blare, its trumpet soaring with the horn of the yellow-and-red filigreed pickup. Super Barrio stood on the hood of his chariot, his red arms flung out, the yellow cape billowing.

"Everyone listen to Super Barrio! The masked marvel needs you! Those guys are gang punks! Gang punks make life in the *barrio* worse for all of us! They're kidnapping those two anglos. Those anglos are friends. Those anglos are trying to help latinos in Santa Barbara. Get in your cars, blow your horn, make noise! Block those four cars! Block the street! Super Barrio, the caped crusader, helps latinos everywhere. Gang punks rob latinos. Block the street! Yell!"

The *mariachis* blared, the car horn blasted, and all the people on the street shouted. The noise rose in crescendo, soared out of the street across the *barrio*. Cars swung across the street, blocked it. People came out of houses along the dingy block. People came from the avenues to crowd at the end of the block and see what all the noise was.

The gang members tried to be heard, threatened. Their attention on Super Barrio up on his chariot, on the violent crowd, they forgot us. Anderson jumped the one who still held our guns. He got his, mine fell to the ground. I dove on it. The chunky gang leader shouted an order, his men pulled out knives, clubs, one lone pistol. They waved them in threat at Super Barrio and the crowd.

The sirens began in the distance.

A silence like the end of the world on the side street.

The sirens came closer.

"Noise! Noise! Noise!" Super Barrio shouted.

The chunky leader of the gang kids glared up at Super Barrio. He gave another order. They ran for their cars. The four old cars bounced up over the sidewalks and through the yards and were gone before Anderson or I could stop them if we'd wanted to. We didn't. We wanted Cholo, not trouble, and we didn't want a bloodbath.

Super Barrio grinned down at us behind his gaudy red-and-yellow ski mask as the first police cruiser growled into the side street. He seemed to fly down from his yellow-and-red chariot, the yellow cape streaming out behind him. The police got out of their cars to stare at the masked marvel of the *barrio* flying in the air. Anderson and I went with him to meet the police.

The winter sun was strong over the sea distant below the Conejo grade. Its light through the windshield picked out the red-and-yellow plumage of Super Barrio in the back seat of the Volvo as we started down the grade.

"Hey, look at that view, you know? We see it first, right? Comin' down from the plateau. Don Gaspar de Portola and his brave soldiers from Mexico."

It was a wide view of the whole coastal plain from the mountains to the sea. Green from Camarillo to past Santa Barbara thanks to the irrigation that has made it a rich land. Lemon and orange groves, truck farms, strawberries, flowers, even bananas up at La Conchita. And housing developments. Everywhere housing developments. Still green where it had been brown in the days of the Indians and Spanish, but crowded with houses in wide clusters and endless rows. Until there won't be any lemons or oranges or strawberries or flowers. Only people.

"The Indians saw it first," I said. "They were here."

"So that's okay. We's Indians too."

The ebullient Mexican laughed out loud. We had been half the afternoon explaining to the Los Angeles police what had happened, who we were, what we were doing, who Super Barrio was and why he had caused a mini-riot. The L.A.P.D. views East Los Angeles as enemy territory, any part of the city that is mainly non-anglo ethnic, question anyone and anything that happens there. They had to check with INS on Super Barrio, with the Santa Barbara Public Defender on Anderson, with the Santa Barbara police on me. They had hamburgers sent in, asked more questions.

Even then they still weren't sure of us. Especially not Super Barrio. He rubbed them wrong in every way. A cocky, loud and trouble-making Mexican. There had to be something wrong with him. He had to be up to some scam. If we hadn't been there, he'd have at least spent the night in jail. As it was, they finally gave up and released all of us. But their hearts weren't in it.

"So I guess we're even, you know? I need to go to Santa Barbara, I ride with you, okay? I got to talk to La Casa De La Raza, United

Mexicans, and out at the Hispanic Studies at the university. Then we go on up to Guadalupe, San Luis, finish up in San Jose."

The yellow-and-red pickup followed us north.

"You're on a tour?" I said.

"Got to bring the word to latinos everywhere."

"How'd you get started on this Super Barrio?"

Anderson watched the road as we came down off the grade. "You never take the mask off in public?"

"It ain't important who I am." He laughed again. "Hey, there was this time I'm making a big speech in Jalisco all about housing reform. So the governor he try to rip my mask off. We got into big wrestling match right up there on the platform. Other people they come help, the governor he don' get my mask."

He looked out the window at the flat land of shrinking farms and spreading tracts that is Camarillo. "You don' start being Super Barrio, it happens. You're doing every day what you always done, worry how you gonna support the family if you lose your job, never make enough money to save, drink too much. One day you look aroun' an' it kicks you in the face. Something it's wrong, you know? Some people got more'n they can use ever, most people they ain't got nothing."

25

He is the masked marvel, the caped crusader. In his red tights, gold lamé bikini shorts, flaming yellow cape. He is the defender of tenants and scourge of greedy landlords, appears wherever poor people suffer injustice. He is Super Barrio.

He rises like the phoenix, the plumed serpent Quetzalcoatl him-

self, from the ashes of the great earthquake of 1985. That year he
lives in the great city of Mexico with millions of other poor working
people crowded into the dilapidated tenements and rundown shacks
of the slums. The earthquake destroys much of the poor inner city
slum neighborhoods. He has a wife, three young children, a thirty-
dollar-a-week job in a factory far across the city he must go to by
bus with long hours of waiting. He is one of the lucky. His building
does not fall down. So many lose everything. He has a job. He didn't
always. Jobs are scarce in Mexico. Before he married he was one of
the large army of street vendors who hawk cigarettes, candy,
trinkets, or anything else the middle-class and tourists might buy.
He didn't even have a place to live before he married. After the
earthquake there are many people without jobs or a place to live.

He rides to his job, walks through the destruction of the poor
barrios, knows he must do something more than eat and sleep and
make love to his wife and work and know how lucky he is. He hears
about the Assembly of Barrios movement some people in the slums
have formed to try to make the government listen to the needs and
suffering of the millions in the slums. He joins at once, soon becomes a low-level leader. They do good work, but something is
missing, something isn't working. Nobody knows who they are and
what they are trying to do. The rich and middle-class and successful, the comfortable people with the good consciences who do not
think about the poor, can't even see what the Assembly of Barrios is
doing. Worse, the people of the slums cannot see them. They need
to do something to make everyone know what they are doing, from
the President of the Republic down to the homeless that crowd the
rundown streets of the city.

It is then that he goes to a popular wrestling arena with his
brother-in-law. This is where the working people go, his people.
They cheer and scream, shout, go crazy for their heroes and vil-
lains. He watches them, their passion and involvement and identification with the wrestlers in the tights and capes and rhinestones
and sequins and every other conceivable kind of crazy costume.
Everybody in the arena has their favorite hero and villain, and he
realizes that the key, the way they know them, identify them, relate
to them, are the costumes. That's how they decide who they will
cheer, who they will hate. That is what makes them identify with a
particular wrestler.

The wrestlers parade down the aisle and enter the ring one after the other, each costume more outrageous than the one before. One of the last to fight that night is a smaller and fatter man than most of the others, but the crowd goes wild, he is obviously a favorite. He wears all red with a flowing yellow cape and sparkling sequins all over him. He is masked. No one knows who he is. The unknown hero protecting his secret identity that will be revealed only if he is beaten. The crowd loves the mystery, the thrill of the threat, the danger of revelation. Is he a movie star? The President of the Republic? A sports hero? Who will beat him and finally unmask him? They all talk about the masked wrestler. They remember the masked wrestler.

Some days later, when he sees his children staring at old cartoons on the small black-and-white TV in his tiny living room, Superman leaps across the screen.

"Poor people go to the wrestling, to the movies," he tells the Assembly of the Barrios at the next meeting. "They cheer, they go crazy when their hero beats all those fake enemies—the Green Zombies, the Hulks, the Blue Devils, the Aztec Ghosts, whatever the writers can think of. We can use the idea to fight real enemies—the landlords, the corrupt politicians, the police, the bosses. We can catch the imagination of the working people by using the symbols of what they know to deliver our message."

Super Barrio is born. The red tights, yellow cape, high yellow boots, and red ski mask with the yellow around the eyes and mouth holes comes from the wrestlers. The red T-shirt with the V-shaped yellow outline around the yellow S.B. from the cartoon Superman. The *barriomobile,* covered with the iron filigree painted the same yellow-and-red, from the rich man's love of big cars, from the decoration beloved of the landowners in their haciendas, the wealthy in their town houses. His chunky, pudgy, unheroic figure from his Aztec and Toltec and Maya ancestors and the beans and rice and tortillas of the poor.

He appears everywhere the people of the slums are exploited, coerced, beaten down. When a poor family is evicted, he is there, sometimes even prevents the eviction. When the broken-down and overcrowded buses aren't running, or fares are going up again and again, the *barriomobile* arrives. When services for the slums are denied or slowed down or cut, he flies in and takes up the battle. Once, when the Assembly is protesting a nuclear power plant in Vera Cruz, he gets into the ring and defeats a ferocious "Nuclearsaurus" to the cheers, laughs and delight of the workers. He joins the fight against the ruling PRI, the "progressive" and "revolutionary" party that is neither, has been in power over seventy years, passes the presidency from rich hand to rich hand. But he is invited to meet the President, makes a speech to the National Congress and all the fine PRI politicians with their good consciences.

"Because when the people see my tights and mask and gold bikini and yellow cape, they laugh, but they listen, too, and maybe they start to think."

He is a folk hero, a legend, but Mexico is not alone, no one is alone. There are so many small, poor countries to the south who speak the same language, have the same poor working people and the same rich people with good consciences. There is one big rich country to the north that does not speak the same language. (A country with parts that did speak the language of Mexico once, that were part, once, of Mexico. Parts where many people still speak the language of Mexico, but that are no longer Mexico.) There is a river that says to the north there is hope, to the south there is only pain. When that is the choice, language or no language, one country or another country, the poor working people of all countries go north. Where his people go, he goes, and the people of good conscience who do not see do not live only south of the river.

He gets the proper papers, takes his *barriomobile* and goes north to see how life is for his poor brothers in the big, rich country across the river. To tell the people of the big country what is really happening in his country. As befits a folk hero, he appears first to his people who have come north to work in the fields, to work in the shops and factories, to work anywhere that will hire them. He comforts the homeless, all those who have no work. He stands on the streetcorners with the poor who wait for work in the rich country. He speaks before the City Council of the great city that is named in the language of the south but ruled in the language of the north. He tells them that work is a right of living. That people must have work. A law to stop the poor from standing on corners to ask for work is not human.

"We are not criminals, we are workers. We are not dead, we are alive, and we must be treated as human beings."

He speaks at universities, confronts and insults the local official of his own country who does not work for the poor of Mexico, does not see the poor. He speaks of the rights of the poor and the rights of

Mexicans in the big country, and of why they do not have those rights. He visits the heart of the old city when it was part of Mexico. He walks with his people on the streets of the great city named in his language.

He is arrested.

On the sidewalk of the northern city he is arrested by the government of the big country. He is handcuffed, taken to jail. He is asked questions. What is he doing north of the river in the big country? How did he get into the big country? Who sent him to cause trouble in the big country? Who does he work for? Who sent him illegally into the big country? Has he come north of the river to sell poisonous narcotic drugs to the children of the big country? They can ask him all these questions, hold him in jail, put him in handcuffs, arrest him, because he did not have his papers with him when he walked with his people in the part of the city that was once Mexico. He is not sure that if he had his papers with him it would have stopped them arresting him. They would have to have determined that his papers were genuine, proper, honest. He learns that to be a poor foreigner in the big country is not much different from being poor in his country. That being poor or foreign or both is much the same in all countries.

His papers arrive, he is released. They apologize.

"We had a tip you were illegal."

The chunky masked man shrugs. "There no such thing as illegal human beings."

He goes on. The caped crusader who appears wherever the poor suffer injustice. The defender of tenants and the scourge of landlords. Who lives in a country with the cheapest labor in the world. In a capital city with two million homeless people. A country that is being sold piece by piece to foreign interests, where the people of good conscience say the country is on the road to development, but where he knows his people are on the road to dying of hunger and corruption and violence. A country where violence is permitted by the strong against the weak.

He goes on in a world where all poor countries are sold, piece by piece, to rich countries. A world where the comfortable see a road to development, and the poor see only hunger and corruption and violence. A world of cheap labor and little work, of the armies of the homeless and permitted violence.

The masked marvel. "Under this mask is everyone. Superman

does not wear a mask, his victories are only his. Our struggle is a collective one, does not belong to one man. Together we are stronger than Superman. The millions of poor across the world."

He is a folk hero, a myth. The masked marvel. The caped crusader. In his red tights, gold lamé bikini shorts, flaming yellow cape. He is the defender of tenants and scourge of greedy landlords, appears wherever poor people suffer injustice. He is Super Barrio.

26

In the interrogation room of the county jail they sat as sullen and silent as they had at the defense table in the courtroom, defiance and disdain the only expression on their brown faces.

"You didn't go up to that campus without a reason, something that triggered you," Anderson said. "I want to know what it was. That's the only way we can defend you."

"You have rights," Super Barrio told them, "but you have to stand up for yourselves, tell your side."

One of the tall ones said, "What are you, man? A clown? Make people laugh in that outfit?"

"He sure make me laugh," the oldest-looking skinny one said.

None of them laughed. There were seven, that was all they would let us talk to at one time. Without laughter or expression beyond the sullen defiance in their dark eyes.

"Mr. Anderson only wants to help," Luis Rivera said. "He's working for you. That's his job."

Luis had been surprised when I walked into his office out at the university with Super Barrio. "You sure as hell get around." I told

him he sure as hell did too, all the way from the academic senate to
fronting for Super Barrio in the local *barrio*. We'd stopped in Summerland to pick up my car so we could come to Luis and check
Super Barrio's schedule. Anderson wanted Super Barrio to talk to
the fourteen Westside Rockers, try to convince them to cooperate
without word from Cholo. Anderson went to the county jail first to
arrange the meeting, while we talked to Luis. Luis didn't think it
would do any damn good, but decided to come with us and see if he
could do anything with the Rockers.

"Who the fuck you work for, Tio Taco?"

"You gonna tell the anglos all about the bad *pachuco* gangs, Tio
Taco?"

It's not easy to live between two worlds. Distrusted by both, belonging nowhere. It's a lot easier to come down solid on one side or
the other. For or against, black or white. Know what you want and
who your enemy is. Then it's all simple.

I said, "Tell me what happened in Alameda Park. You hassle the
street homeless, too? Or maybe they gave you trouble?"

All the dark eyes turned to look at me. Flat eyes in brown faces as
masked as Super Barrio in his costume.

"Who the fuck's the cripple?"

"What the hell you talking, man? We ain't never in that there
park!"

"Hey, public defender man! We ain't no place in that park."

It was the same two who talked. The designated talkers. Sub-
leaders. Lieutenants. A matter of rank, status, position.

"Cholo isn't coming back to help you," Anderson said. "You don't
talk to me, no one's going to help you. You'll go down hard, you
understand? Hard and long."

The tall one sneered. "Hey, man, we's real bad, you know?"

Anderson had the second seven brought in. We did no better with
them even though Edgardo Montez was one of them. Anderson and
Super Barrio decided to try with Montez alone after they were all
sent back to their cells. I had another idea. The only reaction we'd
gotten from the Westside Rockers had come on my questions about
Alameda Park. They had not been surprised. Defensive, ready to
deny anything about Alameda Park.

They had been in the park, and they had done something in that
park they didn't want known.

* * *

Gus Chavalas was ready to go off duty.

"Not home," he said, "just off duty so maybe I can get some paperwork done."

"Any ident on the boy killed out in my alley yesterday?"

"Not my case. Ask the Sheriff."

"I did when I was at the jail. He says nothing yet. What do you say?"

He considered me for some time, maybe deciding whether he wanted to pursue this line of talk or throw me out. Or deciding if he wanted to confirm what I was really saying about him.

"Why would I care about a county case with the load here?"

"Because you're a good cop."

He considered me even longer. "Let's get some coffee."

Outside in the late afternoon, we walked to Santa Barbara Street and down to the Sojourner. He likes the fact that few other cops go into the Sixties flower-child-style health-food-and-vegetables place. He likes the café au lait.

"Two," I said to the waitress. "You talked to the Rockers about Cassandra Reilly. Or at least Alameda Park."

"Ninety-nine percent Jerry Kohnen killed her," Chavalas said. He built a pyramid of sugar and Equal packets on the table near the window where he could sit with his back to the wall and watch who passed outside. "I went out and saw the body of that kid killed in your alley, took a look at his clothes, what he had on him, which was nothing. They're digging on him believe me. He's young, white, looks middle-class or better. I got his prints, the labels on his clothes. Nothing so far, nothing from anywhere about a runaway or a missing person."

"So you talked to the Rockers while you were out there."

Our coffee came. He sweetened his, I took it straight.

"I asked questions, they didn't answer the questions." He drank the hot, smooth coffee with its steamed milk. "They were surprised. Hit where they didn't expect anything. Recovered fast, the tall one who does most of their talking got defensive. But he was really surprised by Cassandra Reilly's name. I don't think he ever heard it before."

"They don't read the papers, and the killer didn't have to know her name," I said.

"If they killed someone in that park, Dan, they'd have read the papers."

"But they were in the park, and recently."

He put more sugar in his coffee. "They've been in the park. They did something in that park that makes them worry."

"What else happened there that could worry them?"

"Could be a lot of things. Something we don't even know about, never found out. Maybe that attack on you."

"Why would they attack me if they hadn't killed Cassie?"

"Maybe they just wanted to bash an anglo." He looked at my empty sleeve. "You looked easy."

I didn't believe that. Neither did he.

Almost down over the sea now, the sun shone directly on the front windows of our rented hacienda in Summerland. Kay's car wasn't in the driveway. Anderson's Volvo was.

"We got something out of Montez."

"What?"

"I'll tell you on the way."

"On the way where?"

"The morgue."

We'd been gone all day on a diet Coke and one hamburger. I could have used a beer, a shower, even something to eat. But I left a note for Kay, told her I was home, safe but hungry, would be back as soon as possible, don't wait dinner. She probably would, but that had to be her decision. Anderson made a right out of our street and took the freeway on-ramp.

"Why the morgue?"

"It's finally getting to Montez. Super Barrio talked hard, made him realize he might have made a big mistake, that he has more potential than anything a gang could ever offer. Let his family down, hurt his girlfriend, the works. All a gang does is build a small world of its own that can go nowhere in the bigger world, has no future outside its own narrow streets. Join a gang and it's all the life you'll ever know, and most of that'll be in prison. Quit the gang, if they let you, and you'll be back in the real world years older without any skills you can use. He laid it on thick. The kid's been sitting there for days staring at prison, not even knowing for how long. He's getting scared, wondering what the hell he was doing up there on that campus tearing things apart and kicking anglo ass. He doesn't even really know what it was all about except that the Rockers were mad at anglos and so was he. So when Super Barrio gave him his pitch of all the poor working people getting together, he told us what he does know."

"The morgue?"

We were stopped by the freeway lights at Santa Barbara Street, the construction that would end them once and for all visible all around us.

"Montez says Cholo talked a lot about some guy in the morgue. How the goddamn arrogant hotshot anglos up at the college didn't give a shit about some poor latino lying in the morgue because of them. No one cared about a dead latino or even a live one. Not in this country. The bastards up on that campus didn't even see the people down in the *barrio*. They were going to show those arrogant sons-of-bitches that latinos were real, latinos were people. Stuff like that. Montez says the whole gang talked about this kid in the morgue, but only Cholo seemed to take it so hard. He says over the last year Cholo took everyone in the gang to look at the kid in the morgue. Cholo would sit and look at the dead boy for hours. Montez says the gang told him Cholo even took other latinos there to see the dead boy."

"You think this latino in the morgue was a gang member?"

"Montez doesn't think so. No one ever used a name. Not once, Montez says. Not even a first name."

"Then what?"

"Montez doesn't know. Super Barrio stayed talking to him to try to get more."

"That's it?"

"All we have so far."

The light changed. Anderson drove ahead toward Goleta and the county morgue.

27

It was growing dark when we reached the long driveway between the open field and the Women's Honor Farm. Beyond the beige buildings of the honor farm, the morgue stood behind its parking lot. A sign announced this was a jail facility, anyone who came was subject to search. The sign was all I could see, the morgue itself half hidden by the crowd that encircled the parking lot.

A crowd of mostly women and young children from the family tract across San Antonio Road. They strained on their toes to stare at something farther back. Anderson parked at the far edge of the lot. A flash of yellow-and-red through the crowd gave me a clue. Super Barrio up on the filigree hood of the *barriomobile* making a speech of greeting and brotherhood from the people of Mexico, his yellow cape flying, his red arms waving.

"Never miss a chance to give the message," he said as he walked up to us through the applauding crowd.

"What else did you get from Montez?" Anderson asked.

The portly Mexican shook his head. "The boy ain't with the gang long enough. All I get is maybe Cholo back into town soon."

Anderson said, "Why did he go to the morgue? Take others?"

"Montez don' know. Thinks maybe the dead guy's a relative."

I said, "Wouldn't Cholo know the name of a relative?"

"Maybe he knows, just never used it," Anderson suggested.

"You'd think he'd use at least the first name sometime."

We crossed the parking lot to the one-story flat-roofed building. It's a new morgue, the first built in the county for the purpose. Santa Barbara is growing. The buff stucco, brown trim and open beams looked like any small office building. Only the double doors of the sally port where bodies were delivered showed it wasn't any small office building. They had planted daisies, white and lavender lilies of the Nile, star jasmine and a tiny lawn to soften the walk to the single door into the office.

The receptionist looked up from behind her desk as if to challenge our right to bother the dead. She recognized Anderson, smiled at him. At me and Super Barrio she raised an eyebrow.

"Is this a delegation, Philip?"

"For a boy who's been here a long time, could fit into a case we're working on. Dan's a private investigator, Mr. Barrio is from Mexico."

Anderson's voice implied that Super Barrio was some kind of official, probably police since he was with us. The receptionist looked at Super Barrio. It was a hopeful look.

"The John Doe? You think you can identify him? Let me call the boss."

The boss was Sergeant Dennis Prescott, Coroner's Division, Sheriff's Department. He was as eager as the receptionist until Anderson explained that we hadn't come to identify the dead John Doe, but only to ask questions about our own case.

Disappointment didn't stop him. "What case?"

Anderson told him about the Westside Rockers. "I'm looking for what triggered them. A new kid in the gang says that the leader, Steve Gonzalez, talked about some boy in the morgue. He says Gonzalez comes here all the time to visit the corpse, brings gang members one at a time. You have records would show if a man named Gonzalez had some regular business here? Maybe was a relative of the dead man?"

"Gonzalez?" Prescott looked at the receptionist who began to go through the records of visitors. "We don't keep a body so long most of the time. The family always wants the body fast, the police let it go soon as they can. But this time . . ."

The receptionist looked up at us. "A Steve Gonzalez has been coming here about once a month for almost two years. He always brings someone who wants to identify the dead boy."

"But no one's identified him?" I said.

"Not so far."

Anderson said, "Why keep this one for almost two years?"

"Ask the police, Phil. They told us to hold him, try to get the identification."

I said, "Have a lot of people come to identify the body?"

"Half the visitors we've had the last two years."

"You let them all see the body?"

The sergeant shook his head. "It's embalmed, sealed in a Maxwell

Tank. Most of them only look at the photos in my office. If they insist they can't tell, then we let them see the body."

"How long do you give them?"

"As long as they need."

"Did Steve Gonzalez and the others he brought take a long time, insist on seeing the body?"

Prescott looked at the receptionist.

"I'm not sure," she said. "We get a lot of people over a month, but I have the feeling they did take a long time."

Super Barrio said, "What he look like, this John Doe?"

"You want to see him?"

"I guess we better," Anderson said. "The photos at least."

Is there anyone who gets used to looking at the dead? At death naked. Anyone normal? What was and is not. The face of nothing. So little change and so much.

The John Doe in the photos was as young as he had sounded. A small, thin, Indian-faced boy. Pale in death, but almost certainly brown in life. Black hair and high bones over hollow cheeks, the full lips and Oriental eyes.

"One of my people," Super Barrio said, looked steadily at the young face that would never be old yet was already as old as the earth. "Maybe Mayan, maybe Aztec, maybe Inca or Quechua. Peru, Bolivia, Mexico. Somewhere Indians live but Ladinos rule."

The injuries that had killed the boy were clear on his face and body, but had been cleaned up, repaired. Massive wounds from what I could see from the untouched photos.

"How do you take the photos?" I asked.

"A still camera or sometimes frames from the video camera we have over the autopsy table. Want to see?"

It might tell us something while we thought, questioned. The sergeant led us through a side door into the area behind the double doors of the sally port.

"What killed him?"

"Hit by a car," Prescott said, opened a massive stainless steel door that faced the sally port.

"Where did it happen?" Anderson asked.

We stood inside a large refrigerated room. There were no drawers, only open shelves like the bunks on the old buckets I sailed on in my war. Blue body bags like mummies rested on two of the shelves, a steel tank was on a third shelf. A small morgue for a small county. The tank would be the nameless John Doe so important to Cholo Gonzalez.

"In the city somewhere. Talk to the Santa Barbara police."

We went through another airtight and insulated door into the autopsy room. A video camera and a dictation microphone hung over the autopsy area.

"We've got a pathology lab in the next room. The whole place was built by honor farm inmates, cost the county very little. The doctors still do most autopsies down at Cottage Hospital, but someday it'll all be here."

He was proud of his facilities. Where the dead can serve the living through science.

I said, "Was there anything special about how he died? Anything special about him, or on him?"

"Not that I know, Mr. Fortune. But there has to be something for the police to keep the case open so long."

The early night outside in the parking lot was almost as cold as inside the morgue. Super Barrio looked back at the innocent little building.

"What you figure?"

"I don't know," I said. "If no one knows his name, or who he was, what connection could he have to Cholo and the Rockers?"

Anderson said, "I'll talk to the police. There's got to be something for them to keep the body unburied this long."

"Maybe I go talk to people in the *barrio*," Super Barrio said, "ask if anyone know if Gonzalez come back to Santa Barbara, where I can maybe talk to him."

I said. "I'm hungry, tired, and have a lady I haven't seen all day. I go home."

Anderson said, "If I get anything important from the police, I'll call you. Maybe we should stake out the morgue tomorrow. If Cholo's back, he hasn't been to the morgue since the raid."

As I took the freeway home in the night, I thought about Cholo and the dead boy. I didn't think he would visit the morgue after the attack. Our best chance was that Anderson would find something about the John Doe that would help. The dead youth had been a latino, but what was Cholo's connection to a boy without a name, without an identity? Why had he really gone to the morgue all those times, unable to let the dead boy fade away in peace?

Kay still wasn't home, only the one light in the front room on in our house. My last question echoed in my mind as I drove into the alley. A silent voice in the night that reverberated with the possibilities of the question. A vision of two young latinos, one in the town where he was born, the other probably from some distant place. A boy who could have lived in a language different from that of the rich northern country. The language of *El Cholo*'s heritage but not of his birth.

They were in the alley again. Shadows in the light over the garage door as I pulled it down. I ran.

No shouts this time. No curses. No flailing chains or flash of knives around me as I ran toward the house and the side door into my office. No crashing through bushes or stumbling over each other. I could only mutter a breathless incantation that the side door was open.

Silence and shadows that ran behind me like vague patches of the night itself.

Movement in the night ahead. Small and quick.

Pain sharp and hard against my ankles. Round, hard, painful. Face down, I struggled, pushed against dirt to get up. A club, a broom handle. Pain against my arm. Elbow collapsed. A foot hard and heavy on my neck.

"Don' move, you don' get hurt."

I lay face down. My lone arm numb where I lay. I could cry out, but who would hear? Lay silent, listened for any sound of someone who would hear in the night.

"Get his fuckin' gun."

Hands found the Sig-Sauer in my belt holster, patted me up and down, found nothing more. "*Nada,* Rizo."

"So get him up."

The hands pulled me up. There were four of them in the weak light from the garage. Dark clothes but no ski masks. The four from the Chevy in East Los Angeles. The short, chunky leader in the tight black jeans and L.A. Laker sweatshirt with his face close to my face.

"Like we say before, man. You gonna talk to Cholo."

28

The light was at the far end of the large, narrow garage where two men were seated on armchairs with wornout rugs thrown over ripped upholstery. The squat kid who'd done all the talking at my house and in East L.A. pushed me forward.

"This the guy askin' after Alameda Park, Cholo. Someone got killed over there he says. One of them street bums."

The two in the chairs were like medieval kings granting an audience. That wasn't too far from the truth in their alternate world. The one on the left was as small, thin, and smooth-faced as most of the rest of the Westside Rockers. In their uniform that was more high school than anything else: black jeans, high basketball shoes, black T-shirt with red lettering half covered by a leather jacket, a green military beret over his long hair. He sat stiff in the chair, his hands on the arms.

No taller, the second was fifty pounds heavier in a pair of loose yellow slacks. Muscular, with a black mustache and beard stubble, mid-to-late twenties. A psychedelic black-and-yellow velour turtleneck, black suede shoes, a yellow headband he didn't need to hold his short black hair. He lounged in his chair, turned hard eyes on my chunky captor.

"So what happen with the clown an' the fat cop?"

"They go from the morgue to cop headquarters. We figure we grab this guy, maybe we don' got to grab the other guys." He held out my Sig-Sauer. "We got his piece."

"You figures? Who the fuck says you does the—"

The thin younger one said, "That's okay, Rizo. Maybe we ain't gonna need them other two. This guy—"

Yellow pants swore, "Shit! You got three guys lookin' for you, Cholo, you grab three guys. You don' grab one."

Esteban (Steve) Gonzalez, Cholo, shrugged. "Down L.A., maybe. Here, like I tell Luisa, it don't make no difference. We know who the fat guy is, what he wants."

"That don' stop him."

"Maybe we don't want to stop him, Narco. Okay?" He took Anderson's PPK from his jacket, held it casually on his knee.

The older, heavier man looked at the gun, lounged back in his chair. I had the picture, wasn't sure I wanted it. The thin youth was the elusive leader of the Westside Rockers, the older man was from Los Angeles. From some Los Angeles gang. An older, meaner, more experienced gang ready to show the young Westside Rockers the right way. I should have spotted it. It was the young one who wore the green. They were all the same age, the Rockers. All local friends not yet sunk deep into the isolation, the gulf that separated the subterranean world of the gangs from the middle-class anglo world. Young with a young leader who had to deal with me.

"You think we kill someone in Alameda Park?"

"I don't know who killed the woman in Alameda Park. I—"

"The big guy, public defender, what's he think we done?"

"He knows what you did. He wants to know why you did it so he can maybe help you."

"How's he gonna help?"

"He wants to know why you went up to City College, what triggered the attack."

"What that gonna do?"

"If a jury knows why you all went up there to attack the campus, maybe they'll understand how you felt, take it into account, go easier on you."

The older one from Los Angeles made a noise. "How long you gonna listen to the bullshit, Cholo?"

"You don't like what we do, Narco, you go back to L.A."

He spoke to the older man, but looked at me. His voice, the voices of all the Rockers, had that same uneasy home in three worlds: anglo high school, *barrio* streets, and not-so-distant Mexican old country. His dark eyes were intense, with a depth behind them that seemed to reach back into a deeper dark. Eyes that tried to see what was behind my eyes. Eyes with a question. Maybe a lot of questions back there in the dark. An uncertainty the older Narco from L.A. didn't have. He had answers not questions.

I said, "Why did you go up there, Esteban? What triggered the attack?"

The questions remained in his eyes. "They kill my dog."

"Dog?" I said.

"Shit," Narco said.

"Cholo!"

My chunky captor, Rizo, pointed my Sig-Sauer toward the dark end of the garage. Outside, voices were raised in angry Spanish. There was a scuffle, more loud Spanish, and at the dark end the side garage door burst open. Super Barrio pushed two of the Westside Rockers ahead of him into the garage, yellow cape flying, eyes furious behind the eyeholes of the red mask. The third Rocker caught up with Super Barrio from behind, threw his arm around the caped crusader's throat as the other two jumped to hold his arms.

Cholo and the L.A. man, Narco, were up. Narco swore.

"Who the fuck—"

"Let him go, Tomas," Cholo said.

Narco turned on the Rockers' leader, "Jesus Christ, you crazy, man?"

The Rocker behind Super Barrio released his throat. Super Barrio shook off the other two. The portly masked man strode into the light beside me.

Cholo said, "How you find us out here, Mr. Superman?"

"They all talks to Super Barrio, *muchacho.* You think you so smart no one know what you do? In the *barrio,* amigo, someone always know." And to me, "You okay, Dan?"

I nodded. "Cholo and I were talking about Anderson and what he's going to do to get them out of the trouble they're in."

"Trouble?" He unleashed a torrent of Spanish on the L.A. man, got snarling Spanish in return. I caught enough of the snarl to know it told Super Barrio which one of the two Cholo was. He was obviously surprised. He looked at Cholo who stood stonefaced, and then hit the Rockers' leader with the river of Spanish too fast for me to get more than a word here and there. I didn't have to understand the words to know what was being said. Super Barrio was telling Cholo he was in big trouble, if he wanted to help the Rockers he'd talk to both Anderson and me.

I said, "He talked to me. He told me the Rockers attacked City College because someone killed his dog."

"Dog? *Perro?*"

"Always they drive fast on our streets, them hotshot college guys," Cholo said. In English. He wanted me to hear his story. It was a start. "Hey, nice, easy way they get up to school, you know? Don't have to go 'round with all that traffic downtown an' up Cliff

Drive with all them lights. We got kinda small streets, you know, a lot of kids plays. Cars parked all along so the streets is even tighter. No lights neither, right? Just stop signs you don't really got to stop by, and nothing to worry, the cops they stay outta the back streets westside."

"*Perro?*" Super Barrio said. "A dog? You—"

"Hey, what is this shit?" Narco the L.A. man swore. "What the fuck you think you doin', man? You in a goddamn Mexican circus? What you hidin' behin' that there mask? You a narc? *La Migra?* Mex cop? What the fuck you doin' aroun' here anyways?"

Super Barrio looked through the dim garage with its bare walls and emptiness, looked at the two chairs under the single light at this end. Then at Narco from L.A. "I don' got to ask what you is, you know? Super Barrio know you. Big city gang, hey? Got your own cut in the territory, sell the coca, the big stuff. Run the shit for the real bosses, the *jefe*. Big shot on the street, drive real nice car an' shoot kids an' old ladies. Real tough, long as you stays no more'n two block from your territory. Hey, man, Super Barrio he know all about you, *muy mucho hombre*."

"Fuckin' goddamn freak." Narco stepped toward Super Barrio, looked for support.

Cholo said, "Shut up, Narco. Everyone know Super Barrio down Mexico. You don't like it up here, go the fuck to L.A."

The other three Rockers watched the man from L.A. Rizo had my Sig-Sauer. Cholo sat down again in his armchair and waited. He held Anderson's PPK. Narco didn't sit down.

"Shit, I tol' Luisa you was all wet shitass kids."

He shouldered through the Rockers and out the side door in the front shadows of the narrow garage. We all heard the car engine start, the screech of angry tires, the car fading away into the night outside. Super Barrio sat down in the second chair Narco had vacated. I found a folding chair in the shadows against the wall. No one stopped me sitting down facing Cholo and Super Barrio in the armchairs. Cholo saw me, said nothing, those questions still behind his dark eyes. The three Rockers behind me seemed as interested as I was in learning what would happen with Super Barrio seated beside their leader.

"Punks," Super Barrio said. "Help no one, you know that? Gangs, all they does is pull down. In Mexico they are like the generals that betray the revolution an' the people. They get rich, live in big *rancheros.* They don' remember the people, the Indian, Mexico. Brown anglos, landowners without land, bandits."

Through the silence of the garage I heard the outside sounds of the night for the first time, became aware of the traffic on the free-way. The open freeway. Cholo had said to Super Barrio, *"How you find us out here, Mr. Superman?"* We were in Goleta, or even Carpinteria.

"Alone we got nothing," Cholo said. "Alone is nothing, Mr. Super Barrio. We hangs together we got a chance."

Super Barrio said, "In a gang you're nothin'. Gangs means you're scared, don' know what to do to make it better. You all mixed up. In gangs you're alone, Cholo. You don' help no one. You don' even help yourself. You're no one. We got to be all together against the politi-cians an' landlords an' bosses. You got to be everyone."

I said, "Why did you go to the morgue all the time, Cholo? Who is that John Doe dead in there?"

"Who say I go to the morgue?"

"We've seen the records. You took your troops one at a time to look at the dead latino. Who is he, Cholo?"

His intense eyes had the questions deep inside the dark behind them. "He's Super Nada, you know? Super nothing. Super no one."

29

The last of fifteen children, he is born in a mud-walled house in Chiapas where his mother squats to drop him into the hands of a *parteras,* the first outside human contact he knows. It is a closer touch with others than he will ever have again.

In the thick heat of coastal Guatemala, he is born under a green banana plant on the vast Del Monte plantation. His father and mother both work for Del Monte. They are not married. His mother is killed by a jealous lover, he is raised by his maternal grandparents. When he is eight he goes to work on the Del Monte plantation with his father.

His mother shivers under the thin blanket in the tin hut on the slope of an Ecuadoran mountain when he is born to her. His father shivers in fear. How will he feed another mouth? His mother and father pray he will die and save his whole family from starvation.

A Marxist guerilla, his father is in the Colombian back country fighting the government troops and the *sicarios* of the drug lords when he is born. His mother is killed by *sicarios* when she tries to reach his father in a rebel village. In a massive raid on the village, the government captures and executes his father.

He is born in an unpainted cottage in the *barrio* of a small town in Central California, the youngest of ten children. His father and mother pick in the fields. His uncles pick in the fields. His cousins become garage mechanics, gardeners, day laborers, handymen, pick in the fields, or leave town.

In Chiapas he has no shoes, speaks only the Tzotzil Indian language until he is ten, dreams of becoming a *curandero* like his mother's brother who has the *nahual* of a jaguar and makes people well all through the highlands with his herbs and his prayers. But after ten it becomes clear to him and his father and all the other banana cutters on the Del Monte plantation that he is not the son of his father, but of some *norteamericano* who had found his mother pleasing and he is not Indian but Ladino and he runs away to the city with two brothers so that his family in the mountains of Ecuador will not starve because they have to feed so many hungry mouths.

There is no work in the city, he cannot go home where there is not enough food, so he becomes a beggar and a street vendor and lives in a shantytown built on the muddy slopes of the city dump where he scavenges for food. His brothers go to work down across the Brazilian border in a hidden jungle cocaine laboratory operated by the Medellin cartel, where both are eventually gunned down by a rival cartel. He gets tuberculosis in the mountains and is too sick to live in the city anymore so goes into the San Joaquin Valley to pick in the fields with his mother and father, has no time to go to school while the picking season is on so falls behind and often has to repeat the same grade.

By the time he is sixteen his mother has ruined her back and cannot work in the fields for the San Joaquin Valley landowners, his father has run away, and he has left grade school to work for a gardener to make more money for the family. The landowners of the coffee plantations in the Chiapas Mountains pay day wages less than minimum, there is rarely money to even buy shoes for the men, the Mexican government has passed a law that makes it hard to become a *curandero* and there is little hope for his dream. He almost dies of his tuberculosis in the hospital in Guatemala City, when he is released he has lost his shack at the city dump, must live on the streets while he begs enough money to buy goods to become a street vendor again.

He cannot beg enough money on the streets of Medellin to buy goods or even live, goes to work as a runner for the cocaine and emerald cartel that killed his mother and brothers. He is caught by the police, escapes, and runs to hide in the cold rain of the Ecuadoran mountain village where he was born. His father has drunk himself to death, his mother has remarried an old man who has a tin shack where she can live out her old age after thirty-five. There is no room for him, no work in the village, no food except what he can plant and scrape from the thin, rocky soil of the mountains, but there is a strange foreigner come to build better houses in the village who tells the villagers of his distant country where there is food and work and everyone lives longer than sixty years.

It is a long way from Chiapas to the United States of North America. He takes his money from work on the coffee plantation, borrows a pair of shoes from the *curandero,* walks down from the mountains to the paved road he has never seen that leads to a Mexico City that he has never seen. The tuberculosis of the mountains has made him weak, there is no way he can walk from Ecuador to the country where there is food and work for everyone. He has no money, rides in a cart down to the banana plantations, hides in the train to the sea and the ships that take the bananas north.

On the road through the mountains of the Mayas to the Mexican border the *kaibiles* anti-guerilla patrols shoot anyone caught walking without proper papers, he must be very careful, move only at night or far from any roads. Careful when he crawls over the fences and across the night to hide in the baggage compartment of the great jet that will fly from Medellin to the great city of the United States of North America, must fight another man for the space that will only hide one. Shivers in the cold as the great bird flies, escapes while all the men in blue and white are taking the other man from where he is frozen to death on the wheel of the great jet. He is sad for the dead man, but he is glad he escapes and is in the rich country of the north. In Central California his mother dies, the gardener does not need him when the winter comes, his uncles and cousins have much trouble of their own in a year of bad money. He leaves to find work and a new life in the cities.

In the great City of the Pueblo of Our Lady the Queen of the Angels he sleeps with two other men who look for work, stands on the streetcorner for men in pickup trucks to drive past and give him work, finds a job washing dishes in a Mexican restaurant where they let him sleep in a back room but do not pay him much. He knows no one, and when *La Migra* finds him at the restaurant he runs and cannot go back, stands again on the streetcorner, sleeps in a room with four men he does not know. He fears *La Migra,* finds no work, is told by another man there is work picking on the ranches to the north.

He falls in with drug dealers, goes north with them to deliver a shipment of cocaine.

He meets some *yanqui* men without homes who tell him Santa Barbara is good place to live, where work can be found.

He is hired by a man who must deliver a load of plants to Santa Barbara. When the truck is unloaded, the man drives away without paying him.

He is afraid of *La Migra,* knows that if he is caught he will be sent all the way home. The men on the streetcorner tell him it is safer in Oregon or Washington. He walks north.

On a back street in Santa Barbara he is hit by a speeding car as he crosses the street in the dark. The car is driven by a City College student who says that he was walking erratically, stepped out in front of the car without looking as if he was sick or drunk. He is dead when the police arrive. The young driver is cited for speeding, but no other charges are brought. He is taken to the morgue.

At the time of his death he is wearing grimy work pants without labels, a cheap rayon shirt with the mark of a homeless shelter in Oxnard, worn espadrilles, a torn straw hat with no label. He has no jewelry, no money, nothing in his pockets, no identification. Blood tests reveal no alcohol, no cocaine, no drugs of any kind. He had not eaten that day, has tuberculosis scars on one lung, no traces or marks of any other disease or injury. He is estimated to be between sixteen and twenty years old. Small, thin, underweight. Latino. No scars, birthmarks or moles.

The shelter in Oxnard does not remember him, has no name and no paperwork on the shirt.

His fingerprints, dental charts, and measurements are fed into computers nationwide in the rich northern country. There are no results. Because he is obviously latino, his statistics are sent to the police and armies and social authorities in all Spanish-speaking countries as well as the United States of North America. There are no results. He is known to no one. He remains in the refrigerated morgue drawer unclaimed and unnamed.

Because of his youth, the police do not bury him, keep him in the morgue in the hope that some family member will come forward to name him and claim him. No one does. Over the years many people come to view the body, parents and police, but no one knows him. The police continue to keep him as if they cannot let go and admit that here is a life no one wants, a human being who never existed. They know that somewhere there are a mother and father, sisters and brothers. They will not believe there are parents somewhere who don't care, or are even glad he is gone. They cannot believe he has no one, has nowhere. Was no one.

30

"Super *Nada*," Esteban Gonzalez, Cholo, said. "Mr. No One."

In the rug-covered old armchair, picked from some sidewalk where it had been waiting for the trash truck to take it away, his eyes with the darkness in them looked past me and Super Barrio and the other Westside Rockers at the shadows of the narrow garage outside the circle of light that held us. A thin youth very much like the nameless dead latino boy in the morgue.

"You don' know the dead kid?" Super Barrio said. "Why you go to that morgue?

"No one, nothing." He talked to the shadows not to us. "No one give a shit if he's dead or alive, you know? That college kid hotshot that killed him don't care, it ain't his problem, right? The fucking beaner was crazy or drunk or maybe dumb. He only a beaner, it no my fault. They don't even put him in jail. Hey, what's one dead beaner no one even knows his name?" The distant questions far back in his dark eyes looked at me and looked at Super Barrio. "Where he come from? How'd he get here? Maybe he was born here, a *chicano* like me. From someplace they got too damn many kids an' no one even know he's gone, you know? I mean, they cares, sure, but they got too many kids, too much trouble, no money."

"You didn't know anything about that dead boy," I said, "but you went to the morgue. What did you do at the morgue, Esteban?"

"What I do? I talk to him, you know, man?" A sudden cloud of anger covered the deep questions in his eyes. "I talk. I say, who was you, where you come from? Up here, or somewhere down there, you know? Maybe Mexico, maybe Guatemala, maybe Ecuador or Colombia or Peru or Chile or even Brazil. Down there they think even us *chicanos* live like *padrones* in the great big country of the *norteamericano,* the *yanqui.* They don't know it's all the same shit up here like down there. Anglos they don't give a shit we lives or is dead, up here or down there. Them goddamn college punks don't care, drives our streets like they don't know anyone else is around. Cops don't care, the city don't care, no one care we even got a name, got born somewheres."

"They let you do that? Go into the morgue and just sit with the body?"

He shrugged under the single light of the empty garage. "I take someone, tell them he maybe know who the kid is. They don't know the difference. What they care anyway? Hey, it's two lousy beaners, what the hell."

"They must care about something. They've kept the body there almost two years. They should have buried him, forgotten him years ago."

He shrugged again. "They think maybe he's a *coyote,* a dope run-

ner, some kind of crook. They maybe want to find out who he is, get
the drug boss sends him up here. Maybe they think he's anglo.
Maybe they don't like it they don't know something. It don't look
good they got a dead guy they can't find out nothing about. They got
to look good. They don't give shit about a dead latino."

"You don't believe all that," I said. "You just want to believe it. You
want to hate the cops, the anglos. You—"

"They don't know we's alive!" Up on his feet, the depths and
questions in his eyes replaced by a wall of anger. "Them fucking
college hotshots drive on our streets like they ain't nobody else
there 'cause there ain't nobody else there! We ain't there no more
than my dog was there. That's what that kid in the morgue told me.
He ain't got no more name or goddamn place in the anglo world
than my dog. In that morgue he ain't no different from my dog. Not
to the anglos. Not to them college fucking guys."

In the dim garage with its solitary light at one end, he stood with
the wall of anger behind his eyes like a black mass that allows
nothing to escape. The dead youth in the morgue without a name,
without a place in the world, had become an obsession. An obsession that, triggered by the death of his dog under the same wheels,
had sent the Westside Rockers up to the campus on the hill that
night. Because when a carrot is there for all to see, and some who
see it cannot have it, then they have to destroy it so they don't want
it anymore.

"A dead man got no name," Super Barrio said, "an' a dog."

Cholo, Esteban Gonzalez, poor latino with all the same dreams as
anyone else in the rich country of the north, but so few of the same
paths to those dreams, had found in the morgue the symbol of his
anger. A dead youth of his own age, of his own language, of his own
people. Killed on his own streets by indifferent anglos. A youth with
the same confusion, the same questions. The same dreams but
maybe even fewer paths to those dreams. Who had come from nowhere to die as nothing and talk to Esteban Gonzalez, Cholo, in the
silence of the morgue. It was enough to take him up the hill with his
gang to attack the enemy. Was it enough for an anglo court to
understand why he had gone up that hill to attack the enemy that
was them and us?

"You are a big fool," Super Barrio said. "All of you are big fools.
Estupido! Not because you go to that college for a dead *muchacho*
and a *perro*. Because you go there to fight a war. That is not our

way, that is the anglo way. The way of the landlords and landowners. The way of big power. The soul of our people is not that way, it
is the way of growing. We can grow all together against the power of
the landlord, the boss."

Cholo dismissed him. "Super Barrio, super crazy! The anglos
they ain't ever gonna give us nothing. The only way we get is we
take."

Super Barrio shook his head. "We teach the landowners an' the
anglos, not fight them. Everybody got a tribe wants to win and keep
everybody else outside. That fight we always gonna lose, Cholo."

"Bullshit."

He snapped his fingers. The Rockers in the garage produced their
blades, my Sig-Sauer. Cholo pointed Anderson's PPK at Super Barrio. "You're in or you're out, *Señor* Superman. We're out, we're
gonna get in."

I said, "By all of you going to prison for an obsession and a dog?
Sounds pretty dumb to me. Sounds like the anglos and the police
are going to win this one."

Cholo said. "They sends us to jail, they knows we're here. They
knows they ain't gonna push us around any time they wants."

"Did some homeless people try to push you around in Alameda
Park, Cholo? You and your troops?"

"Shit, man!" He turned on me. "Get the fuck off my back, hey? We
don' do goddamn nothing in Alameda Park. So—"

"A woman was murdered. A homeless woman who went there to
sleep. A woman playing a radio, alone, minding her own business.
She was stabbed fifteen, twenty times. There were signs like a military attack. Witnesses heard voices speaking Spanish. Since then
I've been attacked in the park and at my house by four men all in
black with ski masks. I got away both times. Your gang was in the
park, and—"

"We jump you in that park, you don't walk away!"

"Cholo—?" It was my chunky captor, Rizo. "Them private school
jerks give us a hard time over there."

I said, "Private school jerks?"

Cholo nodded. "I remember the assholes. Nothing happens,
okay?"

"Who are they? What kind of hard time?"

"Shit man, I don't remember every crappy anglo kid figures he
got to rag a *chicano* so he feel *macho*."

Super Barrio said, "Maybe you send some anglo to jail you tell Fortune what he got to know."

In the shadows behind us Rizo said, "We run into the jerks outside a movie first time. They—"

"—was five, maybe six," Cholo picked up, motioned Rizo to let him do the talking. Rank is rank in any tribe. "Over by Plaza de Oro. Me, Rizo and Tony was coming out of that movie about the anglo guy covers the war down El Salvador. These anglos all got Marine flattop hair, shirts got them loops on the shoulder, chino pants pressed real sharp, boots all shined. They starts talking loud how *spics* are dumb, got no guts, Americans got to show 'em how to fight. How America oughta let all the goddamn *spics* kill themselves off, make all them countries down there part of the U.S. and shit like that. So we tells them they's full of shit. One guy acts tough, I got to slap him down. Rizo an' Tony goes after two guys. They runs, the movie security an' some cops shows up, we splits."

Another of the Rockers, one of the two who still held knives back toward the dark front of the garage, said, "Me an' Tony was over aroun' Alameda Park a couple days after an' them same anglos sees us and we got to run. They chase us across State an' we ducks through yards an' loses 'em. Cholo says—"

Cholo said, "—I say we got to find out more about the guys. So we watch the park. We spots three some night, tails back to this private school. So—"

"What private school?"

"What the fuck they call it, Rizo?"

From the shadows Rizo said, "Western Service Institute. Somethin' like that."

Cholo nodded. "It's a goddamn school, maybe a couple hundred anglo kids. I figure we forget it, stay away from the eastside a while. That's it."

"That's all?"

"Like I say, it ain't nothing."

Rizo in the shadows said, "That ain't all, you know, Cholo. Remember that night I was in Alameda Park an' I spot them guys? Got to get lost fast?"

"What night?"

Rizo said, "Maybe a week ago. Tuesday, yeah. I goes to see Carmen, so it got to of been Tuesday night."

The Tuesday night Cassandra Reilly had been murdered.

"What happened?"

His face was half hidden in the shadows. "I got a girl down on Cota by Milpas. She works late, you know? I goes to see her late. Aroun' midnight, I cut over the eastside. I'm in that park, I see maybe four of the same guys. I figure they spot me. I dives in the bushes, works my way out of the park, takes off."

"Then what?"

"I don' see 'em no more."

"Did you see anything else in the park? A woman," I described Cassandra Reilly. "Did you hear voices?"

"I hears some singin'. *Nortegna,* Tex-Mex, you know? I likes that stuff."

"In Spanish?"

"Sure in Spanish, what else?"

"How could you be so sure it was them?"

" 'Cause they wearin' the same goddamn black outfits, got the same black stuff on their goddamn faces like the time they chase us an' the time we tails 'em."

"Black clothes? Masks?"

"Don' see no masks. See their faces pretty good. Same assholes."

I faced Cholo. "Do we have to fight our way out of here, or do you want our help?"

Super Barrio said, "You gotta go in, Cholo, tell the cops the story. Hide out an' you gonna prove nothing. The guy from the public defender, he's outside. Him and me we come together. He hear any trouble, he calls the cops on the phone he got in his car, okay? He want to talk to you guys, help out."

Cholo's dark eyes looked at the other four Rockers. None of them said anything. Super Barrio walked back into the shadows, opened the side door at the front. There was a silence, and the massive figure of Anderson came into the garage.

They were still talking when I left. They had their jobs and their needs. I had mine. I needed dinner, a night's sleep, and some talk with Al Benton.

Anglo kids with Marine haircuts and military shirts had been in the park that night, dressed in black, with lamp black on their faces.

III
THE HEROES

They hunch in the dark room of the empty house. On the floor, knees up to their chins. All but Wolf. He sits easily, relaxed.

"They don't have a clue." Wolf laughs. "No way they'll ever figure it out. We're too fucking smart for those boobs."

"They'll find out about Roach. They'll come here."

"So what, for Christ sake? No one connects us to Roach."

"I'm scared."

"Jesus, Spider, shape the hell up. Wolf says we're okay, so we're okay."

"So what about that P.I.? We missed the bastard twice, he's not going to just quit and go away."

"Shit, Spider, he hasn't got a clue. He even went down to L.A. looking for us. Right, Wolf?"

"Him and that fat public defender's investigator. They don't know anything, and they never will."

"What if he does, Wolf? What if he finds us?"

In the dark room with its flickering candlelight, they look at each other. Four of them do. Scorpion looks at Wolf. Wolf walks around the room.

"We set up observation posts, divide the day into watches. Half of us are on duty at all times. I'll command one squad, Scorpion the other. We keep total line of communication. We maybe booby-trap HQ, set tripwires, stay armed. If that P.I. finds us, this time we don't try to just bang him up and scare him off. This time he doesn't walk away."

"What if he brings the police?"

Wolf shrugs. "Then we take to the hills. Go underground."

31

Far back from the quiet upper eastside street, the low buildings looked more like some cottages and a modernistic brick church than a school. That is probably what they were before someone bought them, combined them with covered walkways, and hung a wooden sign with raised gold letters over the front porch of the first cottage: *Western Service Institute*. The front walk led to the door of the first cottage through oak and pepper trees, and a low-maintenance ivy ground cover instead of grass. An unofficial dirt walk cut through the ivy to the open covered walkway between the third cottage and the brick ex-church.

I took the unofficial walk, found the school larger than it looked from the street. On the far side of the covered walk a longer wing of the brick building on my right, and a row of more cottages on the left, reached back to another red brick building, and formed a "quad" crisscrossed by the usual X-shaped concrete walkways. The second brick building was two stories with outside stairs and a white wooden gallery around the second floor. Beyond it a high hedge and a row of towering blue gum eucalyptus trees separated it from the houses on the next street. As with much in Santa Barbara, most of the school was invisible from the street.

At ten in the morning, the quad was empty. The only sign of life was a head at an upper window of the rear two-story red brick, and the sound of voices from various places. Single voices lecturing, multiple low voices and the sense of a mass of many people shifting and moving close together. As I walked around the deserted quad, the single voices were in the cottages where teachers paced in front of small classes of heads bent over notebooks and hands writing down every word.

The low pulse of multiple voices, more felt than heard like an insistent C-pedal in a large orchestra, came from an open door in the single-story brick wing on the right. A weight of many people shifting and breathing together, that, inside the open door, became a

165

large study hall almost full of young men and a few women. Seated in rows at long tables, they were deep in study, most with open notebooks writing laborious notes on what they were reading. There was no horseplay, no laughter, no one reading a magazine or novel or comic book. No one slumped over the tables asleep, no one stood outside the door smoking, as there always were in the study halls of high schools I'd seen.

No one inside the study hall even turned to look at me in the doorway. Either they were under discipline as rigid as a reform school, or they were driven by a desperate need to learn. At least to memorize what they were supposed to know, to succeed at what they were doing. To reach some goal they were afraid would be denied them. A visible intensity, tangible, that was also missing from the halls of most high schools these days. A distance from most high schools made visible in the clothes I saw in the gloom of the hall. Ties, neat dress shirts and short haircuts. Creased slacks and shined shoes, jackets over the backs of some chairs.

Prep school clothes. Prep school grooming. The children of the elite. Or those who wanted to be. The children of the elite don't usually go to unknown schools, or study with the intensity of this study room. The dress but not the manner. The intensity of those who want to be what they are not quite. Not yet.

"Sir?"

He stood behind me, a paradigm of all the students bent over their books in the silence of the hall. A striped regimental tie I recognized as authentic but couldn't recall the regiment. White buttondown oxford shirt. Gray herringbone sport jacket a lot like mine. Gray slacks and a leather and fabric belt striped in the same colors as the tie. Shined cordovan loafers. Tall and smiling, his blond hair short and neat and brushed.

"May I help you?" Polite and confident. An upperclassman and campus greeter.

"I'm just looking around."

"Yes, sir. Our headmaster, Doctor Jovanetti, would be glad to talk to you if you have any questions about our school."

I glanced up at the second floor window in the two-story brick building at the rear of the quad where I'd seen the man's head looking out earlier. It was still there, still looked out toward me and the tall, polite youth.

"I can take you to him, sir."

"Sent you to shoo me off or reel me in, right?"

"Sir?" Caught, he was suddenly unsure despite the smooth confidence. He looked and tried to act twenty-five, but he wasn't. The headmaster had seen me on his quad, didn't like people on his quad he didn't know.

"Okay," I said, "take me to Doctor Jovanetti."

He walked ahead across the concrete "X" of the quad, the low hum of the study hall and the isolated voices of the lecturers in the classrooms the only sounds in the winter morning sun. But not the only movement. Halfway across the open space I knew I was being watched. Not by the headmaster at the second floor window that was empty now. Someone else. A quick movement in a cottage doorway behind me. At the corner of the front walkway between cottages. A flash of color that was a tie. A white shirt, there and gone.

"Up here, sir."

We went up the outside stairs to the second floor gallery of the rear red brick. My guide opened the door of the headmaster's office, let me go in first. Before I did, I looked back and down over the gallery rail. Two figures half in shadow, looked up at me. One wore a jacket, one didn't. I went into the office.

"The gentleman said he would like to talk to you, sir."

I said, "Dan Fortune, Doctor Jovanetti."

He stood, waved me to a high-backed leather chair with wooden arms that faced his desk. "Thank you, Mr. Evans."

The overage twenty-year-old closed the door when he left. Dr. Jovanetti sat down behind his desk. "Are you interested in our school, Mr. Fortune?"

He was a tall, heavyset man in a gray flannel suit and the same buttondown shirt and regimental striped tie as his students. Balding with a brush cut and only a touch of gray. The desk itself was as clean and neat as a parade ground. Pen set, lamp, blotter, appointment calendar, telephone, and a single yellow notepad with writing on it. A man who did his work, was probably as quick and efficient as he looked. Erect behind the desk, not tense but a shade alert. Strangers on campus did not relax him.

"Looks like you have a nice school here. Good, hardworking students."

"We think so. Are you interested in schools in general, Mr. Fortune? Or us in particular? Perhaps a son who is thinking of coming to us?"

"No, I really never heard of the school. Not very well known, is it? Not even here in town."

"We're here to educate our students, not make headlines or re-cruit football players. May I ask—"

"All schools have to attract students, don't they? I'd guess your students aren't especially local."

"We get a certain number from the local schools." He wanted to know what I was doing at his school, but didn't want to push too hard and offend me in case I was a prospective customer. "Our students mostly find us. We do most of our advertising with the advisers at other high schools and colleges." He nodded to my empty sleeve. "Were you a military man, Mr. Fortune?"

A man's assumptions and questions can tell you a great deal.

"Merchant Marine. World War Two."

"Ah."

His reactions to answers can tell you even more. He did not con-sider the Merchant Marine, in or out of war, military.

"You were in the military?"

"The Army. World War Two and another twenty-five years."

"You must have liked it."

"I found it interesting and rewarding, yes."

"Colonel or General?"

He smiled at last. "Never quite made my star, I'm afraid. Now, Mr. Fortune, what *is* your interest in our school?"

I had thought of making up a story about being a reporter writing a story on private schools, but the questions I needed answered weren't the kind a reporter would be likely to ask.

"I'm investigating a murder in Alameda Park, Doctor. It's possible some of your students could be involved."

"That's ridiculous! Utterly ridiculous!" His chair crashed back-wards into the wall. For a long few seconds, he stood livid behind the desk. Then he regained his control. "I'm sorry, Mr. Fortune, but that is totally absurd."

"If it is, Doctor, I'll go away. But I need to ask some questions."

"May I see your credentials?"

I showed him my license with its color photo.

"Are the police coming here too?"

"Not until I talk to them."

He retrieved his chair, sat down again. Played a little for time while he thought. "Alameda Park? You mean that homeless person?

The police solved that case, caught the man who killed her. I mean, I'm sure I read that. I followed the case quite closely. It was so near our school."

"Very near," I said. "I don't believe the police have the right killer."

He let that sink in. "And something brought you here. What would that be?"

I told him about the Westside Rockers and their trouble with some of his boys. Not about the attacks on me, or the Spanish music and talk from the bandstand. He would be defensive anyway, too much too soon could make him a roadblock.

"Any students have some trouble with latinos?"

He stood more carefully this time, walked to the window that looked out and down at the quad. The window he'd seen me from. A window he stood at a lot, surveyed his school. Proud of his school. "Our students are often misunderstood in the community, Mr. Fortune. The school is misunderstood. People call us a military school, but we have no military training, no military officers on staff, except me, and no uniforms."

"I don't see anything military. Why do they think that?"

His head moved to watch someone or something cross the quad below. "Because every student here is hoping to be appointed to one of the military academies. That's what we do here: try to raise the academic abilities and test scores of young people who want to attend one of the service academies."

"That accounts for the formal clothes and the discipline."

"We've got good kids here. Goal-oriented kids who want to face a challenge. The academies tell us, 'Get their grades up, we'll do the military training.' Our academic demands are rigorous. We have a nine-hour academic day, four hours of quiet, supervised study every day. Including two each night from eight to ten. How many kids do you know today would do that? These are kids with a goal, who had a difficult time academically in their former schools. Many of them are over eighteen. They're all serious. They want to serve their country, be soldiers, officers." He motioned me to the window. "Look down there."

The students were streaming out of the cottages and study hall, going to their next classes or to their two hours in the study hall. They were all dressed alike even the few women in their tweed skirts and blouses, low shoes and wool dresses. They moved briskly, purposeful, with little of the loud horseplay common to most campuses I'd seen.

"Have you ever seen students quite like them, Mr. Fortune? We have one hundred and ten registered this year, twenty of them women. They are young people with a dream who are, perhaps, not as academically gifted or oriented as many, but are ready to work hard and accept the challenge of meeting and measuring up to the mental and physical demands of the military academies, the rigors of duty in the services later. We should be proud of them, not sneer at them as militaristic, as 'Rambos' and snobs."

We each looked down at the students and saw something different. What I saw was what I had seen in the study hall. Preppies, the elite. Those who wanted to be the elite. That was what they were here to become. The future leaders of men, rulers of the status quo. Children who wanted to be adults, have the status and rewards, the power. Leaders and rulers of the status quo. Maybe we both saw what we wanted to see.

"Is that how they're misunderstood, Doctor? As elite snobs, militaristic Rambos, gung-ho patriots?"

"Usually. A lot of it is our dress code, their sense of order and discipline. But I can't help that, those things are important for the right attitude. Officers, leaders, must have standards, codes."

"They all board here?"

"Yes. We feel that is necessary for proper supervision and work. We aren't inexpensive, our work is intense, we try to guarantee results. These are all kids who need to raise their academic levels or they wouldn't be here."

"How much free time do they have?"

"Curfew is eleven P.M. on school nights, one A.M. on Friday and Saturday nights. As I said, they tend to be older students."

"Is curfew strict?"

"Live-in supervisors personally check all curfews."

"Are they reliable?"

"For the most part. Curfews can be evaded."

The quad below was empty again, silent except for the voices of the teachers from the open cottage doors and the pulse of low voices and movement inside the study hall. Dr. Jovanetti walked back to his desk. He sat again, looked up at me with eyes that asked if we were finished, if I'd satisfied myself that his students could not possibly have been involved in murder.

"Do you know of any students in a quarrel with latinos?"

"Not specifically. There have been some, I admit. The community often misunderstands our boys, finds them arrogant and belligerent when they are only being confident and standing up for themselves. We do teach them to value themselves."

"Are any of your boys missing? Say for a day and a half? Two nights?"

"Certainly not. I would be the first to know."

"Would you check, be sure everyone is where they should be?"

He didn't want to, but he nodded. "It will take some time, we trust our students."

"Okay. I'll be back later."

I had him worried. Murder wouldn't do his school much good.

32

As I crossed the empty quad they appeared ahead of me. Two tall boys in blue blazers over gray slacks, brush haircuts so short and shaved their scalps showed pink, eyes hidden behind dark airforce glasses. In the covered walkway between buildings I had to use to reach the shortcut path to the street. The thin brown-haired one, so thin for his height he looked frail, smiled.

"So sorry to bother you, sir, but we couldn't help seeing your arm. Are you from one of the academies, sir? Perhaps here to evaluate us? Look us over, you might say?"

The heavier, blond and eager, laughed too loud in the quiet quad. "We all bet you were a military man here to look us over."

Four more had come from different directions to stand around me. Only one, a shorter, dark-haired youth, wore a jacket. The other three were in shirts, ties and slacks. Almost triplets. Seventeen or eighteen, brush-cut nondescript hair, the striped ties, one with dark glasses like the older two. They ringed me, pressed close. The tall, skinny one went on talking as he moved closer, almost breathed on me.

"Are we right, sir? You can tell us. We are, aren't we? You have military man written all over you. You can always tell a military hero. What war was it, sir? Korea? World War Two? The big one, right, sir? World War Two. That was one tough fight, wasn't it, sir?"

"Dogfaces crawling up the mountains of Italy."

"The hedgerows in Normandy."

"Omaha Beach."

"If we're going to die, we might as well die inland as on the beach."

"Tree bursts in the Huertgen."

"Desert Rats against Rommel."

Ringed, I watched them as they crowded around me, sometimes touched me. Pushed me toward the street and then back into the quad like puppies leaping around someone with food, eager and unable to stop themselves. Bold and daring, but behind the bravado the four younger ones were nervous. Playing a game, and not quite sure of the game.

"I'll bet you were with General Patton, sir. Or perhaps you were General Patton?"

Cool and bold, the skinny older one sneered behind the smile, not at all nervous. His eyes were invisible under the dark glasses like a blind man who blunders ahead into what he can't see or know, bold and daring. On an adrenalin high.

"No, he was General MacArthur!" the big blond older boy laughed.

Our children, teenagers, can be damn fools, but they're not stupid. They perceive that they live in a power world but have no power. They are a minority, and as any minority they take what power they can by breaking rules, posturing, challenging the icons of adults, never cleaning up the kitchen or their rooms, living in chaos that drives adults crazy. Crossing the street slowly so adults in their power machines must wait.

"I shall return!"

The blond put his hand over his heart. Behind the dark glasses the skin around his hidden eyes moved, twitched. His fingers opened and closed in a spasm. He balanced on his toes, edgy. There was more to this game with me than teenage need for power. That was the root, the real cause, but not what they thought they were doing.

I said, "No general, boys. Just a poor doggie, you're right about that. The mountains of Italy. G.I. Joe. So you're going to be soldiers, eh? Officers and gentlemen. Heroes. Well, now, that's a really fine ambition."

We can all play games. Their game was to ridicule, sneer at me, get a rise. Mine was to patronize them, needle, find out what they hoped to gain from their game.

"You really think so, sir?" The skinny one still smiled. "A fine ambition, the military?"

I smiled at him. "Yessir, son, I'm really proud of you. All you fine boys."

He was bright, the skinny one, had seen my game. "Ah, but you're not from the academies after all, are you? Our mistake. We apologize. But you must be here for some reason, sir. If we knew, perhaps we could help you?"

"Actually, I'm investigating a murder. Can you guys help me with that?"

"Murder?" The voice behind me had a small tremble. It could be simple surprise, shock at the word.

"Wow," another behind me breathed.

The third back there said nothing.

"Hey," the skinny one said, "did someone finally get the math prof?"

"Yeh, I'll drink to that," one said behind me.

"I'd go for the English tutor."

The big blond also said nothing, bobbed up and down on his toes, smiled at me from under the dark aviator glasses. They didn't ask me what murder. That could mean something, or it could be simple teen indifference to anything in the adult world.

"Gosh," the skinny one said, "I guess that's kind of heavy for kids like us. It must be exciting work, though, right, sir?"

"Usually," I said, "it's just sad."

I got no reaction. They only went on smiling at me.

"How about trouble with a latino gang? Help me with anything about that?"

"Trouble, sir?" the skinny one said, his eyebrows rising over the edge of the shades. "You mean ethnic prejudice, sir? Why, that would be wrong, wouldn't it, sir?"

The big blond said, "Half the enlisted men in the services are black or brown, a commander can't have any prejudice if he expects to succeed."

It sounded like a lecture he'd memorized.

"We'll have to lead everyone," one said behind me. "Regardless of race, creed or color."

"We love our brown brothers," the skinny one said, and then looked up over my head toward the buildings behind me. "Well, sir, it's been pleasant to speak with you, you should return to our campus sometime. But now we must attend to our studies."

I glanced behind me. Up at his window, I saw the face of the headmaster again. Coming toward us across the quad was the student monitor, Evans. When I looked back at the six boys, they were all disappearing in different directions. By the time the monitor, Evans, reached me we were alone. He looked around at everywhere the six had vanished, frowned.

"I hope they didn't bother you, sir. Donner can be a pain, but we don't get many visitors here so I guess they were curious about you. The headmaster sent me to shoo them back to study."

"You know them?"

"Oh, yes sir. Not all of them that well, of course. I guess I know Donner the best, he's been here longest. Whitaker too, even if he's new this year. He's in most of my classes."

"They're the two older ones? Skinny and the buff blond?"

"That's them. They're not much older, not seniors like me."

"Which is which?"

"Donner's the stringbean and Whitaker's the weightlifter. Donner was going for pilot, but he's too tall now. Whitaker still is. Going for pilot I mean."

"What are you going for?"

"Air Force fighter pilot if I can make it. That's why I know Whitaker pretty good. A lot of us want to be pilots. Marines and Army Airborne are probably next."

"You come from a military family?"

"No, sir. A lot of the guys do, but not me. I just want to fly fighter jets, I guess. And meet the challenge, you know? I guess I like the idea of a real challenge, being one of the few."

I said. "You like the school?"

"Very much, sir. I'm not good at self-discipline, setting my own program. I like the rigor here, the demands on me."

"That's what you like the most? The demands?"

"And my classmates. That's the really great thing about this school. Everyone here is alike, we all want the same thing, all have the same dreams. That's nice, you know? Not like all the different dumb ideas in a regular high school."

"No," I said, "not like that."

Anderson met me at the county jail.

"How's it going with the Rockers?"

In the interrogation room, he looked tired. "Cholo's come in with the other four. We talked him into it, I hope to hell we were right. We sent Super Barrio door to door over on the lower westside to ask the whole community to testify for the Rockers, tell how bad the shortcut traffic to the college is over there."

"Will that help?"

"You never know about juries. It should help that Cholo came in voluntarily, gave the media their story, but you never know."

We waited for Cholo and Rizo to be brought in. Anderson had arranged to talk to them after I called him. If they could help solve a murder the police had already closed, it might do their public image a lot of good, show them helping the community not ripping it up. Law today is too often a matter of safety and security, of advantage, appearance, persuasion. It can have little to do with truth, right or justice. Maybe it never did have much to do with truth, right or justice.

"How is Gonzalez feeling about it all now?"

"Nervous and surly. Not sure if he's been given good advice or conned."

"It's a big club. Includes most of us these days."

"He's got a bigger reason than most. The major job of the police is to keep the citizens soothed, content and unworried. The powers that be don't like the peasants to get worked up. When there's a crime against the public peace it has to be solved fast so no one worries about it hurting them. Nobody wants to know the reasons for a riot or a bombing, they want to believe it won't happen again, so the police have to give them the culprits signed, sealed and stashed in jail."

"Is that what's going to happen?"

"I think we've got a fifty-fifty chance of getting suspended and probation. I hope so anyway."

"That's not good odds to come in on."

"If the five don't come in, we had no chance."

"Cholo knew that?"

"He knew."

A leader takes care of his men, even in a gang. Especially in a gang. I thought about that as the door opened and the jail deputies brought Cholo and Rizo in. The two Westside Rockers didn't look on top of the world. It was Anderson they turned to as the deputies left us alone.

"Nothing new," Anderson said. "The lawyers are working on the district attorney and the judge."

Rizo nodded. Cholo looked at me. If Anderson had nothing to tell them, the meeting must be for me. That was why he was the leader.

"I need some more help, Esteban," I said.

"Look like it's us needs help," he said.

"You think you can identify those kids from Western Service Institute you had all the trouble with?"

"I don't know. Maybe." A thin smile. "They all look the same to us, you know?"

"How about you, Rizo? The ones you saw in the park both times? Those you both followed back to the school?"

Rizo said, "I was runnin' fast, man. I don' stop to take a good look, you know? Maybe them two we tail to the school, and the time they was at the movie."

I described the tall, ultra-skinny and talkative Donner, the blond and muscular Whitaker, and the four younger students. They listened and thought hard, discussed it with each other in their rapid Spanish. Cholo shook his head.

"Them two you says is older sounds like the punks at the movie. Rizo figures some of the others sound like the guys chases him, but we ain't sure. Maybe if we sees some pictures."

"But they sound possible?"

"Yeah," Cholo said, "they sounds possible."

33

In a Santa Barbara January the sun goes down early behind the Mesa to the west. It wasn't yet six but already dark when I came out of the jail, called Dr. Jovanetti.

"Anyone missing?"

"No one unaccounted for, Mr. Fortune."

"What does that mean?"

"We do have students away from time to time. Usually for illness or some special need of their parents."

"Have you checked on all of them?"

"I have. They are all where they're supposed to be."

The boy Anderson and I had found stabbed and dead in the field at the far end of the alley behind my rented hacienda had to be someone. But no one was missing from the school.

"Do you have pictures of your students, Doctor?"

"We request a snapshot with each application."

"Is that legal?"

"We don't require it, Mr. Fortune."

"But a kid with bad grades and desperate to get into the Point or Colorado Springs wouldn't want to take a chance, right? I'll bet they all send photos."

"Mostly, yes."

Which served the same purpose, more or less.

"I need to borrow some of the photos."

"What photographs?"

"I only know the names of two: Donner and Whitaker. I might be able to pick out the others."

There was a silence. "Donner? He's one of our brightest students. A local boy. He really shouldn't even be here."

"Why is he then?"

"There was a problem of attending more to his studies. A matter of too many friends, too much popularity in his regular private school. His father felt he was a bit immature for his age and intelligence, could profit by some more controlled supervision. Matthew apparently agreed, has adapted very well, is one of our best students."

"And Whitaker?"

"Oddly, also one of our few local students. Not one of the best, I'm afraid. He has attention span problems, is too easily distracted. Something of a big puppy, I'm afraid. I wouldn't have thought of connecting those two."

"They're not close?"

"I've never noticed them associate that much on campus or off. Whitaker is a new boy, only here since summer."

"Did they know each other before they came here?"

"I rather doubt it. The parents don't live in the same area of the city. Matt Donner is from Montecito. Whitaker attended San Marcos High School."

A new boy and a big shot on campus. A leader and what had the sound of a follower.

"Will you be there for a while?"

"Is it really necessary tonight?"

"I think so, Doctor. I can be there in ten minutes."

"I have a faculty meeting, it's sure to last until past eight-thirty perhaps even past nine. Are you sure this can't wait until morning?"

"I'd rather not."

An audible sigh over the phone. "Very well. Nine o'clock. Sharp. I'll have the photos ready."

In Summerland Kay wasn't home yet. I opened a Mackeson's Stout from our cool closet, sat with it in my office. I could open a few more, wait for Kay to come home, and we'd make dinner. I could make dinner on my own and hope she came home before it got cold. Or I could leave her a note, suggest we have a late dinner after eight-thirty with maybe a bottle of wine, go out now and do some more work.

Dr. Jovanetti had said Matthew Donner was from Montecito, Alan Whitaker from somewhere in the San Marcos High School attendance area. No Donners were listed in the phone book for Montecito—you don't need an address to know someone lives in that elite and rural suburb of Santa Barbara, the telephone exchange is enough: the world of 969. There were no 969s for Donner, which meant that either their phone number was unlisted, he lived with his mother who had remarried, or they'd moved and not told the school. In Montecito, these days of twenty-six-year-old rock, screen, junk bond, and computer millionaires who came and went like the wind, the last was more than possible. Whichever, I wasn't going to find them tonight.

Alan Whitaker looked a better bet. Four Whitakers were listed in areas that could be in the San Marcos district. None were named Alan. People who encourage their children to go to the service academies often have senior and junior, it goes with the mind set. With no such luck, the only thing to do was call them all, ask for Alan. The second call worked, a nervous female voice told me that Alan was away at boarding school, what did I want with him and could she help me. I told her I was selling subscriptions to *Air Force Magazine,* did she think he would be interested. She didn't think so.

I called the last two numbers to be sure. Neither of them had an Alan.

The house was small for Hope Ranch, close to the narrow rustic side road and lower, shake roof almost level with the road. A short driveway went down to a blacktop turnaround in front of an attached two-car garage at the side of the standard California ranch-style house. Two cars were parked in the turnaround under the outside light, one of them with a Marine Corps insignia decal in the rear window. Where there should have been a wide door into the garage had been filled in with a stucco wall. Standard Southern California— turn decks, garages, porches, into additions or separate apartments.

Windows in the former garage showed light and curtains. A lighted kitchen was visible in the main house, a living room beyond with the large colored picture of a television. The only path to the front door was from the driveway turnaround. In suburban Southern California where no one walked, why would you need a path from anywhere but the driveway? The outside light over the front door was off. In the entranceway, I rang, heard that momentary shock of silence.

"Yes?"

She stood with the door half open and a hint of fear on her small face. The twentieth century once more. The unexpected knock at the door brings fear even in the U.S.A. Even in the world of the comfortable minority. It could be a drunk and crazed street person, one of the homeless desperate with hunger, an ethnic gang killer at the wrong house.

"Mrs. Whitaker? Can I talk to you about your son Alan?"

"Alan?" Confusion replaced the fear but not the surprise or the question. "Why, he's away at boarding school. You're the second person this evening—"

"I don't want to talk to him, just to you and Mr. Whitaker. Could I come in?"

Some fear returned as she noticed the empty sleeve of my duffel coat, but it didn't stop a sharp snap in her voice. "Mr. Whitaker lives in Virginia. I . . ." She glanced over her shoulder. "Well . . . I mean, yes, all right, come in."

She walked ahead of me past the lighted kitchen to the right, down a short entry hall to the living room with its TV set. A small, slender woman who had thickened in the middle, she walked with her arms folded across her chest. In a brown dress that looked expensive but not new and fitted a shade too tight. Her legs below the skirt were too thin, and ended in a pair of unexpected brown leather pumps with three-inch heels. She turned to face me as we entered the living room, unfolded her arms and gestured as stiff as a robot at a big, square-faced man who sat on the couch and watched a baseball game on the TV.

"Nolan, Mr. . . ." She realized she hadn't gotten my name.

"Dan Fortune."

She nodded. "Mr. Fortune wants to ask some questions about Alan." Before he or I could say a word, she hurried on. "Nolan, Mr. Rochberg, rents my extra apartment. George, that's my ex-husband, pays child support, of course, some spousal support, but in this town, with a boy to send through school, it was never enough. Mr. Rochberg has lived here ten years now, isn't that right, Nolan?"

I realized part of her confusion. She had told me, with a touch of bitterness, that she had no husband in the house or even in California, before she remembered Mr. Nolan Rochberg sitting in her living room in his shirt sleeves and obviously at home. The two glasses on the coffee table in front of the couch showed where she had been sitting with Mr. Rochberg having a drink, and watching a Dodger nightgame from San Francisco.

"Almost eleven," Nolan Rochberg said. His voice and manner had neither fear, confusion, nor surprise. Only easy confidence and a certain interest in my missing arm. The owner of the car with the Marine Corps insignia, and obviously more than a tenant in Mrs. Whitaker's house.

"You must have watched Alan grow up then, Mr. Rochberg."

He nodded. "Mr. . . . Fortune, is it? What do you—"

"Watched and helped very much," Mrs. Whitaker said. She stood with her back to the TV, her round face animated. "A boy needs a man to emulate, a role model. Out here in Hope Ranch we have few neighbors and most of his teachers at school never seemed to be the kind of men to help a boy without a father who needed a father perhaps more—"

She was a chatterer. Probably compulsive and overprotective of her son, and, I sensed, probably confused and ineffectual to her son. A woman for whom the loss of her husband many years ago had shattered something inside her that had never been put back together. Rochberg stopped her with a big hand raised and a smile. It was a gentle smile, indulgent, a friend.

"Mr. Fortune probably isn't interested in the past, Shirl. Why don't you ask him to sit down, turn off the TV and sit down yourself."

He didn't push it, didn't act like the husband or even the drill sergeant. She smiled and calmed, turned off the ball game, and sat on the couch beside him. They liked each other.

"I could be very interested in the past, Mr. Rochberg," I said. "For instance, why did Alan decide he wanted to go to one of the service academies? Which one is it, by the way? Annapolis?"

"Why, yes," Shirley Whitaker said. "Have you spoken with—"

"Is that where you went, Mr. Rochberg?"

He nodded. "Class of '63."

"Vietnam?"

"Yes."

"You came out okay?"

"More or less." He nodded at my empty sleeve. "World War Two?"

"More or less," I said. "Where were you hit?"

He tapped his left leg below the knee. It was artificial.

"I had a company," he said. "Far as I went."

It wasn't far for an academy man, especially with his war. He was telling me that a big wound had ended his career, and maybe he'd wanted to pass it on to someone else. Like Alan Whitaker. His career and his beliefs, his faith and his loyalty, his codes and standards. That isn't unusual. Normal, the way of most people. Shirley Whitaker listened politely to the military talk, but her focus and interest was still where it had been when we began.

"You seem to have been at Alan's school, Mr. Fortune. Are you from the government? Have you talked to Alan?"

"Not the government, Mrs. Whitaker, and I haven't spoken to Alan yet. You spent a lot of time with Alan, Mr. Rochberg? Taught him Marine Corps techniques, maybe? Hand-to-hand combat? Knife fighting."

Shirley Whitaker said, "Nolan was always so nice to Alan, so good with him. I was so lucky to have him here so soon after—"

Nolan Rochberg said. "Why are you asking about Alan, Mr. Fortune?" He leaned forward on the couch. "You have some kind of identification? Is Alan in trouble?"

If I told them about my suspicions, they would probably tell Alan and maybe blow the whole thing. Not to mention put Alan in a lot of danger if I was wrong. It was beginning to look like not such a good idea to have come here. But I'd gotten the start of a picture of Alan Whitaker, and I needed more if I could get it without telling any more than I had by being there.

"I'm a private investigator." I showed them my license. "I can't tell you who for, or what for. I don't know if Alan even could be in any trouble. That's what I'm trying to find out."

Rochberg faced me. "You tell Mrs. Whitaker who sent you here and why, and what trouble you think Alan could be in, or you walk out of here right now."

I said, "Who I'm working for wouldn't mean anything to you, why is—"

"Try us."

"A homeless man named Al Benton."

Shirley Whitaker said, "Homeless? Alan has nothing—"

"What does this Benton think Alan did?"

"Benton never even heard of Alan," I said.

"What do you think Alan's done? What has it got to do with teaching him hand-to-hand combat and Marine fighting techniques? Other than making him want to be a Marine?"

"I don't know what he's done, Mr. Rochberg, and I'm not going to scare Mrs. Whitaker for nothing."

"Then you better get out of here."

He got up, and it wasn't easy. My stump hurt in sympathy. Shirley Whitaker didn't get up, stopped us both.

"Wait. If Alan is in any kind of trouble I want to know and I want to help. Mr. Fortune isn't going to stop whatever he's doing. I think he's here as much to help Alan as to harm him. Am I right, Mr. Fortune?"

"It's always better to know before anything worse happens, before Alan is in danger himself."

"Could he be?"

I thought of the dead boy in my alley. "It's possible."

"Then what do you want to know?"

"Has he been acting odd, strange, when you've seen him recently?"

"No," she said. "Well, perhaps he—"

"I'd say he's been acting better since he returned to school, Shirley," Rochberg said.

She nodded. "I suppose you're right. We don't see a lot of Alan when he's in school, Mr. Fortune. That's one of the purposes of a boarding school. Alan has trouble keeping his mind on studies. He's always had attention span problems, is easily distracted. He's a terrible daydreamer."

"That's not unusual," Rochberg said. "I dreamed of glory and all that. I guess it's why I got into the Marines."

"It depends what you do with the daydreams," I said. "What do you mean he's been acting better?"

"We had a difficult summer." Shirley Whitaker smoothed her dress over her lap. "Alan's father left us when he was nine years old, moved to Virginia and made no attempt to contact Alan until he graduated from high school last year. Not any Christmas, birthday, or anytime. The money arrived each month, that was all. Then, when Alan graduated, George suddenly wanted him to fly to Virginia. Alan was terribly excited at the thought of seeing his father after ten years, and then it turned out that George expected me to pay for the trip. I can't afford that kind of money, and, I won't be used and conned by George, so the trip was canceled. It upset Alan a great deal. He even thought of not going to Western Service Institute."

"But he did," Rochberg said, "and when he came home at Christmas he seemed better."

A boy who needed a father maybe more than most, who had been upset enough to think of giving up one of his daydreams.

"Does Alan have any history of violence, reacting violently to stress? Anything like that?"

They were both silent for what felt like forever. Maybe a full minute. Rochberg broke it first.

"You don't have to tell him, Shirl."

She smiled at the big ex-Marine, then looked at me. "It happened before Nolan came here. After his father left."

34

Alan is a happy little boy, always making friends with people and dogs and cats and once even a snake owned by an older youth, much to his mother's horror and his father's amusement. A gregarious child who as he grows older is always part of a gang of kids who play together every day after school. If for some reason all the gang except Alan are busy on any given day, he hangs around the school playground and tries to join some other group in their games. If there is no one at the school, he plays alone, throws the baseball up and catches it, even tosses a football in winter and runs to receive his own pass. But he always runs to his house to be there when his father comes home from work.

The day his father doesn't come home from work, Alan waits long after dark while his mother keeps his dinner warm and hides her tears both for herself and her son.

She has told him, "Your father is going away, Alan. For a long time. It's something he has to do. He can't help it, he wants you to understand that."

"Can I go too? Can I? Please?"

They have both told him. "I'll be going far away, Alan," his father says. "I'm sorry about this, but your mother needs you here. You'll have to be the little soldier, eh? Do what your mother tells you, work hard in school, get good grades, you'll be fine."

Alan runs home from his games and waits for his father all that week. And the next week. His father does not come home from work. His father doesn't call or write. Alan doesn't seem to have understood, or doesn't want to understand, or refuses to believe, or is sure they are both wrong or that there will be a wonderful change and he will see his father getting out of his car and coming to ask him if he has been good today and done well in school.

After a month, when his father has still not called or written, his mother tells him.

"Your father is never coming back, Alan. Your father and I are getting a divorce. That means we will no longer be married, do you understand that?"

They are in the living room of the house where he has lived with his father and mother all his life. Alan looks at the floor and nods.

"Your father is going to marry someone else. That doesn't mean this other person will be your mother. I'm your mother, that will never change. Your father will still be your father, but he will not live here in the same house or even in the same state."

Alan nods.

"This was what your father had to do. Or so he says. He will pay for your schooling and clothes and all that, of course, but it is probable that you won't see him very often. You may never see him again, Alan. Do you understand?"

Alan is nine years old when his mother tells him he may never see his father again. He stops running home to be there to meet his father's car. That is all he does different, the only change anyone can see. Except that he seems to plunge deeper into everything else he did before his father left.

He stays out longer with his friends, plays harder, comes home later. He doesn't cry. His mother cries a great deal. Alan has to comfort her. He is big for his age, seems much older as he becomes her little soldier, the man of the house. When he is home, which becomes less and less. The teachers see him alone in the playground more and more. When all his gang have gone home, he stays and shoots baskets one-on-one against himself. Throws a baseball against the walls, fields it as it comes back to him. Passes and receives his own football. As summer vacation time comes closer, Alan stays later and later, and finds he is not alone in the playground in the early evenings after school.

A group of neighborhood junior high school teenagers come to play a pickup basketball game after everyone but Alan has gone home. Sometimes they don't all come, and they need an extra player to make the sides even. Alan is big enough at nine to not be out of place with the smaller of the junior high kids. Big enough, and practiced enough, to be a better player than some of the younger junior high boys. When the junior high guys start to come to the playground on Saturdays, Alan joins them. He likes these older boys, especially the two ninth-graders who always captain each side. His mother is concerned, likes to have him at home on weekends when she is loneliest.

"Aren't they a bit old for you, Alan?"

"I'm bigger than some of 'em, Mom. I like playing with them, they're better than the kids at school. I like Jeff and Orel a lot, you know? They're neat. They talk about real stuff, not just kid stuff."

This doesn't reassure his mother, but after the trauma of the divorce, the total silence of his father, she is afraid to forbid him. As the summer moves ahead, and school lets out, Alan takes to hanging around with the older boys, especially Jeff and Orel. The two ninth-graders don't live in Hope Ranch, Alan has to ride his bike to their secret hideout in a field toward the mountains not far from his school. He is often late home for dinner. When this happens his mother eats alone at the table with the small portable television set. She doesn't blame Alan, she blames his father who abandoned them.

Jeff and Orel's hideout is a deep barranca at the edge of the field, narrow and totally hidden by thick manzanita that has grown over it creating a kind of cave without the darkness and cold of a real cave. They have made a clubhouse out of it with blankets on the ground, wooden crates for tables, old mattresses, stacks of *Soldier of Fortune* magazines, and their collection of weapons. At first they only tolerate Alan. Many times he finds the hideout empty when he bikes across the field. But when Alan brings the two old bean bag chairs from his room one Saturday, and great junk food he had his mother buy, they make him a full member of their club. Show him their precious weapons, take him with them when they go to hunt trolls.

They keep the weapon collection in a battered World War II footlocker that once belonged to Jeff's grandfather, still has his name, rank and serial number stenciled on the lid. There are various knives from a heavy-bladed bowie to a Japanese tanto and the double-handled Philippine folding knife neither of them can name. There is also an air-pistol that looks like a real gun, two of the special guns that shoot balls of colored dye in war games, a replica *samurai* sword that won't take an edge, two war surplus hand grenades without explosive, and two old World War II helmet liners Jeff and Orel put on when they are in the hideout. The day after he is sworn into the club, Alan takes some of his saved money and goes down to the Supply Sergeant to buy his own helmet liner for the club.

Jeff and Orel hunt trolls with the two war games guns.

"See," Jeff shows Alan out in the field, "they shoot these balls with like colored ink inside. The balls bust when they hit and leave big swatches of color so the trolls know we hit them."

"You should see their faces," Orel grins. "They're mad, and they chase around like crazy looking for us, but they never find us because we're too smart and too fast for them."

"Only," Jeff says, "we're going to fix it so when we hit them they don't do any more running around. Right, Orelo?"

"Right, Jeffo."

The two ninth-graders give each other high fives and laugh. Their eyes are excited. They take out of a hiding place under some thick bushes at the bottom of the barranca what looks to Alan like a long tube wrapped in black plastic. That is exactly what it is: a four-foot length of plastic pipe, with two hand grips and a pair of flashlight batteries fastened to it by metal bands with wires attached to the batteries.

"It's our bazooka," Orel says.

"The Jeff and Orel Troll Blaster," Jeff says. "When we finish the rocket, we're ready to go and kick some real ass, run the trolls out of the town."

"My brother says we should run trolls right out of the country,"

Orel says. "He's in the airborne rangers. He says all the dirty hippies and longhairs and vagrants and street bums and free loaders should be put in camps and wiped out."

"Free loafers," Alan says, "that's what my dad called all those people the government gives taxpayers' money to all the time so they can lie around and have lotsa kids and get drunk."

"My dad was in Vietnam," Jeff says. "He says we'd have beat those gooks easy if the hippie longhairs and all the rest of the traitors like them hadn't ruined the Army."

"Trolls, all of 'em," Orel says. "We got to chase them right out of the country."

"Save the country," Jeff says.

Alan says, "My dad says our soldiers are real heroes, we ought to shoot everyone who's against this country."

"Shoot all trolls!" Orel says.

"Blast the trolls!" Jeff yells.

That is what they do. Jeff and Orel have bought a rocket from a hobby store. They follow the instructions in the kit and make stabilizing fins for it. Orel makes some explosive in chemistry class and they put it in a bottle that fits perfectly on the tip of the rocket. In shop class, Jeff makes a nose cone, and with the rocket and their homemade launcher they bike out to Isla Vista one Saturday to find some vagrant street people.

"You can run, trolls, but you can't hide," Jeff cries.

"The Troll Rangers ride," Alan laughs as they bike.

They find a solitary young man with long, ragged hair and wearing greasy jeans poking through the dumpsters at the rear of a market. While Alan acts as lookout, Orel and Jeff sneak up behind a row of parked cars, aim their clumsy homemade bazooka, and fire the rocket. By sheer luck they hit the man. By even greater luck the narrow rocket hits him in the fleshy part of his lower leg where no major blood vessel is damaged. The rocket goes through, protrudes from both sides, and the explosion of the charge blows outward causing a lot of shock but little real physical damage except the penetration of the projectile itself like a thick arrow.

The victim's yell of pain and surprise from the impact of the projectile, and the explosion, bring people running. Before Alan can do more than shout a warning, the boys have been seen. They are chased, hide in panic in the first place they can think of—inside another dumpster a block away where the foot patrol easily finds and captures them and takes them to juvenile hall where their parents are called. None of the upper-middle-class parents can believe what the police tell them happened. Not their sons. But the boys admit everything—the evidence is overwhelming anyway, from the eyewitnesses to their abandoned bicycles to the shop owners who sold Orel and Jeff the rocket and pipe.

All three have their hearings in Juvenile Court, where they tell their story of *troll* hunting. The older boys are sent to the California Youth Authority for two years, and put on five years probation. Because of his extreme youth, Alan is only put on five years probation. Everyone cries a lot.

Their parents can't imagine where they got such ideas.

35

After nine at night the dark school buildings set back from the residential side street were black through the oaks and pepper trees. Only a few students walked in and out of the school along the unofficial shortcut through the ivy. I picked my way along the worn path to the opening in the walkway between the outer buildings. Inside the quad, light from the rear two-story building and the study hall guided me across. The outside stairs to the second-floor gallery were lit by a single bulb at the top. The occasional groups of students who crossed the quad below the gallery ignored me. They were on their own time.

There was no light in the headmaster's office.

I stopped on the outside gallery. Light came from the office next door, and from another three doors away in the opposite direction.

No one stood or walked along the dark gallery. It was silent and empty, only the sounds of the occasional students who walked and talked below, a radio or stereo that played dark symphonic music in one of the lighted offices. The grinding first movement of the Mahler Sixth, *The Tragic*. As if any of Mahler wasn't tragic.

The door into Jovanetti's office was ajar.

I put my little Sig-Sauer into my jacket pocket, went in. The only windows faced the gallery. A faint light reflected from the offices on either side like the light of the distant pinpoint sun on the surface of Pluto. In the office, darker shadows showed the desk, the high-backed chair I'd sat in earlier, filing cabinets, a long chaise-lounge where Dr. Jovanetti worked out problems or recovered from long hours of not enough sleep.

The darkness neither moved nor breathed.

There was nothing on the floor, on the furniture.

I flicked the light switch, stood in the sudden glare. Dr. Jovanetti wasn't in the office. No one and nothing was in the office. Except a pair of file folders on the desk with the names Donner and Whitaker on them. Their applications were inside, along with their school records and comments of their teachers, but no snapshots. There were paper clips where photographs should have been, but no photos under the clips.

"What are you doing?" Short and round in a baggy tweed suit and a long scarf like Hollywood's idea of a British university professor, the red-headed man stood in the open doorway from the gallery. "Who let you in here? Who the hell are you? Where's Doctor Jovanetti?"

"That's what I want to know. Where's Doctor Jovanetti?" I held my license up for him to see. "I was supposed to meet him here. I'm fifteen minutes late."

"Investigator?" He had a short red beard, full but trimmed close. "What is an investigator doing . . . ? I mean, are you investigating something here?"

"I'll have to let Doctor Jovanetti tell you that, Mr.—?"

"Matteus. Horst Matteus, math prof. You always read other people's files while you wait for them?"

"The files are for me. Which office is yours?"

He nodded to the right, the office next door. "I heard Doug working in here. I was concentrating on my quiz papers, but I may have heard him leave not too long ago. In fact, when I heard you, I thought Doug had returned, came in to ask him a question."

"The light was out when I arrived."

Matteus laughed. "Doesn't mean a damn thing. That's Doug. He turns out any light he sees, even his own when he's coming back in two minutes. It's not at all like Doug to forget an appointment. You could have a son who wants to go to one of the academies some day and doesn't have the grades, right?"

"I'll wait for him then."

"If you need something, knock on the wall."

I sat behind Jovanetti's desk, read the two file folders. The comments on Alan Whitaker were brief. As Jovanetti had said, Whitaker hadn't been at the school long. Matthew Donner was something else. His records and comments filled most of the folder, were all glowing, with a single negative note: a shade immature that led to some arrogance and self-fantasizing. Otherwise, perfect officer material. A budding general. The little there was on Alan Whitaker was considerably less than glowing. At least academically. All the teachers liked him, found him eager and helpful, if somewhat silent and distracted.

Ten more minutes passed. It was now over half an hour past when I was supposed to arrive. That didn't sound like a man who always kept an appointment. I looked down at the folders of my two wise guys of this morning, and the empty paper clips where snapshots should have been. I went next door. Horst Matteus worked over quiz papers with his blue pencil.

"Where would I find two boys named Donner and Whitaker?"

"If they're not out, in their rooms studying. Especially Alan Whitaker."

"I thought Donner was the smart one?"

"He is."

"But he doesn't study?"

"He doesn't have to."

"Lucky him," I said. "Where is their room?"

"Rooms. They don't room together. And I'm not so sure how lucky Donner is to be that smart." He dropped his blue pencil, sat back, eyed me with interest growing in his eyes. "What made you think they roomed together? Are they who you're here to investigate? What have they done? They have done something, haven't they?"

"You wouldn't be surprised?"

He hesitated, calculated the risk to his career if he spoke too far out of turn about students. "They're a bit too big for their britches, especially Matt Donner. Grand ideas of their own importance. Everything they're going to do, what they're going to be."

"Doctor Jovanetti said Donner and Whitaker didn't really hang out together?"

"I guess they're not together all that much. But I've seen them going off to town, head-to-head on campus. It's more that they're a lot alike in their actions, their attitudes."

"What actions?"

He threw discretion to the winds. He didn't especially like Matt Donner or Alan Whitaker. "Small stuff. Arrogance. They're here because they screwed up and didn't get the grades they need for the academies, yet Matt Donner acts as if he already knows all he needs." He patted his tweed suit jacket, opened a desk drawer. His hand came out with two dry cigarettes, the kind a man who has quit smoking keeps around. Like those in my glove compartment. I shook my head. He lit up. "They bully smaller and newer kids. Women don't belong in the services, what are girls doing here? Curfew breaking. Snotty in class . . ."

"When did they break curfew?"

He inhaled, closed his eyes, let it trickle from his nose. He didn't sigh with pleasure, but I heard it anyway. "Off and on the whole year. I don't know days, dates. It's more a general impression than record keeping. The kids cover for each other. They recreate the adult world they come from. They need their own club until they get in the big club out in the real world."

"Is this school a club?"

"Of course, a manifestation of their place in the world. The world we all live in. Teachers, administration, even, I suspect, you, Fortune."

"How about the people not in the club? The students here have trouble with them?"

"All the time. The community kids bust them as tight-ass, toy-soldier snots. Our little officers sneer at the regular high school kids as beer-swilling imbeciles and worse."

"Do they sneer at latinos?"

"As I said, I don't have a log, only impressions, but I'd bet my salary on it. Is that what they did, Fortune? Trouble with latinos?"

"Could be. Where could I find Donner and Whitaker tonight? If they're not in town?"

He told me where in the complex of buildings I would find their rooms, said he would tell Dr. Jovanetti I'd be back. As I left he leaned back in his desk chair and enjoyed the remains of his cigarette. It looked like it had been a long time.

Matteus's directions took me along a dark path past the first row of cottages toward a large three-story Victorian house hidden behind more cottages.

The sound came from the shadows of an olive tree beyond a row of oleanders that bordered the path near the Victorian.

He lay on his face behind the oleanders in light from the windows of the Victorian. The sound was the groan he made each time he tried to get up and fell back down. From the gouges in the dirt around him he'd been trying to get up for some time. The side of his head and face shined in the shadow and light.

"Doctor Jovanetti? Can you hear me?"

Like a blind insect he gave no response, went on trying to get up, groaning. His pulse was ragged, his eyes were closed. I saw bone under the blood of the wound on the side of his face and head. A broken cheek and maybe jaw, a concussion if not a fractured skull. There were some large rocks, and low-hanging limbs on the olive tree that could have made such a wound in some bizarre accident, but the odds were long.

The arm went around my neck out of the shadows of the olive behind me. A muscular arm, hard and lean. I pulled my chin low and tight against my neck, slipped under the arm, bit as hard as I could, tasted the blood.

"*Agghhhhh!* Jesus goddamn shit!"

The arm jerked away. I caught it in my lone hand, dropped straight to the ground, pulled him over my head to slam on his face a foot from the crawling Dr. Jovanetti.

I turned and ran into the second one in the shadows. White eyes caught the light from the windows of the Victorian. I slammed into the shape at the knees, heard the howl as the knees bent back and buckled and he went down. I took a kick on the thigh. Aimed my thumb at the white, staring eyes and gouged.

"*Ahhhhhh.*"

Another shadow. I found a large rock, swung it hard.

"*Owwww!* Shit!"

I shouted as loud as I had the breath for, hurled the rock through the window of the old Victorian, ran from the light and the rising voices through oleander and trees and a narrow break in the high rear hedge.

Into another yard. Across the dark yard out into a new street.

36

An orderly residential street of the upper eastside. Big houses warm with light in the soft Santa Barbara night. Old and new, Victorian frame and modern brick or fake adobe stucco, in the $500,000 to $1.5 million price range, and 1.5 million light years from the *barrio* of East Los Angeles, from any *barrio* anywhere. Light years and dollars the same thing in the end.

A quiet and empty street.

Only a barking dog somewhere toward State Street, the high screaming snarl of an angry cat.

I trotted to the far corner to circle the block, go back into the school the front way. Dr. Jovanetti needed help, if my rock and yelling hadn't brought them out from the cottages and Victorian dormitory to find him.

The black figure appeared at the corner. Black clothes, black ski mask, black gloves. A long, heavy club. Slim and not tall. I knew what I was dealing with, what had been attacking me if not who. Kids. Older kids, but still kids. The size and muscle, some of them, but not the ruthless viciousness of adults. Not yet schooled or trained in violence, inept. They have the meanness, but not yet the abstract and vicious purpose, the controlled violence to inflict total injury and pain. The thumb in the eye. The kick in the face. They hesitate, still have rules. Good kids do, sheltered kids. Kids for whom violence is still alien, not part of their daily lives. The kids who live every day and night with pain and violence are already adults, as vicious and violent as any of us.

These kids were playing games, inhabiting their fantasies. I took my new Sig-Sauer out of my pocket.

"Hold it right there, son."

He vanished.

I ran to the corner. The house at the corner where he had stood was dark. He could only be in its yard. A small, neat yard for a large frame house, hedged on both sides, no shadows to hide in. The narrow path between hedge and house led to a larger rear yard with avocado trees. Nothing grows under avocado trees except dead avocado leaves. A high wooden fence insulated the yard from the street and rear neighbors, reinforced the hedge on the west. I saw no way out of the yard except over the fence, which was a good twelve feet high, but no one was in the yard. There had to be a way out, but I wouldn't find it in the dark.

Back on the streets I walked south to the block of the school and my car.

The next one came out of the parking lot of a two-story medical office building.

The glint of a knife.

I crouched, dug for my Sig-Sauer again.

Then I was alone again.

Footsteps ran away on blacktop. Back in the parking lot I saw the flash of the knife, ran after him. There was a wide entry to the offices from the parking lot. A twenty-five-watt outdoor light for illumination, a dry fountain in the center. My eyes searched the gloom of tiled stairways up to second-floor iron-railed balconies. There was no other exit or entrance. I circled the lower courtyard, tried all the locked doors. Climbed the stairs and repeated the fruitless quest on the second floor. Again, there seemed no way out except the entrance from the parking lot, but the figure in black had vanished.

On the street once more, I continued south to the corner of the school block. My car was still parked up the block at the entrance to the school grounds. No students in sight up or down the long block. Or anyone else.

Then there was.

Three of them, black, masked and armed, stood at my car between me and the school. One held a pistol high where I could see it as they faced me across the distance. The gun they had lost and found in my yard in Summerland.

They moved toward me.

I jumped into the cover of the nearest front yard and a thick old oak with its elephant leg trunk while the sound of their running toward me was still a quarter of a block away. Down behind the oak, Sig-Sauer in my solitary hand. The running stopped. They weren't going to charge into the dark after an armed man. But if they were as deep into living their fantasy as I suspected, they would come into the dark—spread out and low, jungle fighters, commandos, the special forces that had operated so well behind the distant Iraqi lines in the recent far off Gulf War.

I slipped across the yard to another hedge, thick and too high to scramble over. Right, left, the only cover beside the darker shadows of the house and hedge was a tall trellis in the far corner with a heavy bougainvillea that grew over it. The weight of the overgrown vine had pulled the trellis forward leaving a space between it and the corner of a wall. I crawled in where I would have my back to the wall, pulled the vine over the space behind me. Sat and listened, and felt the cold draft on my back.

The wall and hedge met high but not low, a passage to the next yard hidden behind the overgrown trellis.

I crawled through the space into the dark of another yard where there was light in the windows of an elegant dark wood and white-walled Monterey-style two-story. It was set to the left and partly behind the house on the next street where the first one with the long club had escaped. On the far side of the manicured yard a cyclone fence topped by a barbed wire apron blocked me from the overgrown yard of a dilapidated Victorian, an eyesore in the upscale neighborhood. It looked empty, abandoned. Owned by some absentee owner or locked in an inheritance battle.

The long driveway of the Monterey took me to the next street again. This time I looked first from the shadows.

They were there. In the middle of the block and at each end.

The siren began in the distance.

A single siren. Paramedic rescue from the direction of Cottage

Hospital. It came closer, straight toward the next block and the school.

The two in the middle of the block like detached shadows faced toward the siren, the two at each corner vanished. I sprinted across the street and into the dark of the opposite yard. With a big bottle-brush tree as cover, I watched a third come from somewhere to join the other two, heard the paramedic siren growl into the far street and stop. There were still no other sirens.

Under the cover of the yards on the north side of the block I reached Laguna, crossed, cut through more yards to Olive Street and circled back toward the school where the paramedic van was parked behind my car. The paramedics meant that Jovanetti had been found and reported to 911. The single siren meant that no police had been called, Dr. Jovanetti's injury reported as an accident. I needed to talk to the paramedics, to call the police and tell them I didn't think it was any accident.

Two of them appeared from nowhere to stand at my car. One kneeled down to the tires.

Two more materialized in the middle of the block up Laguna, saw me, began to run toward me.

I ran south, turned west toward Garden Street at the next corner.

Two of them were already between me and Garden.

I ran east.

They seemed to be everywhere in the night, blocked every way of getting back to the school. They appeared like part of the night it-self, able to move at will through the darkness. If I could get back to the school, I was certain they wouldn't try to shoot or even attack me. But they were going to do everything to keep me away, and how certain was I they wouldn't shoot? It would be irrational to attack me where others would see, but I wasn't dealing with rational reactions. Dreams of glory, games and delusions, imagination and fear. Fear and unreality can make people do irrational things.

I had no illusions about what they had been doing at my car. A flat tire wouldn't get me far. I could walk down to the police station on Figueroa, but what would I tell the police? A gang of faceless and nameless kids had attacked Dr. Jovanetti and chased me all across the night. I had no proof who those kids were. I had no proof they had done anything. I hadn't seen anyone hit Dr. Jovanetti. I hadn't actually been attacked by these shadow kids. Sorry, Mr. Fortune, but what can we do with any of that? Maybe when Dr. Jovanetti can talk, if he ever can.

I found an open AM-PM Mini-Market at a gas station on Mission and State, called Al Benton to meet me at our house, called a taxi, and went home.

"Kids?" Al Benton said. "Why?"

He'd gotten my message, knocked softly and slid into my office after eleven ready to be annoyed, but sat in the armchair now only shocked, uncomprehending. "What did kids have against Cassie? How did they know her?"

"I'm not sure they did know her."

"What can you prove, Dan?" Kay said. "What connects that school to the murder? What's the motive? There's no connection between those boys and Cassandra Reilly."

She had made a pot of hot tea. We all sat in the office and drank the tea while I told them about the Westside Rockers, Dr. Jovanetti and the boys at the Western Service Institute.

"The connection is the Westside Rockers, the motive is fear, fantasy, delusion."

"Good luck," she said, sipped the good hot Assam.

We all drank in silence. The endless pulse of the traffic on the freeway filled the office like the enormous breathing of a pit full of animals, covered the softer beat of the surf on the beach beyond it. Assam is expensive tea. The Assamese are rich, will kill to keep the poor Bengalis of Bangladesh out of their domain.

I said, "Have any of your street people reported trouble with preppie kids? Military school types? Buzz haircuts, neat clothes, shirts and ties?"

"We always have trouble with kids like that," Benton said, "but nothing definite lately around here that I've heard."

"Tell them to keep their eyes open for kids like that. Especially around Alameda Park and around that school. Tell some of them to hang out up there if they can, tell you if they see any kids like that acting odd."

He drank his tea, nodded. "What are you going to do?"

"Talk to Chavalas. My guess is Jovanetti went to question Donner and Whitaker about the missing snapshots, maybe pumped them about what I'd told him. It was enough for someone to panic and nearly kill him. If he doesn't die from that head wound."

Benton finished his tea, shook his head in disbelief. "What the hell could kids like that have to do with Cassie?"

"I'm not sure, but I'm going to find out."

"Yeah," he said, stood. "You better find out."

He scanned the night outside before he left. I loaded the dishwasher. Kay went upstairs. She was in the bathroom doing her teeth when I heard the car stop in the alley behind the house. Benton come back?

I looked out. It sat in the alley, its lights out. Then it started up and drove away, its lights still out. At the far end of the alley I saw the glow as its lights went on, heard it fade away toward the freeway.

Someone stood in the alley. There and gone. I thought I'd seen someone, and not Al Benton. I went down and checked all the doors and windows. There is no alarm system, I can't live behind bars, even electronic ones. I got my new Sig-Sauer, put it under my pillow.

Kay came to bed.

Later, I held the pistol in my lone hand under the pillow and listened. Fear can make a man do what he never would, an almost insane boldness. A man or scared boys.

I got up, sat in the armchair near the window, watched the night down in our yard and alley.

37

Dawn comes from the mountains and the sea east of Summerland. On clear winter mornings the first rays of sun pick out the peaks to the east, the silver-gold ocean and the distant Channel Islands. It was a peaceful magnificence, except that the freeway was loud with early morning traffic, and I sat in a chair at the bedroom window with a gun in my lap.

I had slept in the chair as well as anyone can sleep in a chair or anywhere else with one hand on his gun. Better than I would have without the gun in my hand. Which says something about the world we have at the end of the twentieth century in America. More than one thing, and I don't like either of them. The violence or the guns. Kay still slept, but I had awakened with the first hint of light, sat and watched the sun and light dissipate the shadows and leave few places to hide down in our yard or alley.

There was no one down there.

There were a few places a watcher could take cover from someone in the upstairs window, but not where he could still see the front and back and side of the house. Another difference between boys and men is patience. If a boy were hidden somewhere out there now, he would show himself sooner or later out of the sheer inability not to look.

"Dan?"

"Go back to sleep."

She moved in the bed. "Is someone out there?"

"Maybe was. I don't think is." I stood. "I'll make breakfast."

I wanted to take a closer look, and I make a good breakfast anyway. The kettle on, I went out and circled the house with my lone hand on the Sig-Sauer in my pocket. If anyone had been watching, there was no one near the house or in the alley now.

We ate my scrambled eggs and toast, drank our tea, with a sense of eyes watching us, an atmosphere of uneasiness. The watcher could have been withdrawn to lull me, another still somewhere close but not too close. It is something you live with in my work. Kay has never become used to it.

"You're sure it's only those boys?"

"No, I'm not sure."

"What do you do to be sure?"

"Look around, ask questions, put on the pressure, stir up the waters. First, I go and talk to Gus Chavalas."

"Good." She finished her eggs, stood up briskly to go and get ready for her work. "Work with Chavalas, Dan, not alone. I like to think you'll be back intact and in relatively useful shape."

At my age that is flattering.

Sergeant Chavalas looked like he was working on the same file folder I'd seen last time. Police work can be dull as well as dangerous, boring as well as unrewarding. It was the unrewarding part that had finally sent my father running out of my life. That and his sense of not belonging either with those who paid him or with those he was paid to control. Not a boss and not a worker like my grandfather. Not a Pole and not quite an American. The tribe runs deep, a changed name can leave you alone. Chavalas escapes what cost me my father by doing his job as he wants to do it, not necessarily how he is told to do it.

"Still Cassandra Reilly?"

"Even more Cassandra Reilly," I said. I told him about Cholo and the Westside Rockers' troubles with the boys from Western Service Institute. "Last night the headmaster of Western Service Institute, Doctor Douglas Jovanetti, was badly injured and taken to Cottage Hospital. He's probably still over there. A head wound, Sergeant, and I don't think it was an accident."

"What do you think it was?"

"An attack by the same boys who've been attacking me ever since Cassandra Reilly was murdered." I told him about them chasing me. "I expect my car is still parked in front of the school, probably with a flat tire or two."

"Why did they attack this Doctor Jovanetti?"

"I'd guess he asked the wrong questions somewhere around the school and someone panicked. Maybe if we talk to him he can tell us more."

He closed the file folder, picked up his telephone and waved me out of his office. I waited out in the hall. Detective Max Miller found me there.

"You're not still taking Al Benton's money? Not that I'd cry a whole lot over Benton getting suckered."

"I still don't think Jerry Kohnen killed her."

"You're smoking the strong stuff. It was one street bum offing another before we even started. Odds on."

"It always comes out with the odds? You find what you expect to find going in?"

"Ninety-nine out of a hundred."

"What happens to the hundredth?"

"Falls through the cracks. If we miss him, we get him next time. If we get the wrong guy, the courts catch it. You got to play the averages and your experience."

"I sure hope I'm never on the wrong end of the averages."

He shrugged, went off to find what he expected. Chavalas leaned out of his office, motioned me back inside. On his desk the file folder was open again.

"The paramedics at Cottage picked Jovanetti up on a call from the school. The guy in charge of the nearest dorm told them he'd taken a fall, hit his head on a rock. They had no reason to question that, the head damage and other bruises were consistent. They even found a big rock with blood on it right near him, marks in the dirt like he'd stumbled and fallen." He leaned back in his chair. "They said there was one funny thing. Someone tossed a rock through a window in the dorm nearest to Jovanetti, and someone made a lot of noise. That's why the guy in charge of the dorm went out to look and found Jovanetti. The dorm supervisor said he doesn't know why the rock got thrown, unless maybe someone was trying to get help for Jovanetti. Maybe someone who wasn't supposed to be on the grounds. Some kids say they did see a man run away. A man, not a boy."

"That was me. They didn't see any boys running around too?"

"Not that anyone said."

"Can we talk to Jovanetti?"

"He's conscious, but doped and disoriented and still in I.C.U. No visitors yet. Come back—"

"We can still do something today."

"You can. I've got work."

"That dead kid in my alley. The county identified him yet?"

"No."

"I think he's from the school."

"Is anyone missing at that school?"

"No," I said, "but kids cover for each other. Any of the teachers should be able to identify the body."

He closed the folder.

* * *

Outside Western Service Institute my Tempo was still parked at the curb. Two tires were flat, the air let out but not slashed. After we talked to Horst Matteus, all I would have to do is call the Automobile Club or use the foot pump I carry in the trunk.

In his sunny office, the math professor stood when we came in. He recognized me, shook his head in sadness and disbelief. "If you're still looking for Doctor Jovanetti, I'm afraid he had an accident last night. Terrible thing. Fell and hit his head. It must have happened before you even got here, perhaps even while we were talking. That's why he didn't keep his appointment. It wasn't at all like Doug to miss an appointment. I don't know what the hell we're going to do here without—"

I said, "We're not looking for Doctor Jovanetti, Professor Matteus. We're here to talk to you, ask you to help us."

In the same tweed suit, he had the look of a startled cherub with his blue eyes and cropped red beard. "Who is us?"

"Sergeant Chavalas is with the police."

"Police?"

"We're not sure Doctor Jovanetti's injury was an accident."

"Mr. Fortune thinks it wasn't an accident," Chavalas said. "I don't know enough to have an opinion."

"I do," Matteus said, "and it sure seems damned odd to me too. Doug is pretty athletic and careful." He shook his head again, then blinked at us. "Help? What help?"

Chavalas said, "Dan wants you to come down to the morgue and take a look at a dead boy the sheriff's department has there. He thinks it's one of your students."

Matteus's round face got as pale under the red beard as a florid, overweight man could get.

I said, "Doctor Jovanetti was sure none of your boys are missing. I think he's wrong. It's a small school, I expect math is taken by most of them, you should know all the students."

His blue eyes processed what I'd said while his mouth moved automatically. "Yes, math is required. I know most of them."

"The Sergeant can drive us," I said.

"I have a class in an hour."

"We'll get you back."

"Yes. All right."

Chavalas took the math teacher with him. I reclaimed my car, pumped my tires and followed.

The unknown latino boy lay lifeless and nameless behind the steel double doors of the Sally port in the one-story, flat-roofed, window-less stucco building on the edge of the Sixties family tract out in Goleta. Behind those same double doors, the anglo boy lay just as lifeless but now he had a name.

"Raymond da Silva," Professor Matteus said. "Portuguese descent. Rich family. My God!"

He turned away more green than pale under the trimmed red beard. He didn't throw up, but if he hadn't had the iron control of a man who had to hide his true feelings and reactions every day in a classroom, he would have. Pale and cold and bloodless in the morgue drawer, the boy's knife wounds and livid bruises looked worse than out in the open of a dark night.

"How could he have been away from the school three nights without anyone knowing?" Chavalas said.

Matteus shook his head. "I don't know."

"He couldn't have been," I said.

Matteus shook his head again. "I never missed him. No one said anything about missing him. Doug should have known."

"The faculty didn't know he was missing," I said. "But the kids had to. Some of them. Someone had to have lied about where da Silva was, and the others covered."

Chavalas said, "Matteus?"

The red-headed math teacher nodded. "It's possible. Especially with these kids. The future rulers of the country and the world, right? Matter of honor. Superiority. Power players just like mom and dad, against mom and dad. The next generation taking care of its own. Loyalty."

"Then let's go talk to the students," Chavalas said.

"There are a hundred and ten of them, Sergeant."

"So we better get started."

Out in the morning sunlight of the morgue parking lot, we walked to Chavalas's car.

I said, "Call an assembly. To report on Doctor Jovanetti's accident. Tell them it wasn't any accident, then let Sergeant Chavalas talk to them."

"It won't be easy," Matteus said. "Especially if they feel it's the police and adults against them."

"You'll have to convince them it's something else," I said.

When we got back to the school, I went up to Dr. Jovanetti's office while Matteus took Chavalas to the assistant headmaster, Dr. Parnell, to set up the assembly. In Jovanetti's office I got Matt Donner's home address. Back down outside the study hall I made my excuse to Chavalas.

"I better have my tires checked and pumped at the station. I'll get back to the school before you even start."

They could handle the assembly. I had another errand.

38

The houses on Montecito's Lilac Drive you can see from your car are far from mansions. One-million-plus and up, depending on the quantity and size of rooms, number and style of amenities: pools, game rooms, saunas, tennis courts, stables, corrals, solariums, guest houses, etc. The landscaping tends to rustic and native, but runs the gamut to manicured lawns and imitation British country manors.

On one of the larger lots visible from the Drive, the Donner house grounds fell into the rustic category with a lot of rock and gnarled old native oaks. They are messy trees, California oaks, with twisted trunks and limbs, coarse bark and small leaves. The leaves are a dusty green, some always dead and brown. The ranch-style house itself had the rough-hewn aura of redwood siding, thick shakes on a low roof, redwood deck and beams, redwood fencing around what had to be a large pool, a four-car attached garage and a rail fence around the entire property. It looked half a mile long.

The red tile driveway was color-coordinated with the house, led to a large turnaround in front of the garage. A cream Jaguar XJ12, license plate *DONNER 2,* was parked inside the garage with the door up. The other three spaces were empty. A large dog barked somewhere. Another took up the alert. No one came out of the house. The beasts sounded penned, the barks came no closer. My solitary hand rested on the Sig-Sauer in my pocket. I don't know what I would have done with it if the dogs had appeared. There was still no sign that anyone in the house had heard the violent barking of the dog alarm. I rang six times before there was movement somewhere inside. Maybe Matthew Donner's parents were deaf.

"Yes?"

A woman of average height, she gave the impression of being tall. In a trim white silk dress with large green dots. A wide green leather belt pinched in her waist, made her seem slimmer than she was. A solid woman, well-curved but not at all heavy. The comfortable late forties, her well-made-up face and pulled-back blonde hair looked years younger. Everything about her was less or more than she really was. That takes time and money. Only her expression and voice were over forty and herself. She wasn't deaf, she just didn't give a damn who was at her door or how long they waited.

"Mrs. Donner? My name is Fortune. Dan Fortune. I'd like to talk to you about your son Matth—?"

"Matthew is away at school in Santa Barbara. You can speak to him there. The Western—"

"I know where he is, Mrs. Donner. I've come from the school. I don't want to talk to him, I want to talk to you and his father."

She was neither alarmed nor surprised. People had come to talk about Matthew before, it was something that could be handled. Tiresome, perhaps, but not a real problem she had to give much thought to.

"I'm sorry, Mr. . . . Fortune, is it? I'm late for a lunch appointment at The Valley Club. My husband should be home soon. You can wait in your car for him."

The Valley Club was the most aristocratic country club in Montecito. An old club. Tasteful and low-key and comfortable. I liked it myself. Most of its members would never drop the name so obviously, even mention it to someone they didn't know.

"A charity function?" I said.

"Some friends," she said. She didn't like me, looked at my empty sleeve. "Do you represent some handicapped organization, Mr. Fortune? I must tell you that neither I, my husband nor my son particularly approve of charities."

"Discourages honest work? Hurts the hardworking who make the country a better place for everyone?"

She reached behind the door for a small green handbag, stepped out and pulled the door closed behind her. "I really must leave. If you want to wait—"

DONNER 1 was the license plate on the white Mercedes sedan that turned into the tiled driveway and seemed annoyed to find my Tempo blocking one of the empty garage spaces. The space for the Mercedes, obviously. The small man in a dark brown chalk stripe suit who got out walked with short, rapid steps toward us at the front door. A purposeful and irritated walk aimed at me and my offending car, and that Mrs. Donner interpreted instantly.

"I'm just leaving Charles, you can park in my space. Mr. Fortune will be gone long before I return. He wants to talk to you. Something about Matthew and the school."

Charles Donner slowed his pace, somewhat mollified, but continued to look only at me as he drew closer. Trim and lean with a narrow face and dark pencil mustache, he walked stiffly erect. The heels of his dark brown oxfords were almost two inches high.

"Actually, I'd like to speak to both of you," I said.

Mrs. Donner didn't answer me, she answered her silent husband. "I'm really very late already, Charles."

Her voice was different when she spoke to him. More tentative. Somehow smaller. She was tacitly asking her husband's permission to leave for her lunch, to leave him to talk to me alone. Direct and domineering with me. Deferential, even subservient, with him. Sexism for the lord of the manor. A sexism that didn't apply to me. Lower-class males didn't count as males to upper-class females.

"Go to your lunch, Margaret. I suppose Matthew's old enough now to be my province."

She had to bend an inch or so to kiss the small man. Her Jaguar rolled from the garage past my plebeian Tempo and the regal Mercedes, almost silent. She had gone to the car without even a nod to me, drove off without a glance. I required no amenities. I didn't exist in her narrow world. Charles Donner went to drive the Mercedes into the space vacated by the Jaguar, nodded when he returned to me. He lived in a larger world, had some sense of public behavior.

"Come in then, Mr. . . . Fortune?"

"Dan Fortune." I followed him into a wide entry hall that led to a sunken living room two steps down, with a glass wall that looked out to a tiled patio, large pool, two tennis courts, and a large bathhouse that served pool and courts. He walked around the living room on the upper level and out onto the patio, sat in a deck chair next to a redwood table, picked a bell from the table, rang it loudly, crossed his legs, and looked up at me. He didn't ask me to sit. His world wasn't that large.

"So, what is this about Matthew?"

"Has he been acting strange? Doing anything odd recently?"

"Of course not."

"Nervous? Uneasy? Maybe scared?"

"Matthew is never afraid. I've taught him the importance of self-confidence, of toughness. He—"

A latina maid appeared on the patio. She carried a silver tray with a single whisky sour on it. Charles Donner took the drink. The maid turned to me. Donner didn't notice. He automatically waved her away. His answers had been as automatic as the wave or his wife's arrogance to strangers.

Now he sipped his drink, knit his thick eyebrows. "Actually, Matthew hasn't been home a great deal. I encourage his self-reliance, really haven't seen much of him lately. Has he done something foolish at school?"

"His teachers say he's immature, has an exaggerated sense of his own importance."

"What? Who says that?" He set down his whisky sour.

"Doctor Jovanetti himself, and almost all the instructors I spoke to. Very intelligent but highly immature and prone to wild exaggeration. Tends to blow his importance and accomplishments totally out of proportion. No common sense."

His long fingers tapped the arm of the patio chair.

"Are you finished?"

"They're not my words, Mr. Donner. The school—"

"All of it is utter nonsense. The local high school failed to challenge Matthew's intelligence. It appears this so-called intensive school for which I am paying an exorbitant fee is doing likewise. That is unfortunate. But more than that it appears they fail to understand Matthew in any way. Or, I might add, me. I had expected much more."

Up to now he had been concerned not with Matthew, but with himself. He was a man who would always be concerned only with himself: his ideas, his views, his plans, his position. So much so that he hadn't asked who I was or why I was there. Hadn't even thought about that, unlike Alan Whitaker's ex-Marine surrogate father. He simply assumed, from what I wanted and his wife's words, that I came from the school about some petty schoolboy nonsense, the way other people had probably come to him from all of Matthew's schools.

"How do you understand Matthew, Mr. Donner?"

"Matthew has self-confidence and pride. He knows who he is and who he will be. He is a strong-willed boy, I taught him to be that. Life is a power struggle, Fortune. The liberals who run our schools don't understand that. They see strength and call it arrogance. They see power and call it exploitation. They think everyone should be equal. They want 'nice' boys. Matthew is not nice."

Now he was concerned with Matthew, but it was Matthew as his image.

"Is he violent?"

"Violence comes from weakness, or from irrational resistance to reality such as in the recent action we had to take against a stupid Iraqi government. My son is neither weak nor stupid." His analysis of Matthew as his image made him feel better. He picked up his whisky sour, his voice became more philosophical. "My father was a weak man. Something of a liberal even though he voted Republican. He worked in one bank all his life, became branch manager before he retired. Never invested, never had the discretionary income. He always had to rent. When I was twenty-five I bought the house I grew up in and gave it to him. I was worth two million when I was thirty. It's all a matter of a clear vision of what the world is about."

"Being white, middle-class, English-speaking, and well-educated doesn't hurt."

He watched a cat stalk a noisy California jay. "Life is neither good nor fair. Some men are better and smarter. I was born better, but had to learn how to make other people work for me. You take any advantage you can get. It's a war, Fortune. That's what all your so-called educators don't want to believe."

"Speaking of war, where did Matthew get his interest in the military?"

Donner looked at his Rolex. "I have no idea. Not from me, but all the academies are excellent schools, cost very little. I saw no reason not to encourage his interest. The military is an excellent start to learn the uses of power. A successful officer will always be in demand. Those coming back from the Gulf War will go far." He finished his whisky sour. "There's an example of what power can do for the world, American strength. Matthew has been excited by the war. I taught him to be proud of his country. Something not popular the last twenty years but back now thanks to the Gulf War."

"Too bad it cost so many lives, casualties."

"A hundred and thirty? My God, that's zero. More people are killed on the highways in a weekend. Unfortunate for the parents of the few who died, of course, but sacrifice is often necessary for greatness. I taught Matthew that too."

"I had the hundred thousand dead in mind, maybe half a million or so casualties. Give or take."

"What are you talking about? There was nothing like—"

"The half a million Iraqis and Kurds, women and children. At least a hundred thousand Iraqi soldiers."

He stood. "I have a telephone call to make. I hope I've helped you, Mr. Fortune. You never did say what the problem at the school was?"

"Has Matthew ever had trouble with latinos? Women?"

"He knows no latins I know of beyond our maid and the gardeners, has no experience with women." He smiled. "He's much too young for trouble with women, they take some age to handle. If you walk around the house that way, the path will bring you to the turnaround."

He walked with his quick steps into his house. Charles Donner wasn't very interested in his son except as his son. I found the tiled path, followed it to the turnaround, drove out of the Donner's red driveway. An older man in baggy chinos and a straw hat pushed a Rototiller around the smaller house next door. Donner's fence was between the two driveways, but the neighbor had no fence around his house. The man stopped his machine, leaned on it and watched me leave the Donner's driveway.

I parked, got out, walked under the twisted old oaks.

"Kurt Peterson," he said. "Saw you back there talking to Donner. You must be thirsty."

I smiled. "You know the Donners?"

"Better than they do."

"A long time?"

"Lived here fifty years. Couldn't afford it if I hadn't. Saw him build that house, probably see him sell it."

I took out my wallet, showed him my license. "I'm working on a case that could involve Matthew Donner."

He nodded toward the Donner house. "You show him that?"

"He never asked to see it, or even who I was."

"That's Charley Donner." He thought. "Is it bad? Your case?"

"Pretty bad."

"You learn a lot about Matt over there?"

"I learned a lot about Donner."

"Same thing." He leaned on his Rototiller, studied his neighbor's big house. "He's a scientist, Donner. Chemist. Got his Ph.D. when he was twenty-two, invented a new instrument at the university, started his own company to sell it, made a fast fortune, makes more now on real estate. Did it all himself."

"You believe that?"

"He does."

"Tell me about Matthew. How does he get along with his parents?"

"Feels superior to his mother. So does Donner." He went on looking at the Donner house. "You see the boy's room?"

"No."

"I did. Once."

39

Mr. Peterson is cutting down a large Monterey pine behind his house that has died of old age. His oldest son is up near the top sawing the large limbs. Mr. Peterson handles the rope that lowers them to the ground one at a time. On the far side of the fence Charles Donner has built between his house and Peterson's, Matthew Donner rides his bike around in circles on the red-tile driveway of the Donner house. He watches the Petersons as he rides, even if he has to look over his shoulder. *"I know you don't like what I'm doing but you can't stop me. I do anything I want to do."*

Peterson has raised three boys, knows how to ignore this kind of game.

"You're not supposed to cut down trees," Matt Donner calls out as he circles.

Peterson and his son continue to work. The younger man is in the tree with the chainsaw, Peterson is below lowering the limbs with the rope, piling them for later sawing into firewood. It is hot work and dangerous. They forget the boy who continues to circle on his bike, swings around the fence onto Peterson's blacktop drive. Peterson pays no attention, doesn't notice that Matt is riding more and more on Peterson's side of the fence until the boy speaks almost directly behind him.

"I bet I could cut that tree faster."

Peterson is lowering a heavy limb, keeps his mind on his work. "Move back, Matt. You shouldn't be over here."

"My dad says I can climb like a panther."

"Two panthers, probably, but you better ride back to the street and your own driveway."

"I'm strong. I could hold that rope just like you."

"I'm sure—"

Before Peterson can react, Matt grabs at the rope, pulls too hard. The heavy limb is almost to the ground. High up the rope slips, the limb drops too suddenly, swings and hits Matt on the left leg. The boy goes down crying out more in fear than in pain, while Peterson manages to steady the heavy limb and lower it carefully to the ground. His son is halfway down the tree as Peterson bends over the fallen boy.

Matt makes quite a fuss: thrashing and gritting his teeth, holding his leg and acting in great pain. It is a soundless fuss, and before his son even reaches the ground to examine the boy's leg, Peterson realizes that the key word is acting. Matt is being brave. The wounded soldier. The racing driver in a crash. Wyatt Earp at the OK Corral. John Wayne on Iwo Jima.

"It feels okay," his son says. "Just a bad bruise. Want to try it? Walk a few steps?"

Matt nods bravely. They help him up. He takes a step, grits his teeth again, shakes his head.

"Maybe it's broken," he says.

Peterson can hear the next line: *You better leave me, save yourselves.'* It doesn't come, but Peterson knows his cue.

"Here, put your arms around us. We'll walk you home."

When they reach Matt's front door, Margaret Donner opens it and stares at them. Peterson winks at her.

"We've got a wounded man here, Mrs. Donner. We better get him up to his room."

"What on earth, Matthew? Where is your bicycle?"

As they help Matt along the hallway to his bedroom, Peterson explains what has happened. He isn't a fool, emphasizes that Matt should never have been near the tree, but is sure the boy is fine, it's only a nasty bruise. Margaret Donner barely listens.

"Look at your pants! And your shoes. What am I going to tell your father. He's told you not to go on other people's property. And where is your bicycle?"

Peterson sends his son for Matt's bike, waits in the room while Margaret Donner finally examines her son's injury. The large bruise on the leg is already discolored, will get worse. Matt's wound isn't what Peterson examines. It is Matt's room. The room is much neater than any of his sons' rooms when they were pre-teens. But that isn't what interests him either. It is what is on the bureau and work table and bookcases. The displays all over the walls.

Pictures of weapons and uniforms and soldiers, military aircraft and naval ships, are everywhere. Some real weapons hang on the walls. A replica of an M-16 rifle and a wooden AK-47. Miniature

tanks, jets, artillery pieces. Color photos of current military uniforms and hardware from almost every Western nation and modern
war. Harrier jets and the British troops in The Falkland War. The
invasion of Grenada. The Contras in Nicaragua. The Afghan guerril-
las in their mountains with their American and Soviet weapons.
Guerrilla forces and regular troops in many nations, all with their
U.S. military advisers.

Historical weapons and uniforms. A World War I helmet and a
frontier Colt. 44. Civil War kepis from both sides. From his own war,
Peterson recognizes the Nazi ceremonial dagger with the swastika
on its polished wooden handle, and replica of a German P-38 pistol.
American soldiers on Guadalcanal, Marines on Iwo Jima, the British
Desert Rats and Field Marshal Erwin Rommel on the sands of
North Africa. Black-uniformed Waffen SS troops on many fronts
from the snows of Russia to the canals of Holland. Two large repli-
cas of the collar-tab runes of the SS above his bureau. Field Marshal
Goering. Adolf Hitler.

"Why Hitler?" Peterson says. "He wasn't a soldier."

Matt is propped up on his bed, ice packs on his leg. "He was a real
great leader. I mean, my dad says he was dumb to fight us, but the
whole world sure knew who he was."

Peterson's son brings the bicycle to the room. Charles Donner is
behind him. After Matt's father has investigated the injury, questioned his wife and Matt, he puts the ice packs back on and thanks
Peterson for bringing the boy home.

"Matt should not have been on your property, Peterson, I apologize for him. I'll speak to him about it tomorrow."

"He was just interested in what we were doing with the old tree,"
Peterson says. "Boys are curious."

Some years later Charles Donner wants to build a bathhouse, pavil-
ion and guesthouse that will serve his pool, tennis courts and visitors. He needs some of Peterson's land, requests that Peterson
come to his production plant in Carpinteria to sign the papers. Peterson, who has gotten his full price for land that is of no use to anyone
but Donner, sees no problem in that, arrives at the appointed hour.
He finds Matt, now fifteen, waiting to guide him. It is summer vacation, Matt is working at the plant as his father's assistant.

"My dad's showing me how to run everything."

They talk as Matt leads Peterson along the maze of corridors among the busy offices and clean production rooms where the instruments are made.

"So you're going to be a chemist like your dad."

"I don't know about that, all those stinks and all," Matt says, makes a face, "but I'm gonna run the plant after my dad. Even if I go into the service."

"What are you going to do in the service?"

"Maybe fly. I like fighter jets. My dad says being a staff officer could be better, real command."

"I think if you go into the Air Force you have to fly or know how to handle missiles."

"I guess. Maybe I'll be a Marine. They get to go to more action. Everyone knows the Marines."

His business with Donner and the lawyers concluded soon enough, despite Charles Donner's last minute attempt to add the air space over the creek behind the land to the deal, Peterson remarks on Matt working the summer at the plant.

"He has a good attitude for management. I have to admit it's gratifying to see that my talks about the need to work hard, build a strong position, are bearing fruit."

"Sounds like Matt's thinking about a different career."

Donner nods. "We've discussed his college plans. I've told him I'll send him anywhere he wants as long as it's practical for his future. Actually, a service academy would be ideal." Donner smiles. "Best executive training there is, and no cost to me."

"He going to work here all summer?"

"We're not sure yet."

"Fifteen's pretty young to be all work and no play. I remember my boys—"

"He has the right stuff, Peterson. His mother was worried he needed more free time this summer, but we scotched that."

"Well, he seems to be enjoying his work."

From his kitchen table in the mornings, Peterson watches Matt get into his father's car promptly at nine. They drive away, Matt looking pleased with himself in the front seat. Sometimes Peterson sees them arrive home, usually toward six o'clock, but otherwise he sees little of Matt the first half of that summer. Later in the summer, Peterson runs into him seated in the bank with his mother. It is mid-morning on a weekday. Peterson greets Margaret Donner, nods to Matt.

"Not at your dad's plant today?"

"My dad's showing me about real estate and investments now."

Peterson remembers how his boys announced grandiose plans for their future lives, only to change their minds to some completely different vision in six months.

"How about the Air Force and Marines?"

"Oh, I'm going to do that. But I have to know all about the estate, you know? We're going to look over Mom's portfolio. I'll maybe take over running it from Dad."

"Well, perhaps someday, Matthew," Margaret Donner says.

Matt laughs. "I'll take good care of you Mom, even better than Dad."

Then Matt does something unusual. He winks at Mr. Peterson, man to man, obviously feels vastly superior to his mother who is smiling beside him.

Matt Donner is seventeen when he starts workouts at the Montecito YMCA. Peterson has been a member since it opened. He notices that Matt has joined when the boy appears in the Nautilus room one day. A classical music station plays on the radio. Matt glances around the room full of machines, spots the radio, walks to it and reaches up to change the station.

"Just leave that station on, all right?"

Matt looks at the man who spoke. He is a large man leaning on one of the machines. Matt, tall now but still skinny in all-white tennis shirt and shorts, stares at him for a moment, then rolls his eyes, shrugs, and turns away to the first machine.

Some weeks later, Mr. Peterson is on one of the Lifecycles in the weight room. Matt is on another. Matt reads a magazine as he cycles. Most people read something while they cycle or tramp the Stairmasters, it makes the boring exercises tolerable. The vast difference between twelve and seventeen shows. In over two weeks, Matt has not noticed Peterson at the Y. A difference even between fifteen and seventeen. Peterson watches the sweat pour off the boy's thin body as he cycles. He guesses that Matt has been told that a cadet at the academies has to be in good physical condition.

Peterson finishes the Lifecycle program, crosses the weight room to sit on the stool and lift some weights. He can still see Matt sweating and reading on his cycle, decides that the boy must be six feet tall now and tower over his father, but probably doesn't weigh much more than the father. Matt finishes his test program, does not get off the cycle. He has not finished the magazine he is reading. He remains seated on the Lifecycle, in his sleek white Sergio Tachetti shorts, doing nothing but read until he does finish the magazine, doesn't notice if anyone else is waiting for the cycle or not.

Mr. Peterson is again on the Lifecycle in the weight room the Saturday afternoon Matt comes to the Y with two friends. Matt wears the same white shirt and Tachetti shorts, or identical ones, but has not come to exercise this day. He has come to show his friends the Y and its pool and sauna and machines. They decide to play ping pong out on the patio between the weight room and the gym where group classes are held. Peterson watches the three youths in fascination. Especially Matt Donner.

They play two at a time, but one is always Matt. It looks like a real game, but isn't. They act casual, but aren't. Each one serves, the receiver then tries some flamboyant stroke that invariably fails— goes off the table or into the net or sometimes is missed entirely. The one who misses pretends shame while the other two hurl loud taunts. Sometimes there is an actual rally of serious shots, and Peterson thinks a real game is about to start. It never does. The moment one of them makes a mistake, or sees he won't be able to return the shot, he begins to clown.

But it is Matt Mr. Peterson can't take his eyes off. On every shot that flies past the friends, Matt taunts them, pumps his fist in the air in imitation of every athlete on television. Each smash they can't handle, he stabs his finger skyward in the high sign of Number One. Number One in the world, the best, the greatest. He falls to his knees with fists clenched and looks up at the heavens just like John McEnroe, or raises both arms in a wide V-for-victory gesture à la Becker or Agassi or any of twenty great tennis players. He struts and whirls and slams balls and does a dance of victory.

And all the time, he watches himself in the glass doors of the weight room or gym.

He watches himself make each gesture of imitation triumph, often repeats the gesture in a different manner as he studies his own movements in the windows. He mimes the facial expressions of a McEnroe, a Boris Becker. All the famous tennis players current on world television. Often he freezes in a pose that seems to please him either because it is a good mime of one of the famous, or because he likes how he looks. When both his friends are chasing the ball, or watching something else, he stops moving at all and poses openly, his dark eyes fixed on his image in the windows. He stands tall, serious-faced. With his brown hair cut in a kind of military bowl cut he is the image of Lt. Col. Oliver North of the White House staff in full uniform with medals defying the congressional committee that accuses him of illegal actions for the President. Or Gregory Peck acting the ramrod Brigadier General trying to save the squadron from its own battle fatigue weakness in a movie whose name Peterson forgets.

Mr. Peterson on the Lifecycle is frozen by Matt watching himself as much as Matt is frozen by his own image. Until Matt looks past his reflection and finally sees Mr. Peterson on the bike inside the weight room. They look at each other. Peterson smiles. Matt does not smile. He looks at Mr. Peterson the way he looked at the man in the Nautilus room who told him not to change the station on the radio. He comes to attention, salutes smartly, stands with both thumbs hooked into the waistband of his Tachetti shorts.

Now he is not looking at Mr. Peterson. Or the weight room through the windows. He is looking again only at his own image in the glass. Before he turns and swaggers away, shouting over his shoulder at his friends to follow him.

40

The quad of Western Service Institute was empty as an abandoned outpost on some frontier. Empty but not silent. A swell of sound came from the dining hall on the ground floor of the two-story brick building across the deserted open space.

Inside the long hall the dining tables had been folded and stacked against the walls, the chairs lined up in rows that faced a raised platform at the front. All one-hundred-plus students were seated in the chairs. They talked, looked around at each other, wondered why they were there. At a table on the front platform, Sergeant Chavalas sat alone. The rows of students stared up at him, whispered, speculated. I stood against the side wall at the rear near the entrance, looked for Donner and Whitaker. They weren't anywhere in the long room.

Horst Matteus and a tall, sallow man in a well-worn gray flannel suit came from the right of the platform and climbed the two steps up to it. The murmur of the students rose higher. Matteus sat down next to Chavalas, the tall man remained standing. He raised his hand no farther than his shoulder. The hum of sound stopped instantly. The tall man looked sad.

"You all have, I know, heard of last night's most terrible accident suffered by Doctor Jovanetti, which explains my presence up here. As assistant headmaster, that is my duty. We have few assemblies at Western, as you all know, which makes this a most important duty for me. Your duty is to listen to what Doctor Matteus is going to tell you, and to think very hard. To think hard and clearly. Very clearly. Doctor Matteus?"

Matteus stood and walked around the table. Gus Chavalas remained seated. The assistant headmaster walked back and sat down at the table beside Chavalas. Matteus stared out at all the young faces. His thick red hair and beard caught the platform light as he surveyed the students. His voice was solemn.

"Thank you Doctor Parnell."

Whoever had choreographed the platform actions, Chavalas or the two teachers, it was all intended to impress the students with its gravity, make them wonder more what was up and who the silent stranger on the platform could be. The reference to Jovanetti should scare some of the kids in particular and all of them in general.

"One of your classmates is in the county morgue." Matteus paused to let his gaze move across their silent faces in the hush that filled the hall. "Raymond da Silva is dead. Murdered."

An uneasy silence now, more scared than shocked. They were all young, death did not sit heavy on them. Concerned less with death and Raymond da Silva, more with what his death would mean to them, to their futures. If I were right, some of them should be very concerned with their relation to the death of Raymond da Silva. I looked again for Donner and Whitaker, and saw them now far across the room.

They stood against the far wall with what looked like the four other boys who'd been with them when they'd confronted me on the quad. Matt Donner was smiling, whispering to Whitaker and the other four. Alan Whitaker's face was as blank as a human face can get. The other four seemed nervous, looked constantly at Matt Donner, at the two teachers and the stranger up on the platform, at the faces of their fellow students in the dim room.

Matteus said, "If any of you are wondering who the guest up here on the platform is, he is Sergeant Chavalas of the Santa Barbara Police Department. He is here to find out who murdered Raymond da Silva."

I watched Donner, Whitaker and the other four across the long room dim in the afternoon sunlight. A dusty light through the high and curtained windows in the wall over my head that picked out the six boys in long shafts like spotlights. Only Matt Donner still smiled, grinned, whispered to the others. He seemed to be clowning, mocking the adults on the platform, posing for his friends. As I watched them, there was something familiar about them in the narrow light beyond the rows of chairs. As if I'd seen them there at the edge of the crowded faces before.

Matteus said, "Raymond da Silva has been missing from the school for three days. Some of you had to know that."

Chavalas walked to stand beside Matteus. "Some of you had to have covered for Raymond da Silva, fooled your teachers. To help a friend or friends. Friends who lied to you . . ."

A low murmur began again in the narrow dining hall. A murmur that flowed like a soft wave through the rows of faces on the chairs in the dusty light that could have been dusk or dawn, the interior of some medieval cathedral.

". . . friends we think murdered Raymond da Silva. Your friends and his friends who were pretty bad friends to him and to you."

The murmur continued like a pulse in the hall, the pulse of a single large animal with a hundred faces. They sat in the dim light as an entity that Matteus and Chavalas had to somehow break into. Teenagers in an adult world where they feel powerless, where they are out of touch, feel allegiance only to their peers, to the dreams and needs and rules of their friends. A monolith of outsiders who make their own world, even these who wanted desperately to join the adult world.

"Friends," Chavalas said, "who could have murdered someone else. Who maybe murdered Raymond da Silva because he knew they had murdered someone else and they were afraid he would tell your teachers or the police."

The murmur became more ragged, a skip in the monolithic pulse, a break. I heard it and Chavalas heard it. I looked across the room at Donner, Whitaker and the others to see if they had heard it. They were gone. One moment they had been there, the grotesque smile of Donner, the blank of Whitaker's face, then they were gone. There had to be another way out of the hall on that side. Somewhere out of sight to the right of the platform. Maybe from the kitchen that had to be back there somewhere.

Chavalas said, "Doctor Matteus and I will be in his office. For any of you who want to tell us about your friends and Raymond da Silva."

Outside, I ran around the building. Behind the two-story red brick two low sheds stood among bushes between it and the high hedge at the rear. Both sheds were without windows and padlocked. There was no one among the bushes. No one anywhere behind the dining hall turned into an auditorium. Chavalas's detective at the foot of the stairs up to the offices had seen no one come from behind the building.

On the second-floor gallery above the dining hall, Chavalas's two men stood at the corners where they could watch the quad below, be close to the second-floor offices in case Chavalas needed them. Inside Horst Matteus's office Chavalas sat behind the desk. Matteus leaned against a filing cabinet in the corner.

The assistant headmaster, Dr. Parnell, stood between the door and the desk. "I don't know, Sergeant. It won't be easy. They'll be too afraid to break ranks."

"You heard the break in their voices down there, Tom," Matteus said.

"They'll be afraid to lose their protection, the solid front," Dr. Thomas Parnell said. "Just as their parents are, all we happy adults."

"They're younger," Chavalas said. "Not as scared. These kids have adult ambitions. Some of them'll tell us. With kids, fear doesn't decide everything they believe."

I said, "I heard it down there too, Doctor Parnell. Some of them don't like what Chavalas told them happened, what they know they did, maybe who they covered for."

Matt Donner and Alan Whitaker and the other four had heard it too. The break in the clan. I was sure now they had killed Raymond da Silva and Cassandra Reilly. But sure and prove are not the same. We needed the students, waited in the office of the math teacher until the first light footsteps came along the balcony outside.

She came in alone, stood between the door and the desk where Dr. Thomas Parnell had stood before he'd joined Matteus across the office. I closed the door behind her.

"Most of us knew he wasn't in school."

Chavalas said, "Why did you cover?"

"For him. Ray. We thought it was for Ray. They told us it was for Ray."

"Who told you?"

She wasn't ready for that yet, looked at the floor. Chavalas picked up on it, switched. "How was it for Ray?"

"They said he was in love with a girl in town and his folks didn't like it, wanted to break it up. They said it really meant a lot to Ray to have time with the girl. Ray was ready to quit school if he had to, and then he wouldn't have a chance at the academy. It's important to us to get into the academies. They said Ray and the girl had to have a few days to decide what they were going to do, work out their future. So we all agreed to help cover for him."

"How?"

"Some of us did his homework and papers. Some guys took his tests, answered when his name was called, said he was in the head or in town or studying or anywhere except where whoever asked about him was."

"The teachers never noticed other people answering for him?"

"They don't pay a lot of attention when they call roll. Let the room monitors do any checking up on where we are and what we do outside their class."

Matteus said, "It's a special school. We know they all want to be here so we don't worry much about anyone cutting. We get lax. If one hasn't been here long, doesn't make us notice him in a class, we can hardly know him."

"Lack of teacher involvement with the students is a problem Doctor Jovanetti and I often discussed," Thomas Parnell said. "I'd say the faculty shares a certain guilt in all this."

Chavalas nodded, but his attention was fixed on the girl between him and the door. Then on the two boys who opened the outer door and stepped into the office. The girl turned to look at them. Three more boys came through the open door. The girl smiled at them.

Chavalas said, "Okay, which one of you guys wants to tell me about it first?"

Without words, the boys decided who was their leader faster than any computer could ever have. There is a natural hierarchy, pecking order, in all human groups. It seems to be part of our genes, but children understand and accept it quicker and faster. The chosen one took one step forward as if he were about to salute. He didn't, and he told the same story as the girl in entirely different words but identical details.

Chavalas nodded. "We can get all your written statements later, one at a time. I thank you all for coming forward. I know it was a hard move. But I'm going to have to ask for one more move that is even harder. Who?"

It was the girl who spoke. Maybe because she'd had a little longer to come to terms with it. Or maybe because she was a woman in a world where the rules are still made by and for men.

"The Seven."

"Seven?"

She nodded. Chavalas looked at the boys, both interest and question in his eyes.

I said, "A secret society?"

"Just sort of a group of guys who hang around together," one of the boys said. "Mostly off campus."

Chavalas said, "Any of you in the group?"

"No," they all said at once. The leader added, "We don't even like them all that much, Sergeant."

Matteus said, "Then why, Kurland? Why cover for them, do what they asked?"

"We don't rat," the leader boy said.

The rest took it up like a Greek chorus.

"It's the biggest rule."

"You got to stick together."

"Adults and teachers don't feel the same, you know?"

"I mean, he could have been thrown out of school."

When they stopped, I could hear a lot of students down on the quad. The loud voices of teachers ordered them to class and study hall.

I said, "Was Ray da Silva one of The Seven?"

"Yes," the girl said.

Chavalas said, "Who are the rest?"

"Matt Donner," one of them said.

"Al Whitaker," the leader boy said.

They rattled off four more names. Horst Matteus looked at his feet where he leaned against his filing cabinets, shook his head. Thomas Parnell got up and left the office. Chavalas went with him. So did the kids. I didn't. He wasn't going to find Donner or Whitaker or any of The Seven.

Matteus said, "We haven't done much of a job teaching our morals and values, have we, Fortune?"

I said, "Those are our morals and values."

41

The early winter evening turned to dusk on the jacaranda outside Chavalas's office window. The Seven had not been found anywhere on the grounds of Western Service Institute. I'd put in a call to Al Benton. Maybe some of his street people had been around the school, seen them slip away through the yards to the next street, could tell us something.

They had not been found at the houses of the Donners or Mrs.

Whitaker. The Sheriff and the S.B.P.D. had the houses under surveillance. The other four were from out of town.

"They killed Cassandra Reilly?" Chavalas said.

I told him about the encounter of the school kids with the Westside Rockers outside the Plaza De Oro theater, the chase of the two Rockers from Alameda Park a few days later, the Rockers' stakeout and location of Western Service Institute, and Rizo's night in the park the Tuesday Cassandra Reilly died.

"They have to be The Seven, some of them were out like an army patrol in that park that Tuesday. They spotted Rizo, knew he was one of the Rockers, tailed him but probably lost him, and found Cassandra Reilly under the bandstand. They crept up on the room, soldiers on a daring mission. Some of them kept watch, others went inside and killed Cassandra."

"Why?"

"We won't know for sure until they tell us. Maybe not even then. I'm not sure they really know."

He looked out his window. "Jesus, it has all the sound of the truth, but not one goddamn shred of evidence or facts a jury could believe." He shook his head. "We can't touch those boys for the Reilly woman. You have no evidence it was any of those kids, and sure as hell nothing to prove *which* kids. No way we can get them."

"They'll get themselves. When you catch them, one or more will tell you. Maybe all except Matt Donner. And maybe I do have some evidence."

"What?"

"You still have that crime scene video?"

"Far as I know."

"Can we look at it?"

"You can't tell me what you've got?"

"I'm not sure what I've got."

In the glare of the floodlights the white faces of the police were again as pale as the painted faces of actors in an old silent movie from the Twenties. *The Cabinet of Dr. Caligari.* Motion stiff and angular, slow and deliberate under the trees that looked like painted backdrops in the garish day of the floodlights. It was colder in the room this time, the night outside instead of the afternoon sun. Or maybe it was what I knew this time that made me feel colder. The chairs we sat in were the same, but Miller and his popcorn were gone. Only the two of us in the room with the flickering light of the grainy video of the morning park where Cassandra Reilly had died.

In the distance on the TV screen, beyond the wide perimeter of tape and the uniforms of the patrolmen, rows of black eyes and featureless faces like masks. A crowd of masks that stared at the gingerbread bandstand, its filigreed conical roof topped by a weathervane, as artificial as a stage set in the flood of white light. *Masque of the Red Death.* Detectives, paramedics, coroner's deputies in and out the door beneath the high floor of the bandstand. Detectives, paramedics, coroner's men on the white glare stage inside the tape looped from tree to tree: *Crime scene . . . Crime scene . . . Crime scene . . .*

"How long do we watch it?"

In the video-taped park the painted faces of the detectives, the glare of floodlights on the dark green wood of the bandstand began to fade into the dawn. The trees emerged with the real day, and the faces of the crowd drawn to the blood even at the crack of a weekday dawn. The faces of the curious beyond the crime scene tape and the trees took shape with the dawn. There was an unreality again, like watching the news on television. I knew this was real, as real as if I had been there that morning, but I felt detached, watching a movie about some distant place I couldn't be sure existed at all. Until I saw what I had seen in my mind across the dim dining-hall-turned-auditorium at Western Service Institute.

"There."

On the screen the dawn light was full over the park. A yellow wash of sun behind the crowd of watchers that had grown with the coming of morning. Once more they brought the body of Cassandra Reilly out through the heavy wooden door under the bandstand. Once more the gawkers strained to see while the patrolmen held them back and the detectives cleared the way to the morgue wagon, and I saw their faces as they stood at the rear of the crowd of curious. Matt Donner and Alan Whitaker and some of the others who had ringed me on the quad.

"Turn it back. Stop. Now forward, and . . . stop." I sat back as the frame froze on the small screen. "Meet Matthew Donner and Alan Whitaker. At that hour of the morning they're in bed, or in the dining hall. But not that morning."

Chavalas and I watched the faces of the two tall boys where they stood behind all the other faces as Cassandra Reilly's body was put into the morgue wagon. Chavalas started the tape again, and we watched as Matt Donner talked and laughed at the back of the crowd, preened for the other boys the way he had for the windows of the Montecito YMCA, put his arm around the shoulders of an unsmiling and silent Alan Whitaker. Chavalas and I sat until the park was empty and the screen went blank.

"Whitaker," I said. "He'll tell you."

All the students on the campus of Western Service Institute waited in the crowded study hall while Chavalas's men searched every room and inch of the grounds. Al Benton called me back. I took the call in Dr. Thomas Parnell's office in the study hall.

"One guy was working the trash cans on the next block from the school. Says he saw a tall, skinny kid come out of a yard, get in a car, drive off."

"No one else?"

"No."

"When was this?"

"He ain't sure. Two, maybe three hours ago. The kid was in a hurry."

The deputies on stakeout at the Donner and Whitaker houses had reported no sign of any of the missing boys. At the school, Chavalas came up empty.

"Donner and Whitaker are both local," Thomas Parnell said in his office. "They know the city. They could be anywhere in town or around it."

I said, "When I talked to Doctor Jovanetti about Donner and Whitaker, he said he wouldn't have thought of connecting the two. He said he'd never noticed them associate much with each other, that he doubted they'd known each other before they came here."

Parnell nodded. "When I think about it, I'd agree. I never noticed them together much myself. Matteus?"

"I knew they spent time with each other, I didn't know how much or about any Seven."

"Then," I said, "where did The Seven meet?"

"Meet?" Chavalas said.

"You ever hear of a kids club that doesn't hold meetings?"

"So they could've met in someone's room where no one saw them."

"No," Matteus said. "We control room visits or the kids wouldn't get any damned homework done. They're here to cram, know they have learning problems. If they'd met often in any rooms we'd have known it."

I said, "When they tried to attack me after I found Doctor Jovanetti, they appeared from everywhere around the school. Materialized out of the night like magic."

"Like they've got secret passages through all the yards," Chavalas said.

"They were in the hall until you dropped the bombshell. When I looked again, they were gone. The only door on that side opens out of the kitchen behind the building. I went after them but they'd vanished. The only way out from behind the building is the way I went in. They didn't come past me or your man. But they were gone."

"So they went a different way."

"The only other way is through the hedge to the yards and houses on the next block."

"Okay. That took them out to the next street up. They were free, clear and on their way."

"But haven't shown up anywhere."

Outside we could hear the students as they walked, talked, shouted to each other as they crossed the quad. The young bounce back fast.

Chavalas said, "You think somewhere back there is where they hold their meetings, that they're still back there?"

I nodded. "And I think I know where."

They sat in the big, bare room of the empty house between the back of the school and the next street. The abandoned house I'd seen the night they appeared like magic to chase me.

They sat on the floor behind boarded windows, a circle of candles in the center of the room the only light. The candles all different colors and sizes, set in small glasses and jar caps. Hunched near the light, or back against the walls of the big ground-floor room that had been a living room, lost in the gloom of flickering shadows. Empty cans and food wrappers littered the floor: taco chips, Oreo cookies, pretzels, beef jerky, 7-Up, Pepsi.

Alan Whitaker and the four others.

"Where's Donner?" I said.

Chavalas motioned to his men to search the house.

"The Seven were his idea," I said. "It was all his idea."

One of Chavalas's men stood in the doorway between the living room and the kitchen, another in the arch of the dining room. Chavalas himself leaned in the entrance to the room from the entry hall. I sat on the floor beside one of the smaller boys.

"Wolf took to the hills," the boy said. "He went ahead. We go out and meet him tonight."

"Wolf?"

The boy nodded. "I'm Spider. Whitaker's Scorpion."

"What was Ray da Silva."

"He was Roach. He was going to talk. To the enemy."

Another said, "He was going to break, talk to that detective."

They were bright, privileged, educated kids with problems. Individual problems. The kind of personal problems that led to trouble in school despite their brains, their advantages. Elite misfits, a shade out of the norm of their world. Intellectually smart, but psychologically immature or damaged. Whitaker abandoned by his father. A problem that got a lot worse this year. Matt Donner a grandiose kid who demanded to be important. They all had dreams of glory, believed they were superior, yet could not perform up to that superiority so created a super-elite club to prove their own importance.

"Matt Donner, Wolf, got the idea for The Seven? The black clothes, the ski masks, the weapons? Going out after latinos?"

"We should never have listened. We were crazy."

"Ray was right. We should've gone to the police."

Someone started to cry.

So Matt Donner could be the leader of something, the general. An elite little club like some army unit, and like Hitler and the Third Reich and every military society ever formed, sooner or later the leader had to do something with the club or watch it fade away. So Matt Donner went around looking for trouble, at least unconsciously, and ran into the Westside Rockers at the movie house.

It was Alan Whitaker who cried.

He sat alone almost in the center of the room close to the circle of candles where the light flickered on his heavy face.

Cried, his voice almost too low to hear. "It wasn't latinos. It was everyone who gave us trouble because we believed in our country, wanted to be in the military. We had to take back our country from the bums and foreigners and liberals."

Chavalas said from the entrance to the room, "You didn't go out specially to attack latinos? Or the homeless?"

"They all want to take it away from us," the one beside me said. "Look at Desert Storm, we saved the world. They all hate us because we're the best."

I said, "All the weak and the jealous are always attacking. They have to be stopped, don't they? We have to show them we're not afraid. Show everyone who we are. They came to the school, those latinos. They came to attack. They had to be stopped, so you went out to find them in the park. You—"

Alan Whitaker cried in the center of the empty room, hunched over in the light of the candles as if he had a terrible pain inside.

42

Wolf knows the latino gang will come after them to destroy them. That is what the enemy always does.

"A home field attack," Matt Donner says. "We have to be ready, prepare."

They gather weapons—knives, clubs, bicycle chains, water-sodium bombs. They talk about building homemade grenades and rocket launchers, mortars and booby traps. How to set tripwires around their hidden headquarters in the empty house. They sleep in their clothes even on campus, stand guard on the dark quad all night in four-hour shifts. They practice self-defense and knife-attack techniques. They go out on a late-night patrol, run into the enemy gang in Alameda Park not three blocks from the school.

Whitaker, Scorpion, says. "They're moving in on us, we've got to go out and protect ourselves."

They all know that the best defense is a bold offense, make their plans, decide on a patrol in force that Tuesday night. One has to do homework, is left to guard their secret headquarters. One doesn't feel well, has been confined to his room. Five of them, led by Wolf and Scorpion, dress in black, take their weapons, and slip off the campus after all the room monitors have checked curfew. Once away from the school they blacken their faces, move ahead in protective formation: Scorpion on point, Spider at the rear, Wolf in the command center with Roach and Wasp on his left and right.

When a car passes on the late-night side streets, or people come toward them through the dark, they slide into the shadows of the front yards and dark driveways. No cars stop. The few night people they see are all older and anglo. Until they reach the far corner of Alameda Park. Wasp sees the solitary latino who takes a shortcut through the park from the northwest corner toward the distant southeast corner. They know the latino.

"He's one."

Wolf decides, "He has to be a scout. The rest are somewhere near. Be careful."

They draw their weapons and hurry into the park after him. It is darker inside the park, the weak lights on the path only make the shadows blacker. Somehow they lose him.

"Stop," Wolf whispers.

They freeze and listen to the night of the sleeping city. There is the far-off freeway. Cars from time to time on State Street a block away. An occasional voice somewhere on the quiet upper eastside. Nothing else. No footsteps, no movement, no sounds inside the silent park except the winter night wind and the faint movements of small animals among the trees and bushes.

"Where did he go, Wolf?" Scorpion wonders.

"He must be hiding," Wolf decides. "We'll move ahead with caution, be alert."

They move on deeper into the park, stumble over unseen objects, grow nervous. They stop every few yards to listen, become even more nervous.

"Where the fuck did he go, Scorpion?"

"The bastards'll hear us!"

"Shut up! All of you!"

When Wolf speaks, they freeze and listen to the silence. They all freeze in the dark night under the shadows of the palm trees, the oaks, the maples with red leaves. All the weird trees from alien countries.

"Jesus, Wolf, we could be walking bareass into a trap."

They move on, invisible in their dark clothes, only their alert eyes white in blackened faces. Afraid of a trap, seeing a trap behind every tree.

"Maybe we should get the fuck out of here."

"You want to sleep in your clothes another goddamn night, Roach?"

Wolf's sharp voice. "Down!"

Weapons at ready, each faces away to cover front, rear and both flanks.

"Over there, Wolf!"

It is a voice, voices. The voice, voices, are singing in Spanish. Speaking in Spanish. More than one voice. Wolf, Matt Donner, is excited. His voice seems oddly high, almost shrill.

"Scorpion with me. Roach and Spider cover our tails."

Matt Donner and Alan Whitaker move through the dark trees toward the Spanish voices that seem to sneer at them. The high-pitched, exuberant Mexican singing. The rollicking accordions and guitars, the heavy bass guitar.

"We got to rag one, Scorpion," Wolf says. "We don't, they never stop hitting on us."

Scorpion, Alan Whitaker, nods. His throat is dry. He holds his combat knife low in his right hand as Wolf leads them through the dark park toward the Spanish voices and music. They realize the sounds are coming from under the bandstand that looms ahead, a giant shadow in the silence broken now only by the voices and music that cover all other sounds.

Wolf orders them to put on their ski masks, sends Wasp to climb up on the bandstand and watch from above. Roach and Spider spread out, take cover among the trees. When Wolf and Scorpion move ahead, Roach lights a cigarette with his nervous fingers, smokes. On the bandstand, Wasp does the same, cups the cigarette to hide it from the enemy.

Near the door under the bandstand, Matt Donner motions to Scorpion that they will get down and crawl up to the low door. Commando style. Arm and hand signals.

They see that the door opens outward, can't be locked. Wolf stands, bent low, puts his hand on the latch, points to Whitaker, pantomimes that he, Donner, will pull the door open, and Scorpion will go through first. Whitaker licks his parched lips, but he nods and stands crouched and ready. Wolf's smile in the darkness is rigid. Donner pulls the door open, Scorpion dives through, rolls the way Mr. Rochberg has taught Whitaker and The Seven have practiced, comes up on his feet knife out low, left hand ready for defense. Wolf jumps in to the right, his club held high.

"Lie flat! Don't move!" Matt Donner's voice breaks as he shouts the commands.

He and Alan Whitaker stare at the enemy at the far end under the single light. He lies on a sleeping bag, a book in his hand. A large portable radio stands next to him. He has dark skin and eyes, full lips pink under the single small bulb, wears a wool navy cap pulled down low to his ears. A heavy plaid shirt, jeans and a baseball jacket. Work boots. He sits up.

The latino's voice is low, rough. "What do you kids want?"

The music and voices are coming from the radio. The enemy looks older than they remembered. An important leader? A decoy? To trap them in the small room! The rest of the gang outside, waiting to attack.

"Is he . . . is he one of—?" Whitaker stammers.

"Go on out of here, both of you."

Donner's hands shake. He nods, excited. "Yes! He's one of them."

"What do you two—"

The enemy starts to get up from the sleeping bag. Whitaker hears them all outside. The whole gang! The enemy at the far end of the room is moving at them attacking.

"He's got a knife!" Wolf cries.

Outside they have killed Roach and Spider. Their feet pound in the night out there as they run up to the hidden room under the bandstand. Donner's voice is thin over the pounding of the running feet.

"He's coming after us!"

Whitaker sees them as they pour into the room. The enemy. They attack Donner. The enemy. They come toward him. He leaps, thrusts and slashes. They are all over him, smothering him. The knife is wet in his hand. He cuts and slashes at the enemy. The knife is red, sliding in his hand. He can't breathe but he won't let them hurt him. They won't hurt Donner. They won't destroy The Seven. They . . .

The small room under the bandstand is silent.

A single dim light.

The ghetto blaster sings in Spanish. Talks in quick, bright Mexican accent.

"You got him, Scorpion!" Donner exults.

The man, the enemy, lies motionless in the blood of the sleeping bag. The book lies on the dirt floor. The radio still sings and talks.

"Now they'll know we mean business," Donner crows. "We bagged a Mexican."

Whitaker stares down at the dead man, the blood everywhere, the baseball jacket and shirt ripped open, and sees.

"Matt? It's a woman, Matt."

Donner looks at the dead woman.

"What do we do?" Whitaker asks. He needs to know what he should do. "We bagged a woman."

Donner shrugs. "Hey, innocent people get killed in a war. They won't mess with us anymore."

"Matt . . . ?"

"We better get the hell out of here. Pull back to the command post. The gang could counterattack at any time. We got to pull out now."

Alan Whitaker turns to leave the small room. He has his orders. Matt Donner looks down at the dead woman in her wool hat and men's clothes. He spits on her. "Bitch!"

He follows Scorpion out into the night where they all rip off their ski masks, hurry out of the park.

43

His face in his hands, Alan Whitaker cried. "I saw them all attacking us, me and Wolf. They had knives, guns, everything. They were going to kill us. Me and Matt. They were all around us. They . . ."

Chavalas said, "Then you came back here."

In the shadows of the big, empty room Whitaker nods. They all nod.

"But you went out again. To the park?"

Alan Whitaker still cried, sobbed in the silent room.

Another boy said, "We went back to the school. Matt listened to his radio all night. He heard about the police finding . . . He said we had to see what the police were doing at the park."

I said, "That's all?"

One of the boys against the wall said, "He wanted everyone to see what he and Alan did. Prove it to us."

"So you'd all be proud," Chavalas said. "Good soldiers."

"I guess," the boy said.

"You went back to your rooms," Chavalas said.

Whitaker cried over the flickering circle of candles almost in the center of the room. "I was numb. We were all numb. Matt made us go out every night. On patrol. Watch for the latinos, watch that one-armed detective. We didn't know who he was. Matt found out he was a detective. We had to scare him off."

I wasn't even there. Or Alan Whitaker was somewhere else. Somewhere inside his own fear. I said, "You had to attack the head-master?"

The boy against the wall said, "We took our photos out of the files. He found out, called the room monitor to see if Matt and Alan were there. Matt heard. We were scared."

Chavalas said, "Where are you supposed to meet Donner?"

None of them spoke. Against the wall or out in the room. They sat silent. Whitaker cried harder. Another one started to cry. Low and trying not to.

"It's too late for that," I said.

"Alan?" Chavalas said.

Whitaker held his wet face in his hands, in the flickering room, his knees up to his chest.

"The . . . the teahouse in Montecito."

"It's closed off," I said.

"We climb the fence by the old gate. At night no one knows."

"When?" Chavalas said.

"Ten . . . Tonight."

Chavalas read them their rights. "Did you think you'd get away with it?"

"No," Whitaker said.

"Before or after you killed her?" I said.

"After."

"What did you do before?"

"What Matt said we were going to. Wolf."

We went back to the school and our cars. Chavalas would talk to the school staff, contact the Sheriff, go out to the teahouse. He didn't believe Matt Donner would be there any more than I did, but he had to go out in case. I had another idea.

The freeway isn't the best way to Montecito from the upper east-side, but it's the fastest.

The Seven had not gone out to attack latinos that first time. Any minority would have done. Any outsider not in their tribe. Any infe-rior. Anyone weaker. They didn't know Cassandra Reilly, had noth-ing against homeless people. They didn't hate anyone in particular. Only everyone who wasn't them. They loved themselves. They were superior, the destined winners. The death of Cassandra Reilly had been an accident and inevitable. The three groups that had made it happen were unrelated, except by chance and the world they lived in. By the chance that they were all in Alameda Park that Tuesday night. The haves and the have-nots in the same space, separate and unequal. The Poles, Russians, Jews, Cossacks of my grandfather.

The Sheffield exit took me up the dark roads of Montecito to East Valley Road and Lilac Drive. The world of the comfortable voting majority with the power and the fear. The fear of losing that power and that comfort. A self-perpetuating world that reproduces the peo-ple and conditions that preserve it, defend it, continue it. But sometimes there is a mistake, an aberration. Someone is produced who does not believe, or who believes too much. Each is a danger, a disaster waiting to happen to Lilac Drive and Charles Donner.

"What do you want, Mr. Fortune?"

"Is Matt here, Mr. Donner?"

"Since a deputy has been sitting in his car in front of my house all afternoon, and is still sitting there, I should think you would know the answer to that."

In the open doorway he did not invite me in. He stood in the rectangle of light, a corner of his sunken living room and his wife behind him, his small mustache trimmed and neat, not a hair out of place. In a three-piece chalk stripe blue suit, polished black oxfords, a white shirt, reserved blue tie, a glass in his hand. Another whisky sour. After-dinner drink time.

"Do you know where he is?"

"I do not."

"Do you give a goddamn?"

His lips pinched under the thin mustache. "Matthew has been foolish. When he comes home I will deal with him and whatever he may have done."

"Don't you know what he's done?"

An eye twitched like a tic. "I know what the police say he may have done. I have heard no proof, do not care to know the speculative details until I do."

"I've heard proof, and so have the police. I know what he's done, what he and all his friends have done. Do you want me to tell you?"

He turned and walked inside his house. He didn't close the door, tacitly invited me into his living room to tell him and his wife what their son had done, but he didn't want to know. Matt had been foolish, he would handle it, but he didn't want to know. It would all be told to him, but he would not want to know. He would hear but he would not know. To know would be to ask questions and he did not want to ask questions. He didn't want to lie awake and wonder, he wanted to sleep.

"Where would Matt go in the hills?"

He sat in his living room, watched me over his whisky sour. "In our mountains? Anywhere. He always walked in the mountains. It's good exercise."

"What hills?" Margaret Donner said. She stood at the top of the steps down to the living room where she had been when Donner opened the door.

"The hills above Mountain Drive," I said. "Was there some special place he went? A secret place. Some favorite spot he loved since he was a kid."

Charles Donner drank. "I don't think so. I don't know of anywhere he—"

"Why?" Margaret Donner said.

"Because that's where I think he is. He's taken to the hills. That's what he told the others in The Seven. Retreat to the hills. Guerrilla war. He's scared, Mrs. Donner. He's retreated into his fantasies. If he doesn't come out of them, he hasn't got a chance."

Donner said, "The Seven?"

"Matthew doesn't have fantasies," Margaret Donner said. "It's that Whitaker boy. I never liked that one."

"Whitaker, and Matt, and all of them," I said, and I told them.

They sat and listened. They watched me and said nothing. They heard what they could. They heard, and maybe soon they would think about it all, but there wasn't time to let them think. To let them decide what and where their best interest was. I didn't want to let them think about that, they might decide it lay where I didn't want it to lie.

"The police are going to the teahouse where Matt is supposed to meet the others. He won't be there, but he won't be too far away. They won't find him at the teahouse, but they will find him sooner or later, and if he tries to fight, to live out more of his fantasy, he'll be killed."

Donner's eye twitched again. He put his whisky sour down on the coffee table.

I said, "He had a gun. He may still have it. They won't have any choice. If I find him first, I think I can make him surrender."

Margaret Donner said, "Somewhere near the teahouse?"

"That's what I think. A place where he can see the teahouse. At least see lights at the teahouse."

"The old Parsons Trail. Near Cold Spring Trail. There's a big rock where you can see almost to Catalina. Some bare outcroppings lower and higher. You can see the teahouse from any of them. He used to love to go to that rock where you can see the whole channel."

"Give me twenty minutes, then call the police and tell them."

All kids posture and pretend, dream of being heroes, imitate their idols. What counts is who that idol is, what they see as heroic. I always wanted to be, not the dashing leader, the lord or king or general, but his second-in-command, his hard-bitten professional lieutenant, the gunbearer who was smarter and more skilled than the white explorer. The one who knew more than the boss, saved the day and let the King have the glory. I don't know what that says about me except that I wasn't cut out to be the daring thief, the flamboyant freebooter, the leader and money-maker in this world of ours, which, in a very real sense, are all the same things.

Matthew Donner's posing and pretending and imitating told me a lot more. The important and the famous. The hero is the winner. The tough, elite and famous. Image was everything.

44

In the mountains it is beautiful at night. The stars are clear, higher yet closer, the moon casts silver shadows. Long, soft shadows, muted and indistinct, like dark mirages with shapes that shift and change, can be imagined as almost anything. Giant rocks and cliffs are white and smooth, the crags and hollows and deep fissures of the day are smoothed into a single surface, a soft night skin. Motion is slower, the nocturnal pulse moves on the light feet of the night creatures.

There is danger in the mountain night. The sudden heavy beat of an owl's wings, the stealth of the coyote, the lumbering, looming shape of a sleepless bear, the soft footfalls of hunting cats, even the last of the mountain lions. But it is a different danger, an older and simpler danger, without the hate and malice and blindness and stu-

pidity of the dangers of the day. Without the arrogance of a danger
that would destroy the night itself.

Higher on the coastal slopes the sweep of the night opens wide
over a black sea and in winter the blacker islands far out. The shape
of the land curves the mountain shadows north and south against
the sky of stars and the silver path of the moon across the black sea.
If you stand with your head high and your eyes upward you can
almost escape the intrusion of that day world below in its defensive
carpet of lights. You could turn your back, look away and up to the
dark peaks painted with the path of the moon. But there is no escape, and it is better to look down and find the beauty of those lights
so small and stubborn under the moon.

City lights as artificial in the wide night as the image of Matt
Donner in the YMCA windows. As Matt Donner who watched his
own image in the windows. As the powerful and famous and important whose image he saw as himself in those windows. So insignifi-
cant in the infinity of the sky and beyond the sky. The lights and the
images and Matt Donner. Only Cassandra Reilly had significance
under the black sky, a small part of all that might be real.

I climbed the silver and shadow trail up the steep slopes along the
path of the moon to find Matt Donner. To find Wolf, the famous
leader of The Seven. A hero in his own time. A leader of men. A
force. Known to the whole nation and far beyond.

"Stop! Don't come any closer, shamus."

He stood high on top of the giant rock above the dark trail.
Nonchalant, legs spread easily for balance, one hand on his hip. In
the path of the moon like a spotlight. Wearing his black clothes,
without ski mask, and something in his hand that could be the
pistol.

"Who told you I was up here?"

An edge of hysteria in his high voice. I kept my eyes on his hand
that held what could be the gun.

"Your father and mother."

"No way. He'd never tell. Maybe her, but not my dad. How would
you know to go and ask them anyway?" He laughed. He was too
smart for me, had seen through my feeble lie.

"You don't think your clever little setup for meeting The Seven
fooled anyone, do you?"

High on the rock, he dropped to a crouch. "They caught them?"

"All of them. Whitaker told us the whole thing. I went out to your parents and they told me where your favorite hideout was. From where you could see the teahouse. What did you do, leave a message there for Whitaker and the others? Sort of like a game, a treasure hunt?"

"She told you! He wouldn't remember. Stupid fucking women. Hitler was right."

"You don't like women, Matt?"

"Wolf! Call me Wolf." I heard the hysteria build in his voice. Crouched low on the rock he was out of the path of the moonlight, a shadowy shape on the pale surface of the stone. The gun, if it was a gun, in both hands now like some aid to prayer.

"Is that why you spat on Cassandra Reilly?"

"Fucking men's clothes. They want to take everything we have, the goddamn women. Old Scorpion wasted that streetbum. Fucking bloodsuckers all over the streets."

"You didn't even know who she was, anything about her. It could have been anyone, couldn't it? You—"

"Anyone gets in our way! Stay out of Wolf's way."

"Out of your way to where, Matt? You've got nowhere to go. Not anymore."

"Shit! Shit!"

He held out his hands and what was in them. I fell flat. The two wild shots echoed from rock to rock, canyon to canyon through the night. Up behind a rock, I waited for more. None came.

"Not smart, Matt. That'll bring the police. They have to be over at the teahouse waiting in case you show up. They'll come here fast now."

I hoped it would be Chavalas, and that they were closer than the teahouse across the canyon. An hysterical kid with a loaded gun, on a rock where I couldn't reach him, was something to worry about. The shots could hurt me more than help me. If it was the Sheriff's people they could barge in and get me killed. Chavalas would know I was here, would hold back for fear of getting me killed. I was on my own until I could get the gun away from Matt Donner.

"Shit! Shit!" He slid down the slope of the giant rock, stood between me and the trail out, the pistol in his shaking hands aimed at my belly. "You stay right there! You hear? Turn around. Now!"

I wasn't going anywhere. Not without him. That wasn't anything he would have thought about. It wasn't part of the fantasy of the hero who escapes from the bad guys and takes their boss as hostage as he backs away and warns them not to follow if they want to see their boss alive again.

"Walk up the fucking trail!"

I walked up in the moonlight, stumbled over unseen holes and rocks. A one-armed man doesn't have the balance of the normal two-armed, it's harder to climb a steep slope. Donner stayed far enough back to prevent me from trying for the gun, but not so far I couldn't see his death grip on the trigger, the shaking of his hands. It would be as hard to climb with both hands on a pistol as with one arm. A stumble . . . I stumbled, went to one knee.

"Ahhh—"

An upper-middle-class boy, he came to help. I went for the gun.

"Wha—!"

My lone arm missed. He slipped going back, went down, and fired. The bullet spun me against a boulder, bounced me off on my face on the ground. I tried to breathe without air to breathe. Only the pain. The ache of a pain that couldn't find a breath. A burn of pain under my missing arm. Wet and black. Black on the rock. Something pulled at me, turned me over. A twisted face in my face. The gun in my face.

"Shit, you son-of-a-bitch! You . . . fucking bastard son-of-a-bitch. You . . ."

Breathed in my face, his voice like a shrill scream in the wide night of the mountains. The pistol hard against my chin. Gasped for breath, his mouth working like something with its own life, the high hysteria of his terrified eyes. The fear behind everything he did or had done. His father's fear of the end of power. The fear in his hand that still shook out of control. I had maybe ten seconds.

"Matt! Stop it. Stop!"

The fear in him that needed everything to stay the same. The order of the fantasy, the promise of the image. The need to know what he wanted was right and true and possible. Scared and isolated, he stepped away, his eyes like those of a confused dog that doesn't know what it is supposed to do so does what it has always done. His mouth still worked, the gun aimed in both hands at where I got up, bleeding, and leaned back against the rock. A smaller rock at the edge of a sheer drop. With three other rocks that formed a circle at its base. The refuge of a boy.

"Turn it down, Matt! The gun. At the ground."

Another of his hideouts, the circle of rocks with the small space among them hidden from the trail and all sides except up. My hand came away from my left side wet, dark. He looked at his haven among the rocks. Lowered the gun with his shaking hands. My hand on the wound, I stumbled inside the rocks. He groped in behind me, his eyes on the ground to feel his way in the shadows of the rock. He was, in the end, only a boy.

My solitary hand caught the pistol, jerked with all the weight of my shoulder, flung him across the small space and against the far rocks. The pistol was in my hand.

"On the ground! Now!"

He leaned spread-eagled against the pale rocks, his arms out and down in the silver shadows of the night like the broken wings of some large bird. Silent and motionless, a crucified statue. The prisoner-of-war tortured for his country. The heroic political martyr who has held out for his beliefs to the end against the rack and the whip.

Then he was crying.

His legs collapsed.

He sat on the shadowed ground, his arms over his head, and cried in the sudden chill of the winter night. Cried as if he could never stop. "Why . . . why . . . why . . . ?"

He dropped his arms, looked up at me, his eyes as bright and empty as the eyes of the bird with the broken wings. "What did we do wrong? We did everything we were supposed to do, but it all went wrong. How did it all go wrong? Scorpion knew hand-to-hand and knife fighting. We had to fight them, the goddamn *spics* trying to hassle us. If you don't go out and stop them they come in after you. Attack is the only way to defend yourself. You have to win or you're nothing."

I leaned back against the low rock, the wet trickling down inside my shirt, under my belt. Lightheaded. How long would Chavalas be? How long could I hold Donner here without the gun dropping from my hand? A small revolver, blue and black in the night. Colt or Smith & Wesson. A .32. How many? Three fired. I felt two rounds with my thumb, the third under the hammer. If it had been loaded full. Or had not been fired earlier.

"Why?" His eyes stared up into my face as if looking for weakness, but they were eyes that saw only his own question. "They weren't there. The *spics*. That fucking woman. Why did she have to be there? Why did you have to come looking for us? What did we do to you? Why are they all against us? That fucking Jovanetti. Fucking Roach. The police." Crying again without even knowing he cried. "They're all against me. Everyone. Why are they all against me?"

I breathed slowly against the pain in my side. Leaned the wound against the rock to feel the pain and stay alert and on my feet. I listened to Matt Donner cry in the night where the moon washed the shadows with its soft silver. Listened to his high, thin voice that questioned the night.

"They were going to hurt us, the *spics*. We didn't mean to do it. She was talking Spanish. She had men's clothes, you know? An accident, you know? We made a mistake, we're sorry. We're sorry we hurt anyone. We went crazy with Roach. It was his fault, he scared us, we couldn't help it. Hey, we wish it hadn't all happened, but it won't ever happen again, Dad. You can get a good lawyer, he'll tell them how it happened. We just wanted to do something big. We . . ."

I heard them then. Chavalas and the Sheriff's deputies out of the moonlight all around us. The rocks and me and Matt Donner who still talked to the night. They helped Matt Donner up. His hands were behind his back. He talked to the police and the deputies. He cried. Someone talked to me.

"You're goddamn lucky," Chavalas said. "Nasty goddamn flesh wound, but a flesh wound. You shouldn't—"

I walked down the mountain. Cassandra Reilly had died of power and illusion and need. She would have understood more than most. Cholo, Rizo, the Westside Rockers would find a way. There were lawyers who understood too. Wolf and Scorpion, the rest of the surviving Seven, would have more expensive lawyers. I looked up to see if there were any bombs bursting, any rockets glaring red, but the wide and clear mountain sky was quiet. Only stars and the blackness.